PRIVATE UNIVERSE

Cornelia Feye

D0359499

Konstellation Press

San Diego

ISBN-13:978-0-9987482-0-7
ISBN:099874820X

To Katherine,
thank you for helping to
get Konstellation Press off
the ground! *[signature]*
                              March 2017

FOR GLEN

For all his patience and support

ACKNOWLEDGMENTS:

It takes a village to create a book. The myth of the lonely writers at their desk is just a myth.

To complete *Private Universe* I needed help from many people.
My husband Glen deserves thanks for his patience and support.
Members of my writing groups have contributed enormously to this book with their advice, their questions, their suggestions and their book reviews. Kudos and gratitude go to Mary Kay Gardner, Tamara Merrill, Edda Hodnett, David Porter, Katherine Porter, and Glen Vecchione. Mary Kay also helped with proofreading.
Katherine Porter was a sensitive editor, who selflessly tried to bring out the best of the book and clarified my intentions.
I am very pleased with the book cover, because it conveys a sense of the art and the vastness of our inner life. The amazing artist Pat Kelly, whose superb technique is en par with the old masters, allowed me to use her painting of the *Ramona Grasslands* as a background.
Graphic designer Scarlet Willette put the pieces together to create a truly stunning and striking cover. Thanks to Amber Sykes for providing the first draft of the cover.
Beta reader Lidia Rossner gave me valuable feed-back and marketing advice. She is a creative spirit, whose ideas just flow generously, when prompted.

Finally my sons Sebastian and Max always inspire me and keep me going. Aspiring screenwriter Max gave me two excellent pieces of advice that helped me finish *Private Universe* after struggling with it for years. He told me, "Mom, never let the truth get into the way of a good story". And: "Don't be afraid to feature a morally compromised main character." I followed his advice. It was a good one.

Part I

Microcosmic Traveler

Cornelia Feye

Prologue

"Our planet, our society, and we ourselves are built of star stuff."
Carl Sagan, *Cosmos*

Our bodies carry elements that go back to the birth of the universe. Every single atom in our bodies—the calcium in our bones, the carbon in our genes, the iron in our blood, the gold in our fillings— were created in a star billions of years ago. We live because stars died.

Astrophysicist, Peter de Grasse Tyson, explains that we are a walking galaxy of fossil stardust, originating from the big bang. For millennia, great minds of the East and West have believed that the entire drama of the universe repeats in our own bodies.

"In each atom of the realms of the universe, there exist vast oceans of world systems," declared the ancient Buddhist scriptures of the Great Flower Ornament.

In the 19th century, the German writer and thinker Johann Wolfgang von Goethe, pondered the connection between microcosm and macrocosm. "In the inside, there is also a universe." Search for the whole truth within, he suggested, so you may fathom the basic reality of the cosmos.

If we could understand our bodies and minds completely, these philosophers say, we might comprehend the entire universe. Unfortunately, it is difficult to reach this level of understanding. Often, we treat our bodies as we do our cars. We refuel and wash them and expect them to function without much complaining. We don't think about the inner workings of our bodies or the mechanics of our car engines until a pebble hits the windshield, or the red warning lights begin to blink

Chapter 1: The Power of Hair

"If my hair were shaved, my strength would leave me, and I would become as weak as any other man."
Samson and Delilah, Judges 16, *Old Testament*

February 1976:
The light of the last-quarter moon and a few distant stars struggled through the puffy cloud layer covering dark houses like a down blanket. The street called Filderstrasse had been quiet for hours. Squat multi-family homes with red tiled roofs and small windows had been built rapidly and without imagination in the recovering Germany of the 1960s. Bare lilac and berry bushes in the front yards fulfilled their purpose of separating the properties, rather than decorating the gardens. Orderly sidewalks, swept by housewives every Friday afternoon, glistened wet under the streetlights.

Inside their houses, the inhabitants slept deeply. Only the sound of pebbles pinging on a windowpane disrupted the quiet night.

Vega tried to ignore the noise, but the stones hit hard enough to damage the glass. The gravel's signal got louder and more persistent. There went another one. What if Vega's mother and brother woke up? What of the family living right underneath Vega's room? She imagined the lights going on and Mr. W getting up in his doubtlessly striped pajamas. What if he yelled out the window? Other sleeping burghers would awaken and then she'd be in deep trouble.

Vega carefully peeked through the curtains. She knew what the thrower of the pebbles wanted, and she had no intention of giving it to him. Tom grinned and looked up at the window. Of course, he'd seen the orange curtain move. He knew she was watching. The light of the street lantern reflected off his long mass of hair, which reached halfway down his back. That thick wavy hair first attracted Vega to him. It was one of the reasons she constantly forgive him—but that was much later.

Right now, she was furious. How dare he make such a racket? Just because she let him walk her home? Just because they missed the last tram? Did he expect her to let him in? Resigned, she pushed back the flimsy curtain and opened the window a crack.

"Shush, be quiet!"

"Let me in. I'll be very quiet," Tom said. His grin was wider now.

"Go home!"

"It will take me all night to walk home."

"I don't care. You figure it out."

He hesitated. Vega suspected that finally a small doubt had crossed his mind.

"When will I see you?" he asked.

"Friday. Go now."

"Friday," he said as he turned and walked off. The metal-tipped heels of his cowboy boots clattered loudly on the sidewalk of the empty suburban street. He didn't look back to Vega's six-family apartment building but only slowed for a moment to light a cigarette. The glow from his lighter outlined his tall silhouette. His tight jeans and black leather jacket didn't fit well into the quaint street scene. Tom didn't try to soften the noise of his bold footsteps. Although Vega was relieved to see him go, she knew that she would see him again. His pushy behavior annoyed her, but she sensed that this was just the beginning.

**

"Where are we going?" On Friday evening, Vega sat in the back of a taxicab.

Seated in the front seat next to the driver, Tom smoked a cigarette. He wore Levis with a denim shirt and had tucked his hair behind one ear, baring a silver earring. "It's a surprise," he said.

In the seventeen years of her life, Vega had never ridden in a taxi. She couldn't afford it, and neither could her parents. They went places using the streetcar, the bicycle, or they walked. Tom could not afford a taxi either, she was sure of that. But he liked irrational gestures, extravagant, and unreasonable. Taxis were part of his image.

He never drove—he was driven, had never even owned a car. His hair hung over the backrest and draped in front of her. So thick and wavy, she couldn't help herself—she had to touch it. Gently taking a handful of his mane, she let it slide through her fingers. It felt cool, soft, yet strong at the same time. One handful was not enough. His hair, not silky and pliable but slightly coarse and untamed like horsehair, was so abundant that her hands disappeared within its bulk.

Tom sat very still. The smoke from his cigarette hung suspended in midair. Unable to stop herself, Vega kept playing with his hair even though she knew she was crossing a threshold. Touching what should be left alone. Now, she was in danger of becoming entangled, as if she had stroked the fibers from a magic spider whose threads would draw her into a dangerous web—never to be released.

Tom turned toward her with a little smile. He understood what was happening and savored the magic of the moment, which stretched like a strand of his hair in her fingers.

Falling for Tom was Vega's offering to Samson's descendants: a surrender to the power of long hair.

**

The taxi dropped them off at an inner-city park. They planned to smoke a joint to enhance the experience of Tom's surprise, a Jethro Tull concert. Alas, they ended up staying on a park bench. Between drags, their hands and mouths explored each other. Tom clicked his little golden lighter again and again to relight the joint and to warm their hands. Vega had goose bumps on her arms, not just from the cold, but also from the charge they shared at each point of contact. The attraction drawing their lips and hands together was like opposing poles of a magnet—soothing but electrifying. A strange energy pulsed through Vega's veins. Was it Tom's presence or the joint they smoked? Tom was the most physical being she had ever met. And he seemed to know it. When he looked at her over half-closed eyelids, she felt lightheaded.

"Shouldn't we go to the concert?" Vega asked.

"Maybe in a little while. How is the concert hall?" Tom said lazily.

"You've never been inside?"

"No, I just moved here."

"From where?" Vega had never left her hometown except for short family vacations to Austria or Switzerland.

"I spent some time near Basel. And before that, I lived in Cologne for a while, in rehab. But I'm all good now."

Rehab? She had never met anybody who took hard drugs, let alone attended rehab. Vega imagined rehab as an intriguing place in the country populated by exotic, fascinating inmates dressed in black, discussing deep and existential problems. In contrast, her life was sheltered and predictable. She attended the local all-girls high school and existed in her small dysfunctional family of three, where nothing ever happened. Her divorced mother and younger brother led quiet lives. A little too quiet for Vega's taste. She felt stifled and craved adventure. Tom's life sounded exciting. Exactly what Vega was looking for.

She did not know it yet, but her infatuation would have extensive consequences – dramatic and destructive consequences.

The chill of the February night enveloped them. A white mist rose from the grass and appeared like a veil in the diffuse light of the street lamps. It mingled with their breath and the smoke from the joint, which hung in the air. Vega looked at the sky and unsuccessfully tried to find her namesake star in Lyra among the few celestial lights able to break through the spotty cloud cover. Almost full that night, the pale moon did not radiate a warm glow. Instead, it looked small and cold and very white. In German the moon is male, *der Mond*, because there is nothing soft or female about it. Vega thought it looked distant, no brighter than a small bulb in the cold night sky.

She did not mind the bareness of their surroundings, the barren branches of the birch trees and beech shrubbery. Tom held her tight, and she felt his body heat through his leather jacket. They sat close, sharing what little warmth they had, and thrust their hands into each other's pockets. Around them, swaths of smoke from their faintly glowing joints began to spin the fabric that became the foundation of their invisible fantasy. They sat suspended in their own private world. There, they ruled as king and queen, separated from the rest of humanity by a flexible, but durable membrane.

After missing the last tram and with the taxi money for the day already spent, they had to rely on their feet to carry them through the wet, empty streets. Stiff with cold, they entered a disco called Mousetrap. Inside, a warm, noisy, and busy space greeted them. They danced to loosen their arms and legs. Vega watched Tom move effortlessly like a large cat. She found herself swaying in unison with him, as if he were her puppeteer. She did not mind. Other dancers shared the floor with them, but the others seemed to be part of a large backdrop. Vega and Tom remained separate. They stayed untouched on their observation post. They were two three-dimensional creatures in an otherwise flat world.

Chapter 2: Doors of Perception

"By its very nature, every embodied spirit is doomed to suffer and to enjoy in solitude."
Aldous Huxley, *Doors of Perception*, 1954

Lisa, Vega's mother, lay in the dark on the narrow sofa that transformed into her bed at night. Lisa slept in the living room, leaving the two bedrooms to her children. Since the departure of her husband, she did not need her own room anymore. Or so she thought. She wanted to give Vega and her younger brother Daniel their own spaces. She hoped this would make them feel more comfortable at home. This strategy had not worked on her daughter. The green, glowing numbers of the alarm clock showed two o'clock in the morning, and Vega was still out. Lisa could not sleep until both of her children were safely in bed. She listened for noises outside from footsteps or passing cars, but all was quiet. The last tram had come and gone, without her daughter.

This flat represented Lisa's safe haven, and she could not understand why this should not be true for her children. Since their father had left, she had struggled to provide a comfortable and healthy place to come home to.

Streetlight shining through the curtains faintly illuminated the dark outlines of the furniture; her rocking chair by the tiled oven, a round dining table, a shel   h books, and a television. The cheaply built post-war ap   )uilding had low ceilings and walls so thin she could hear th   or flush his toilet. From a narrow hallway, doors opened or   bedrooms, the living room, a small bathroom, and a tiny kitc   ch was just big enough for one person. Brown speckled   covered the floors, and two layers of curtains hung in the v   one for daytime and a heavier one for nights.

Lisa felt proud of this apartment, the only place she could call her own. Her father had given it to her. He predicted her marriage would fail, and it had. Her husband left her for a younger woman even though Lisa was fourteen years his junior. Now she clung to this place. She had nobody to talk to because even her church had turned its back on her. Catholic marriages are forever, so as a divorced woman her congregation shunned her, no matter that she was not at fault.

Lisa heard the key in the front door, and careful footsteps tiptoed in. She sighed with relief. Vega tried to close the door quietly.

"I'm awake," Lisa called. "Come sit with me."

Vega entered the dark room and sat down on the floor next to her mother's bed. She listened patiently to anoth[er of] her mother's wartime stories. Lisa had been evacuate[d to the] countryside from the heavily bombed city. She was separated [from he]r family and placed with German farmers, who took her in bu[t abuse]d the city girl. They had made Lisa work in the fields, some[times un]til she fainted. They had even intercepted her letters to [her m]other, so her complaints had never been heard.

"One day I saw my school burn down. It ha[d been h]it by a stray bomb. We kids were so happy and ran around th[e buildin]g laughing. We did not understand the danger. We only kne[w we hate]d school and our teachers, and now we didn't have to go back." Lisa said with a little laugh. She hesitated and her smile disappeared. "I was never a good student and never finished high school. I feel ashamed that I know so little."

"Your grandfather was a POW in a Siberian prison camp in Russia. Your grandmother lived in a bombed-out house with three small children, together with refugees flooding in from the East. My mother had nothing to feed us, so one day I stole potatoes that fell off a truck when it hit one of the many potholes." Lisa was proud of this incident when she had provided food for her little family.

Vega listened, patted her mother's hand, then crept away to her own bed without saying where she had been or what she had been doing. Lisa finally fell asleep.

**

Vega felt sorry for her mother and wanted to show her a good time. Once, at least, she did. In the summer of 1976, Vega owned a little, gray Volkswagen beetle, fourth-hand with 130.000 km on its back. She called it Little Feet, after the Rock Band, and painted red and black footprints all over its roof. It looked as if a small army of elves with muddy feet had trampled across. One Saturday morning, Vega packed her mother, a picnic basket, and their bathing suits into the car. Lisa had never learned to drive, and Vega did not tell her where they were going.

"It's a surprise," she said. She had learned a thing or two from Tom.

They drove out of the city into the nearby woods to a secret spot, which was known only to Vega and several thousand other people. Surrounded by dense beech trees, a lake had been created by using dredged-out sand and rocks for construction projects. Grass and moss grew on the wooded banks of the gravel pit filled with water.

After driving on small roads winding through the forest, Vega and Lisa found a peaceful spot by the pond and put on their bathing suits. Mother and daughter launched into the water to swim all the way across. They took their time covering the distance, and talked, while they swam. On land, Lisa was timid and anxious. In the water, she felt relaxed. When they reached the middle of the lake, green water surrounded them on all sides. Along the distant rim, the shady surface reflected the foliage of dark trees. People splashed close to the banks, but nobody else was venturing out this far. The water's soft texture touched the skin of their legs, invisible within the densely green pond.

Vega and Lisa kept floating along, their strokes becoming easier and more fluid. Reaching the other shore, they sat on the slippery slope in the sun, wet and out of breath.

"We did it. We swam all the way across," Lisa said and smiled proudly at her daughter.

"We did it together," Vega agreed.

The outing with her mother remained an exception. Usually, Vega left Lisa alone in the apartment with her grief, her helplessness, and her misery. With Tom, she silenced her guilty conscience with another joint. She did not want to be her mother's confidante, did not want the responsibility for her happiness. Vega was tired of hearing about the war that was over long before she was born. She wanted nothing to do with her mother's past and the sins of her elders.

When the tentacles of her mother's trauma wrapped themselves around Vega's legs too tightly, she ripped them off determined not to let them tie her down. She felt sorry for Lisa, and her whole generation who had been sacrificed to the crazy vision of one madman. But Vega was young and brutal in her rush to fulfill her own desires and to feed her own demons, without holding onto the monsters emerging from her mother's past.

Chapter 3: Vertical Time

"This is how one ought to see! This is how things really are!"
Aldous Huxley, *Doors of Perception*, 1954

Tom and Vega frequently returned to the forest lake. The lake appeared to be transformed into a jade pool of life after they had taken LSD. Lying on its verdant shores, Vega noticed each water droplet turned into a crystal, reflecting all the colors and transmitting a rainbow to those who had eyes to see, meaning people on acid like herself.

Vega loved floating in the water, her face turned toward the sun, listening to the crackling stillness of the underwater sphere. Her body had no weight, and her hair grew longer and longer until each individual strand became a sentient sensor, reaching down into the furthest depth of the lake, tickling the bottom-dwelling creatures into action, connecting her with each and every living being, making them all one great organism. When she dove into the lake, she thought she could stay there, stop moving, gently sink to the bottom, and dissolve. She became green. She did not need air.

Somehow, she broke the surface again. Tom must have pushed her up, providing her with a tentative link to the real world.

"What do you want? Let me be. I am green-ness," Vega snapped at him. Then she forgot about the green-ness and became content to lie on the shore next to him, observing vertical time.

People usually experience time in a linear fashion. One moment follows the next. Events, thoughts, and observations happen one at a time, in an orderly sequence. During vertical time, each second is splintered up into a myriad incidents all happening at once.

Simultaneously, a dragonfly flaps its blue metallic wings while hovering over the surface of the lake; a drop of water, lodged in

Vega's belly button evaporates with an almost inaudible *plop*, spraying minuscule rainbow-colored droplets onto her skin; sound waves from the voices of playing children reach them from the other side of the lake; rays of sunlight warm her wet cheeks; a flickering shadow from a branch overhead falls across her eyes; a strand of wet hair slides across her forehead; Tom lies besides her, their bodies slightly touching at the thighs; a ripple disrupts the smooth surface of the lake, extending farther and farther outward from its origin, from where a fish burped; a daisy, with a perfectly round yellow center surrounded by white petals, trembles in an almost unnoticeable breeze.

"The daisy is perfectly round," Vega said to Tom.

"The number Π measures the area of a circle and it extends into infinity," he answered.

A fly descended onto Vega's knee, lifting one leg and rubbing it against another in incredibly slow motion, looking at her with multi-faceted, compound eyes.

"A fly has the eyes of an alien," Vega told Tom.

"The pyramids in Egypt contain passageways ascending toward Sirius in the constellation Orion. They point to the cosmic origin of the aliens, who built them," he said.

A pliable blade of grass bends and scratches her skin lightly; it penetrates the surface of her body and causes cracks to run along her calves, covering the surface of her skin with a network of veins that spread rapidly; becomes a brittle surface, covered with a web of lines; underneath that skin, there is an indestructible core at the center of her being, like a multi-facetted shiny diamond.

Vertical time is like a column of moments, comparable to earth-core drillings geologists bore out of rock to demonstrate the various layers of sediment that have accumulated one on top of the other over millennia. Vertical time goes deep but only takes a fraction of a second, Vega realized. She knew her world would never look the same again. How can anybody with an ordinary mind perceive all this? How much do we miss each second, when we go about our daily business? Vertical time is the right way to view the world. Linear perception barely scratches the surface of reality.

Vega now saw the true nature of time. She knew she could not explain vertical time to her mother. Tom knew too, so at least one other person shared the vertical reality with her. The faces of some of the other bathers started to look grotesque as if they had been created with dough and their maker had pinched them too hard in the wrong places, pulling their foreheads too wide and making their cheeks too thin. Fortunately, Tom's face looked the same. He didn't even have cracks running through his skin like she did. Maybe I'm peeling, Vega thought, and have to shed this skin.

"I think we should go," Tom said. "It's getting late."

"But only a minute has passed," Vega protested.

He smiled and started packing up their belongings.

"Am I driving?" Vega asked with alarm.

She always drove. Tom did not drive, and neither did Vega's mother or brother. The only other driver in her family, her father, had left. And his leaving was all Vega's fault—or so she believed, because as a teenager she assumed the universe revolved around her.

**

Vega's father felt comfortable b[ehind t]he steering wheel with Lisa frequently telling him what a go[od driv]er he was. The driver's seat gave him confidence and contr[ol he wa]s otherwise lacking in his life. As the only driver in the family[, he pic]ked up Vega and her brother from school on Saturdays a[nd dr]opped off his whole family at church on Sundays.

A flashback took Vega to one [...] [af]ternoon, after she had just turned seventeen. Her father had p[icked h]er up from a friend's house. She sat next to him in the p[assenge]r seat, sulking. He wanted to know too much about her life, and tried to interfere despite his frequent absences from the family.

"You should be nicer to your mother," he said. "She is complaining that you are not listening to her. You are not telling her anything."

"You should be nicer to her," Vega snapped. "You should tell her what *you* are doing. Do you think we don't notice what's going on?"

"What do you think is going on?" he asked calmly.

"You really think we don't know that you have a girlfriend? You think we don't notice that you and Mom can't stand each other anymore?" Vega raged.

"What do you mean?" He looked at her, slowed down, and

drove around the block. Rain pelted the windshield.

"I mean that you can't fool us. We know you have an affair. We've known for years. We know you don't spend your spa retreats and separate vacations alone."

"How do you know all this?" He seemed more interested than defensive.

"It's obvious, isn't it? Someone embroidered your handkerchiefs with your monogram. Mom would never do anything like that," Vega continued.

"What about your brother?" He didn't even deny anything.

"What about him? Do you think he enjoys living with your lies? You come home and make a half-baked effort at family life. We can't stand all the tension anymore."

"Your mother and I wanted to protect you," he said quietly.

"Protect us from what? Ruined Christmases? Unbearable holidays? The mood in the house is so rotten you can smell it on the street. And Mom is so bitter she can barely eat."

"You really feel this way? We've tried to give you an unbroken home."

"Well, it didn't work, did it? The atmosphere is so poisonous, it's eating me up. It's better, when you're not there."

"You think I should leave?" He gave Vega his full attention, driving around and around the same block. The windshield wipers squeaked back and forth, attempting to keep the rain at bay.

"It would be better for all of us. We should face the truth, instead living a lie."

Vega spoke with moral outrage. She naively took the high-road, practically begging her father to walk out on her family.

"How long have you known?" He seemed relieved that he didn't have to pretend anymore.

"Oh, please. There have been so many signs. The trips, the red underwear you brought back from your solo trip to Spain. You gave yourself away many times."

He sounded delighted now. "So you've known for a while." The possibility of getting away from this family and the oppressive apartment had just opened up to him.

"You want to get away. Just like me," it dawned on her.

That moment was the end of her parents' marriage.

If she had been able to imagine the grief and deep loss this separation would cause her mother and her younger brother, she might have taken back the conversation in the car with her father that rainy day. She could have held her tongue. But Vega only thought about herself. Like her father, she was the center of her own universe. For one instance, one instance only, they both wanted the same thing: to get away. It did not turn out well for either one of them.

**

On their way back from the lake, a deep dip plunged the road down into a valley. It looked like a take-off runway. Screaming at the top of her lungs, Vega gunned the Volkswagen down the steep incline and back up the other side.

"Intergalactic brothers, here we come," she yelled to the universe.

The road rose straight out of the dip, and Little Feet's old engine, even with the gas pedal jammed down to the floor, didn't go anywhere fast. The beetle came out of the dip with a little jump and a thud, landing on the wrong side of the road.

"We almost took off," Vega cheered.

"Maybe we should take another break before we get to the freeway," Tom suggested. He obviously did not want to risk another close call.

"Okay, why not," Vega said.

They stopped in Bebenhausen, a small Cistercian abbey in the early gothic style typical in Southern Germany. Nestled in a valley of green meadows and fertile fields, the abbey was surrounded by the hills of the Schönbuch forest. By the time they arrived, Vega could still feel the acid soar through her nervous system. She hadn't eaten in hours. Her head seemed to expand, almost ready to pop from all the sensory input happening in the vertical time zone.

Tom and Vega drank some water and nibbled a few crackers they found on the backseat. They entered the monastery and sat down on a bench in the shade of the ancient stone arcade surrounding the cloister garden. Looking at foxgloves and coltsfoot through the vaulted arches calmed Vega down. Snapdragons swayed peacefully in orderly beds between the slate pathways crossing the Garth. Stocky Romanesque columns with simple Doric capitals framed the outlook where Tom and Vega sat.

Cistercian monks, who once tended the flowers and vegetables there, had dedicated their lives to extraordinary simplicity and strict adherence to the rules of the order, based on the balance between *vita activa* and *vita contemplativa*, work and prayer. Surrounded by the covered cloister walk on all four sides, the central Garth connected the dormitory, the scriptorium, and the chapel. To get from one place to the other, the monks had to walk through there several times each day.

Sitting on the cold bench, contemplating the slightly overgrown garden illuminated by the golden, fading light of dusk, Vega felt the roots of her vertical time sensors extend further and further back into the past. Back to a time when seven times a day, the stone floor tiles had been worn down by shuffling feet of monks on their way to vigils, matins, lauds, terce, sext, vespers, and compline.

"Can you hear the singing?" she whispered to Tom.

He nodded.

The air flickered faintly as twilight descended. The sound of sandaled feet, accompanied by the rustling of rough robes, approached from the shadows of the cloister walk. A humming sound floated in the air ahead of the movement now becoming noticeable to their right.

"*Gloria patri et filio et spiritui sancto*, sicut *erat in principo, et nunc, et semper et in saecula saeculorum, Kyrie eleison, Christe eleison…*"

A musty smell arose with a slight shift in the air, as twelve monks approached, dressed in gray, stained robes, simple sandals on their calloused feet, tonsured heads exposed. The evening was still too warm for hoods. Hands pressed together, fingers extended straight toward heaven.

Tom and Vega froze, morphed into stone columns like those that had witnessed the *Kyrie Eleison* long ago. The Cistercian monks passed their bench close enough for robes to brush against Tom and Vega's legs. Unaware of their guests, the monks remained enraptured in prayer to God.

Vega hoped He heard them and acknowledged them somehow.

The vision disappeared as suddenly as they had come. The magical moment dissolved.

**

Vega and Tom heard a truck rumble by on the road outside the monastery. Someone slammed a car door. The spell broken, their bottoms suddenly felt cold on the stone bench. The sun had set. They looked at each other, astonished to find themselves in this particular spot here and now, back in the 20th century. They returned to their car. Weary and sober they drove silently into the deepening darkness.

Vega thought about their day. What a journey it had been, from medieval chanting monks, to the origin of the Egyptian pyramids. Then, home to a dreary post-war apartment and the accusing questions of a suffering mother.

"Where were you?"

What was Vega supposed to say?

"I floated in a lake becoming one with the bottom dwelling creatures, and later counted the flaps of a dragonfly's wings? I sat in a late 11th century monastery listening to Cistercian monks sing the Kyrie Eleison?"

She could not face her mother or the apartment. Vega no longer felt part of that world. She snuck out and only came back long after her mother was asleep.

Chapter 4: Stairway to Heaven

"There's a lady who's sure all that glitters is gold, and she's buying a stairway to heaven." Led Zeppelin, 1971

The mother of Tom's friend Pete worked at a hospital. She had gotten Tom and Pete jobs there, which was pure irony. Both had just been released from drug rehab. It was like employing kids in a candy store.

Pete looked like Tom's opposite: short and wiry, with close-cropped frizzy blond hair. Pete seemed tense and tightly wound, while Tom was laid back. Pete had an introverted and earnest personality, while Tom didn't take anything seriously.

Their hospital jobs came with the fringe benefit of attic bedrooms overlooking the roofs of Stuttgart's inner city. The rooms lay next to each other on the fifth floor of an old, pre-war brick house built into the hills. Stairways with wooden banisters, polished by hands over decades, led up there. The rooms were off-limits to visitors, particularly girls, but Tom and Vega learned to avoid the steps that creaked the loudest. Tom's room became their home base—a safe place. It turned out to be the only haven they would ever have.

Cut into the slanted ceiling, a skylight opened and allowed them to stick their heads out to glance over the red, shingled roofs of the city. The attic became their favorite lookout, a nest high above the rooftops. Here they could listen to the music of The Doors and Led Zeppelin, make love, and smoke pot. The smoke of their joint slowly drifted to the ceiling while the riffs from Peter Frampton's guitar rose and dipped.

Even though Tom possessed the presence and look of a rock star, he was a lazy musician who picked on his guitar more out of boredom than inspiration. Vega did not care. She just loved to watch the muscles on his shoulders ripple and his biceps flex.

Vega wanted nothing more than to stay with Tom all night, fall asleep, and wake up in his arms. But she had to go home and go back to school the next morning.

**

When Vega walked the hallways at school the next day, she felt as disconnected as watching a movie. It became harder and harder to come back to reality after she had been with Tom on the other side. She tried to straddle the two worlds she inhabited. Tom's world always won. She didn't want to share her mother's gray existence. On the other side, she discovered an exciting life with Tom, and a whole culture of music and art. Visions from her subconscious began to bubble up from the depths. The world looked new and exciting, though also overwhelming. She wanted to enter this world, but without Tom as her guide she felt lost.

She couldn't talk to anybody about her experiences. None of her girlfriends at school understood.

"What happened to you? You look like a ghost," Vega's friend Isabella said as they walked to lunch.

"I am a ghost," Vega answered. "I don't really live here anymore."

"Where do you live then?" Isabella wanted to know.

"I live in the vertical time zone," Vega answered.

"You make no sense, Vega. You are frying your brain with all those drugs you're taking."

"No, on the contrary, I now see how things really are. You are the one who doesn't understand." Vega argued.

"You're right, I don't understand what you are doing to yourself." Isabella shook her head.

The girls in Vega's class avoided her as if she carried an infectious disease. The boys looked at her with a mixture of disgust and fascination. They did not dare to go where she had gone. Vega bore their contempt and her isolation like a badge of honor. She wore it with pride, like the long, black Moroccan cloak she had found at a flea market. It separated her from the boring, unenlightened people.

Tom was the only other inhabitant on their particular kind of planet. He understood. Vega trusted him to lead her through the confusion of growing up in a time of great changes.

Chapter 5: Round Trip Ticket

"She was a day tripper, one way ticket, yeah. It took me so long to find out!" John Lennon and Paul McCartney, 1965

Soon after their outing to Bebenhausen, Vega and Tom lay on Tom's mattress and listened to The Grateful Dead. The sounds stretched, and the bedroom expanded and contracted and became an organic womb, a breathing organism. Rays of sunlight fell through the slanted window creating a veil of light. A sparrow flew over the skylight so slowly that Vega thought it would fall out of the sky. Jerry Garcia sang about a friend of the devil, who was also a friend of his.

Vega stared at a poster on the wall of a red face, advertising Camel cigarettes. Without warning it became the personification of the devil luring her into hell. The peaceful feeling of a second ago inverted itself like an inside-out glove and turned oppressive, claustrophobic. The red face came alive, jeering, and threatening. It beckoned and mesmerized her, so she could not look at anything else. She struggled to resist, but the devil won. His face turned into a mask, extended out from the wall, became three-dimensional, and stretched close to her face with a triumphant sneer. She tried to turn away, tried to pull back, but her muscles could not obey her, and she lay paralyzed on the mattress within reach of the devil's face. He extended his neck farther to capture and suck her into his realm.

"Help me," she screamed inside, but no sound came out of her mouth. As she tried to gain control over her body, her limbs got away from her, began to melt and turn liquid. Give me something to hold onto, she pleaded silently, then looked up at the ceiling and at the table next to the mattress, but those too would not stay still, her surroundings morphed and buckled. She realized they had eyes staring back at her. You are a table, stay still, she tried to command, but the table's eye just widened as if to mock her. Make it stop, make it stop, she prayed, but the devil sneered, the eyes mocked, and she had become an inanimate object in a world gone livid.

She saw Tom's face above her but was completely cut off from him. Please help, she pleaded. My life and soul depend on it. But she could not cry out, could not move, could not communicate. She wanted to lift her hands, to reach out to him, but they were stuck at her side, bound, even without rope.

The visions pulled her into a bottomless abyss. Her mind drifted unconnected to her body, which she could not control. It was no longer hers. Her soul was about to be taken from her. She thought that this is what hell must feel like.

She tried to remember the vertical time and its peaceful feelings, but she was stuck in the terror, away from grace, separated from the rest of the universe and alone in a hell of her own creation. Wandering through the circles of hell, an hour seemed like an eternity.

Tom sat her down on the sofa and himself on a chair beside her. Close, but not facing her. Looking at him could have terrified her further. Instead he turned his back to her, so Vega only saw his hair falling down halfway to his waist. While she stammered and whimpered, he ignored her panic and remained calm.

He played the Beatles' *Sgt. Pepper's Lonely Heart Club Band* record on the stereo. Slowly, the sounds penetrated and trickled into Vega's awareness—peaceful, harmless, and benevolent. The membrane that had isolated her in a private jail of horror became permeable. As sudden as the horror had begun, the scale tilted, and she found herself in a Sergeant Pepper candy land. Cartoon-shaped words from Beatles songs floated in the air like bubbles, spelling out "Love" and "Glove" and "Submarine" in pink, yellow, and baby blue.

Tom had led her in and out of hell.

**

Going back to school the next morning, Vega realized she had been lucky to return to the harmless reality of high school. After her journey to hell, the classroom appeared like a two dimensional background screen. Her classmates looked like cut-out paper dolls. How could she ever talk to them again? They had no idea of the strange worlds existing right between their eyes.

**

It was an act of rebellion against her father that Vega even bothered going to school anymore. He had suggested she quit school after 10th grade and start working for the postal service, as a mail delivery woman. Mainly, he argued, she could take advantage of the excellent pension plan. Because she was a girl, he assumed, she would get married anyway, and a lengthy education was therefore a waste. Out of defiance, Vega insisted on completing high school.

Every morning, she walked to school through a small park with casually planted trees around the borders and a large expanse of grass in the middle. Crossing the park, she usually lit her first joint. One day, the dose must have been too large, or the fresh, black Afghan hashish was too strong. While entering the hallways of her girls-only school, Vega could feel the chemical fill her head first, and then slowly drain all the blood from her brain. As her circulation collapsed, she observed her surroundings turn gradually grainier and grayer, like the image of an early 50s television set. The picture went from color to black-and-white, and dissolved completely, and she blacked out.

Vega found herself lying on a cot in the nurse's office. The nurse explained that circulation problems were common in girls Vega's age especially if they had low blood pressure.

"You girls are growing so fast, the body can't quite keep up," she said.

Happy to just rest there for a while, Vega grunted agreement. Again, her increasing drug use went undetected, and her journey to the underworld continued without interruption.

Chapter 6: Beyond Good and Evil

"The Christian church has left nothing untouched by its depravity; it has turned every value into worthlessness, and every truth into a lie, and every integrity into baseness of soul." Friedrich Nietzsche, *The Anti-Christ, 1888*

A highlight of Vega's high school education was a philosophy class, which replaced religion instructions. The class gave her an opportunity to write about Friedrich Nietzsche, her favorite philosopher. Vega's teacher regarded her a little strangely, when he returned a paper she had written titled, *Nietzsche and the Anti-Christ*, but he gave her an A anyway.

Nietzsche's anger against the church and his fury in expressing it appealed to Vega. After all, the Catholic Church had dropped Vega's mother after her divorce. Before that, Lisa had spent a lifetime in faithful worship. Vega had endured countless Sundays at her side, kneeling on hard church benches through endless sermons and uninspired services. But Lisa had failed the holy sacrament of matrimony. Of course, if God was an old man, the way he is generally depicted, He would place the entire burden of keeping the marriage contract onto the shoulders of women. With the church community out of the picture for support, the ball fell into Vega's court. She felt terribly guilty for causing this divorce and now for not being able to console her mother sufficiently. She was furious with the church. Why couldn't they comfort Lisa and give Vega some space to lead her own life?

**

At age nine, Vega had experienced her own disappointment with the church. It was the year of her First Holy Communion. Her mother told her, with rare solemnity, that there were really just two important events in the life of a woman: her first communion and her wedding.

"Both are of course related," Lisa explained, "because at the communion, we become little brides of Christ, and at the wedding we become the bride of our husband."

Lisa made sure to celebrate the occasion in grand style. She designated a large bolt of cream colored silk, brought from China by her grandfather, for the communion dress. After studying countless dress patterns, Vega finally chose an elegant, simple design, with a flaring skirt and matching jacket. She went to several fittings with the tailor and felt important and proud.

The grand day arrived, and Vega was ready in body and soul: she had been absolved of her meager sins during first confession; put on her beautiful dress with matching jacket; and in her curled hair sat a white silk tiara decorated with little pearls. The preparations had been elaborate, and Vega's expectations were high. When the priest finally laid the bland, white wafer containing the body of Christ onto her tongue for the first time, she did not dare to bite down. How could she chew on God? She just let it sit on her tongue and waited for the sacred encounter. All the preparation, all the anticipation had lead up to this moment. Surely, she would now be able to experience the presence of the son of God in some profound way. Surely, something important was about to take place. But nothing happened. The wafer just stuck to the top of her pallet like paper, and she had to peel it off with her tongue, after which it finally melted in her mouth. Kneeling in the pew, tears of disappointment stung her eyes.

Lisa enjoyed the day as if it was her daughter's wedding. Of course, Vega could not tell her about her disillusionment. It would have broken Lisa's heart, and Vega was not prepared to admit her shame and failure. Surely, she had done something wrong, which was what prevented her from feeling the presence of God.

After church, the whole extended family and many friends came to Vega's apartment. A great horseshoe-shaped table had been set up, laden with white linen, good china, and cakes and delicacies. Their Hungarian neighbor had baked for days and brought cream-filled pastry puffs in the shape of swans, many layered coffee cakes decorated like big baskets, baking sheets of plum cake topped with whipped cream, and delicate apple tarts in ruffled round forms.

Vega's grandfather was the guest of honor because Lisa had sworn a solemn oath to him. She would bring up her children as Catholics, and now she could make good on her promise. Lisa hoped to soften her father's opposition to her marriage with a man who was not only fourteen years her senior, but also, to the whole family's disgrace, a protestant. The patriarch sat at the head of the table and looked pleased. He approved of Vega's dress, gave her a watch as a communion present, and patted her hair. Vega admired her tall and powerful grandfather, but she felt unworthy of his generosity.

Her aunts, and uncle, and cousins drank coffee and juice and consumed large amounts of cake. They chatted at a high volume and seemed to enjoy themselves. For the entire day, Vega felt like an imposter. Everybody celebrated her communion with Christ, but she had failed by not feeling even the least bit of God's presence.

Church was never the same again for Vega. The altar boys grew up but were not replaced. The old ladies who had decorated the church and the streets with flower carpets died, but no younger women took over the task. The organ was out of tune, and the plaster Madonna in the side chapel and her fake-gold-leaf adorned son in front of his cross, looked sadder and smaller than Vega remembered them. She stopped going to confession because she had real sins to reveal. As soon as she was old enough, she left the church by making an appointment at the mayor's office in the town center to be released.

Lisa begged Vega not to tell her grandfather. It would have added another failure to Lisa's life; a fallen granddaughter after a failed marriage might have killed her father.

**

Vega was through with Christianity. Nietzsche validated her anger with organized religion and justified her move beyond good and evil. She did not want to lead a life like her mother's, stifled by guilt and the inability to live up to church standards. Vega wanted to make her own rules and live life by her own standards. If she made a mistake, she would deal with it and not depend on the church for forgiveness. Hell could not frighten her into submission. Under her desk at school, Vega kept a pocketbook edition of *Thus Spoke Zarathustra* and read it during boring French lessons. With her friend Isabella as a kindred spirit, she memorized whole paragraphs of Nietzsche's books, and they recited them to each other. Nietzsche's writings made perfect sense to Vega because she related to his outrage. He did not think in a linear fashion but instead created thoughts full of poetry. In his writing, Vega found affirmation for her tumultuous soul and validation for her rejection of religion.

Chapter 7: Twilight

"There is a fifth dimension, beyond that which is known to man. It is a dimension as vast as space and as timeless as infinity. It is the middle ground between light and shadow, between science and superstition, and it lies between the pit of man's fears and the summit of his knowledge. This is the dimension of imagination. It is an area which we call the Twilight Zone". Rod Sterling

On a warm September evening in 1976, Vega rang the doorbell to Tom's room, but nobody answered. They had planned to walk downtown and spend the evening together. Pete did not answer either. Vega waited on the stoop while other inhabitants of the house passed her on their way home from work. In the twilight, the last rays of the setting sun lingered in the sky. The first street lanterns, store signs, and living room lamps began to flicker. The lights of the city below created a shimmering carpet of sparkling colors, imitating the stars above.

Something was wrong. Where was Tom? He had never stood her up. Slowly the cold night air crept up her back from the stone stoop, and she felt locked out and excluded from the warmth of the lit rooms she could see in the surrounding apartment buildings, where people sat at supper tables.

Worried, cold, and disappointed Vega went back home. Had something happened to Tom? The telephone number of Pete's mother Martha was listed in the phone book, and when Vega called she answered right away.

"Tom and Pete have been arrested. They were caught stealing barbiturates from the hospital medical supply closet," she reported wearily.

Vega felt the news like a blow to her chest. Her heart pounded.

"Apparently this has been going on for a while." Pete's mother sighed. It was not the first time that her efforts toward a new life for Pete had collapsed.

Vega shook herself out of her shock. "We have to find them. We have to get them out!"

"They have their court hearings tomorrow," Pete's mother answered in a tired voice. "They'll have to spend the night in jail."

"We'll go in the morning," Vega insisted. "We will get them out."

"We can give it a try," she agreed not sounding very hopeful.

**

Pete's mother Martha lived within walking distance from Vega's apartment in a part of the suburb where residential streets turned into an industrial zone. She lived in a trailer next to a manufacturing plant. Both Martha and Vega had taken the day off. Martha's face showed deep lines underneath graying hair. She wore a green blazer with shiny elbows. Vega liked her warm smile and kind welcome. They chatted while they took the tram downtown.

"Pete has been in and out of rehab and prison for seven years," she told Vega. "It is getting more and more difficult to find a job for him. He never had a father, you know. It has made life hard for him."

And for you, Vega thought and felt sorry for her.

Their search started at the police station nearest to the hospital.

"Yes," said the officer on duty. "We have records of the arrest. The defendants have been transferred to the central detention facility in the Haldenstrasse."

As they made their way from one Federal building to another, Pete's mother seemed to enjoy her day out.

"It is fun to walk through the city with you." She smiled. "I get a kick out of the way men stare at you."

Her words surprised Vega because she had not noticed anything, being so preoccupied with finding the defendants. Vega still felt like the awkward adolescent with disproportionately long, skinny legs and acne. The fact that she had grown into a slim seventeen year old, with long blond hair, was still new to her. She wore tight bellbottom jeans and a sleeveless jeans vest as a top. Now that Pete's mom had mentioned it, Vega noticed appreciating glances from passing men on the Königstrasse, the main shopping street in the center of town.

This pedestrian zone of the inner city had been hastily rebuilt after being bombed to rubble during the war. A patchwork of 50s and 60s concrete buildings had been erected as quickly and cheaply as possible, without regard for aesthetics. They now accommodated businesses, shops, and offices. People here went about their tasks efficiently and without pleasure.

The low-security federal building, Haldenstrasse, located in a side street off the main boulevard, was one of the few remaining pre-war structures and had a facade of darkened, rough-hewn limestone. They climbed the dark stairways, prepared for yet another desk cluttered with files in front of another federally employed clerk referring them yet to another agency. After passing floors filled with offices, interrogation cells, and hearing rooms, they reached the top landing. Doors had been left open to catch the breeze on a hot Indian summer day. They could see through a whole flight of rooms to the window at the end of the floor. In the farthest of these rooms, Vega saw a figure sitting on a wooden chair. His back was turned toward her. He wore a blue-jeans shirt, and his thick brown hair hung down over the backrest of the office chair. Tom.

As if on cue, he turned around slightly and looked at her with a crooked, half-apologetic smile, an expression she would see often in the months to come. She had found him. Vega felt relieved, excited, and happy, but as she looked more closely at his face covered with stubble from a night spent in jail, she also realized that things were not going to be all right.

The police released Tom and Pete on bail because they were employed. Pete's mom and Vega could take them home. Except, neither of them had a job to go back to anymore.

**

Vega had to go back to school, and when she arrived in class the next day, she could not believe that life seemed to go on just as usual. Everybody looked so normal and unperturbed.

Don't you understand? Vega wanted to scream at them. A catastrophe has just happened. My whole world is collapsing!

But everybody remained as indifferent as always. Their greatest worries were about which grade they got on the math test, what to have for lunch, and how to spend the evening. The students deliberately avoided Vega in the hallways. They must have noticed her alienation, and didn't want to have anything to do with her. So, although she felt like screaming inside, she just continued silently attending her classes.

Pete's mother, good-natured to a fault, took Pete and Tom into her own house. Now, Tom shared a room with Pete within walking distance of Lisa's apartment.

Without a job, Tom had a lot of time on his hands. Every afternoon when Vega returned from school, he visited. Strangely and fortunately, Vega's mother tolerated Tom. His gentleness triggered her maternal instincts. She saw the lost soul in him—a boy who had to be saved.

**

A few days later, Vega and Tom sat in her room on the white shaggy rug and listened to the Beatles on the turntable. They burned incense, in their little bubble of music and dimmed lights, hoping Vega's mother would not burst in on them. Tom talked about his childhood in a small town on the Rhine. He talked about his parents, his rehabilitation efforts, and how he had started taking drugs. Vega felt preoccupied and tired; she thought about her schoolwork, and about the final high school year ahead. Since Tom had nothing else to do, visiting Vega became the main occupation of his day. For her, being in her bedroom was not as fascinating as Tom's attic room, nor was sitting on her orange beanbag and talking about Tom's past. She had to start thinking about her future.

"One day," he said, sensing that her thoughts had wandered, "you will remember these afternoons, and how we sat here telling each other everything about our lives." It sounded as if their lives were almost over. They had lost their magic and desperately tried to win it back. Of course, the only way they knew how was with drugs. Tom talked often about his time before rehab, when he took the strongest escape mechanism of all—heroin. The drug occupied more and more space in his mind the longer he floated in limbo without anything constructive to do. Heroin slowly took over.

Vega could feel them drifting apart. She realized that she did not understand that aspect of his life. She would do anything to retain their special bond. If she wanted to keep Tom, she would have to follow him down that path.

Chapter 8: The Great Forest

"Mixed feelings, when he entered the forest for the first time. Delight and oppression and what the romantics labeled "Nature Feeling". The wonderful pleasure of breathing freely in open space, and simultaneously anguish at being imprisoned all around by hostile trees. Inside and outside at once, free and captive." Max Ernst, 1926-27, about his first visit to the forest at age three.

The Black Forest began not far from Vega's hometown, but the woods of the Schönbuch, a mixed forest of pines and deciduous trees, stood practically right outside her door. The beeches and elms wove a luminous semi-transparent foliage roof in the spring. During the height of summer, deep-green leaves provided a cool and shady place to rest and walk. In the fall, orange, brown, dark-red leaves, and the yellow of the birch trees glowed against grey skies. And in winter, the pine trees carried their snowcaps with dignity.

Tom and Vega could still escape to the sanctuary of the Schönbuch forest after Tom's life had collapsed. Its tall tree trunks rose like columns of a natural cathedral where rays of sunlight filtered through gaps in the leaf cover as if through stained glass windows. Shadows sprinkled and flecked yellow patches and patterns onto the forest floor. Lighter than the dense imposing pines of the Black Forest, the Schönbuch felt like being inside and outside at once. They walked under its low branches, through intimate rooms whose floors were made of soft carpets of fallen leaves, and velvety moss-covered cushions of stones. The forest became their refuge after losing the attic room overlooking the city.

Despite its enchantment, the forest remained a wild place. They got lost several times amidst threatening sounds of nature. They once encountered an orange fox who noiselessly appeared ten-feet away. They stood frozen. Creature stared at human. Human stared at creature, each with fascination tinged by fear. Then the fox disappeared as quietly as he had come.

**

Vega saw a painting in her art class at school that captured her feelings precisely. The surrealist artist Max Ernst was fascinated with the forest, leading him to dedicate over a hundred of his paintings to that environment. One of the series, entitled *The Great Forest,* from 1927, resembles a fortress consisting of tree trunks in a partially fossilized stage. Some of the trees are in the process of falling over, others have dense foliage still attached. A central tree trunk resembles a totem pole presiding over its crumbling brothers. The great forest is actually a rather small grove. An olive green light emanates from the strangest pale yellow moon imaginable. Maybe one day in the far future, an intergalactic satellite probe will send back images of a cosmic body resembling Max Ernst's moon: a ring-shaped, yellow circle with a hole cut out in its middle, it hangs in the sky like a gigantic cosmic lemon donut. Partially obscured by the central totem pole, the moon forms a bracket, clamping onto the brittle trees, keeping them from falling over, or possibly sucking the last remaining life out of their fragile trunks. Max Ernst's forest looks morbid and devoid of life. Except at second glance, when the faint outline of a bird emerges from the light texture of the trees. This bird is captured, possibly fossilized, inside the thicket of the grove. Ernst obsessed about the forest because in its realm dream and reality meet. A dark dream, close to nightmares, sucks the observer through his paintings, into the depths of the sub-consciousness.

The subconscious can be a terrifying place, as Vega had experienced during her horror trip. Getting stuck there, like the bird entangled in Max Ernst's silent petrified forest felt particularly horrifying to Vega. Mercifully in the painting, the moon looms right behind. Its large central hole now acquired a new purpose: it provided an exit route through which the bird could escape the trap of the trees. Even though the great forest was foreboding, it included a path to freedom.

In the fall of 1976, Vega could not see this escape route. Caught in her desperate wish to save Tom and her relationship, she was not able to freely weigh her options and choices. Like the bird in Max Ernst's forest, she was entangled and caught up. Unlike the bird in the painting, Vega could not see the escape route in real life. As fall neared its end, Tom and Vega's excursions into the forest to escape the unavoidable came to an end as well.

Chapter 9: Traveling the River Styx

"I love those who do not know how to live, except as sinking beings, for they are the transcending arrows of longing to the other shore." Friedrich Nietzsche, *Thus Spoke Zarathustra*, *1883-85*

Preparations for Vega's first shot resembled a dark ritual. The paraphernalia included a belt to tie off the arm until a vein emerged, a spoon, a candle to cook the mixture of heroin and water, and a syringe for the injection. The smell of the bubbling potion made her nauseous. Tom had refused to give her the first injection and wasn't even present, but Pete did not mind. Once Pete had found a vein, he drew some of her blood into the syringe like the offering for an unholy sacrifice.

If she wanted to stay close to Tom, she had to know what it felt like. Either that, or lose Tom, her guide, her only friend, the one who made her heart ache whenever she looked at him.

Vega could not watch as Pete pressed the potion into her vein. Nothing had prepared her for the kick she felt when the mixture hit her bloodstream. The jolt almost knocked her breath out, and her whole body convulsed as if from an electric charge.

Tom picked her up in a taxi, and they aimlessly drove around town. Vega saw blurry lights reflecting in the wet asphalt of the nighttime city streets. Her stomach heaved and she felt dizzy. She experienced no vertical time, no expansion of consciousness, just dull emptiness, a floating detachment from life. By then, her course was set, and its direction was clearly going one way—down.

**

Isabella looked at her friend, Vega, clad in her black, floor-length, hooded Moroccan wool cape, wearing blue lipstick, black nail polish, and sucking greedily on a cigarette. During lunch, they stood in a small smoking area behind the school. Isabella did not smoke. Vega looked as if the sun never touched her skin. In her deadened white face, the eyes burnt like dark holes outlined with thick black eyeliner. Isabella thought about going over to her and saying something. Vega stood all by herself, as though she were contagious.

The infectious disease was called heroin, and within it was the breath of death.

Vega looked in Isabella's direction for a moment. Isabella smiled at her, hoping for a sign of recognition, a nod of encouragement, acknowledging their former closeness. But Vega just stared back blankly with eyes as empty as bottomless wells. Isabella wasn't even sure Vega had recognized her. She seemed so far gone. Goose bumps rose up on her arms, despite the sunshine. Isabella turned to go back into the school building.

**

As fall turned to winter, Vega and Tom crept through their nights like hungry dogs, scouring and hunting for dope. Now, Vega understood what had been happening to Tom because it started to happen to her. They slowly turned into empty shells, their insides consumed by a single desire. This desire overrode any compassion, charity, love, dignity, pride, or decency they might have had. They experienced no insights into the nature of reality, just a dull escape into the stupor of the half-dead. There was no sharpened consciousness or brilliant perceptions. Instead, the world around them turned gray and bleak, and the only way to bear it was more dope, causing them to sink deeper and deeper, withdrawing from everything alive. They became travelers on the river Styx, floating in limbo between Hades, the Underworld realm of the dead, and the border regions of life. They dressed in black leather to reinforce their armor against their surroundings because life and light were their enemies.

A single step could take them all the way across the river Styx.

**

One morning, a sanitation worker found Pete dead in a public toilet, a needle still stuck in his arm. He completed his crossing the week after initiating Vega into the fellowship of travelers who waited along its shores. He had set his golden shot and gone over to the other side.

Pete's memorial service was as dismal as his final hour. Tom, Vega, and Pete's mother Martha stood forlorn in the bland and unadorned Lutheran church. They were the only three mourners. Pete's mother looked as gray as the leaden sky. Her hair seemed to have lost all color. She did not cry. Maybe she had spent all her tears for Pete already, and what was left to drain from her was the color of life. Vega did not dare to hug her since she looked as if she would crack at the gentlest touch. The pastor gave a short speech but none of them listened. They were each absorbed by a private movie playing in their minds. Vega's mind played images of Pete's dead body lying on a wet concrete floor in a toilet stall. Over and over they played. For the rest of her life, she could not enter a public restroom without this image flashing through her mind. Maybe Pete's mother remembered her son as a small child, sweet and innocent as he must have been once.

Tom told Vega that he imagined the other side as a place not so different from the one he lived in already, just populated by more shadows and ghosts in an endless state of disembodied numbness.

Pete's mercifully short and unembellished memorial service concluded after half an hour. Vega and Tom went home with Pete's mom and listened to Elton John songs, *Funeral for a Friend* and *Candle in the Wind*, both about lives cut short. Maybe the fatal shot had been the only logical consequence of Pete's course, the final ticket. Maybe it was Tom and Vega's destination as well. With each shot, they killed a small part of their bodies and souls. The golden shot merely completed the process. For those traveling on the dark waters of the Styx, that last action deposited a weary passenger permanently at the feet of Cerberus, where at last all desires cease. Tom and Vega considered the deaths of people around them as inevitable. It barely penetrated their armor, consisting of dope and dead emotions. They were just part of the ghostly army of half-deads marching on Hades. Nothing could touch them.

**

Shortly after Pete's death, Vega experienced an overdose herself and touched the banks of the Land of Shadows. Emerging as if from a deep sleep, she saw Tom leaning over her frantically slapping her face and splashing it with water.

"Let me go," Vega yelled. "Let me be, it's peaceful here."

Returning reluctantly to this side, she wrote a poem about skirting closely along the shores of Hades.

Death stands behind my left shoulder
I turn around, catch a glimpse
feel his cautious hand
touching me lightly, tenderly, quietly.
When iron-tipped boots bang through the streets
he comes on cat paws
Soothes frayed nerves.
In a time chopped by sirens, he is timeless.
When I stumble, he opens his arms wide.
I travel the endless road where no breath
moves the leaves on the trees.
Let myself fall into clouds of cotton
where fog veils the glaring neon lights
Tears wash my eyes clear.

**

After Pete's death, Tom could no longer stay at Martha's house. For a while, he tried to find another place, but without a job, money, or connections it was hopeless. Vega's former friends, classmates, and acquaintances had turned their backs on her and would not even think of taking Tom in. They were junkies, literally marked by rows of needle scars on their arms and by their pale faces and empty eyes. They were plagued by death, and no one wanted to catch that virus. Her friends' horror and avoidance hurt Vega. She felt abandoned and burdened even though she had chosen her path. The rejection vindicated Vega's rage against a complacent, narrow-minded society. Tom and she lived on the fringes and had only scorn for the burghers and their safe, orderly, and privileged lives. Eventually, though, they ran out of options.

**

For two weeks Tom lived in a shabby motel and Vega paid for it from her allowance. He came to visit every day and often stayed for dinner. One night after he left, Vega's brother Daniel realized that his gold coin collection was gone. He had kept it in his closet in a red leather box. But the box was now empty. Vega's heart sank. She did not want to believe it, but there was no other explanation. Tom had taken the coins. When she confronted him the next day, he gave her his half-apologetic smile and shrugged. He was so stoned he could barely keep his eyes open.

"How could you do this to Daniel? He looks up to you."

"Calm down, have some dope," he said. With a lop-sided grin on his face, Tom slid down on the orange bean bag and fell asleep.

Lisa realized something terrible was happening to her daughter and Tom. She raged and cried and pleaded. "I don't want to see him ever again. He is not setting foot in this house anymore. Stealing from a child, after all I have done for him. I was kind to him, welcomed him like a son."

Vega stared back at her, stone faced.

"What is the matter with you? Why are you wearing this black cape and black lipstick all the time? Why don't you eat anything? Are you sick? Please tell me. I don't understand what is going on with you?"

Vega remained silent. She couldn't explain and didn't want to add to her mother's burden. Eventually Lisa gave up. Vega assumed her mother was too wrapped up in her own private universe of suffering, pain, and rejection. She was relieved that Lisa did not have the strength to stand up to her.

**

Tom had to return to his parents who lived in a small town three-hundred miles away. After he left, Vega felt relieved. He had become such a burden. She had to finish school and her final exams were imminent. Exams Tom had never taken because he had dropped out of school after 10th grade.

Vega's relief was short lived. She knew she had to stop using in order to graduate, and the only way to go was cold turkey. Telling Lisa that she had the flu, Vega coughed, shivered, vomited, and convulsed with stomach cramps. Her throat felt like it was full of feathers, making it difficult to swallow or breathe. As bad as the withdrawal symptoms were, they could have been worse. She had not been using long enough for them to be unbearable. After three days she felt better. Determined to complete her final exams, she went back to school. Her father should not have the satisfaction of seeing her drop out.

Every day, Tom wrote her a letter about how unhappy he was at his parents' house. He had struggled to leave his small town, whose sole claim to fame was the strong beer made in the local brewery. Tom's parents were less than sympathetic. Like Pete's mother, they had seen their share of rehabilitation attempts and botched new beginnings. At this point they had given up hope, and they had lost interest in their son. They had enough to worry about, trying to make ends meet, and caring for their three daughters. Tom was stuck in their dark house with nothing to do and only his own miserable company. His only glimmers of happiness came when Vega answered his letters at irregular intervals.

After the initial relief, Vega started to miss him. She no longer respected Tom, but she still loved him despite his shortcomings. Vega felt the distance had strengthened their feelings for each other. Therefore, she was not prepared for the telephone call that came one evening. Lisa answered the call and handed her the receiver.

"Vega?"

"Yes . . . Hello?"

"This is Tom's father. He wanted me to tell you that he is alright now."

"Well, that's good. Why doesn't he tell me himself?"

"He can't. He is still in the hospital."

"Why is he in the hospital?"

"He tried to kill himself." Tom's father's voice sounded dry and matter of fact.

"He tried to kill himself? Why? How?"

"I can't answer why. I have long stopped wondering why he does what he does. But I know he took sleeping pills. They pumped out his stomach. He will be okay."

He didn't sound convincing to Vega. "When did this

happen?" She felt a surge of blood in her head droning out his voice.

"It happened this afternoon while I was at work. Look, I have to go. Tom just wanted you to know that he is fine. He'll be released tomorrow."

He hung up, and Vega was glad he did because she had to lie flat on her back on the carpet. She felt as if someone had dealt a blow to her chest and knocked the air out of her. It was physical, not just psychological pain. She pressed the palms of her hands against the floor as hard as she could, just to feel the resistance of the surface.

Staring at the dark stains on the ceiling where the heating vents came out of the wall, she tried to concentrate on anything outside of herself, anything that could take her out of this feeling of collapse and panic.

The betrayal was almost too much to bear. How could he do this to her? How could he try to kill himself without reaching out to her first? No call, no letter, no message, no last appeal? Did she, did their relationship, mean so little to him that he would try to take this final step without even considering her? Had she not been enough reason for him to live? A realization flooded Vega with force: she was not going to save him as she had always assumed. He had apparently given up believing not only in himself but also in her, and worst of all in them. During these last few months, Vega had still assumed that their problems were temporary obstacles, delays they had to overcome, and in the end they would succeed being together again. But now, this new insight hit her like a blow to her gut. There was not going to be a rosy future. Not because of the hostile society, not because of their parents' resistance, but because Tom had lost faith and hope. And possibly his love for her.

Should she take a train and visit him? What would she say? Vega did not want to see him right then. She could picture his half-apologetic smile greeting her.

As she gasped, made choking noises on the floor, struggling with her emotions, Daniel came over. Even though he was only twelve, he must have sensed that something terrible had happened. Something to do with Tom whom Daniel adored like a big brother, despite the fact he had stolen his gold coins. He brought Vega his favorite *Rin Tin Tin* comics, to cheer her up. Vega smiled and gave him a hug. For a moment, Daniel managed to pull her out of her personal misery and grief. Through his compassion, he reminded her that the universe did not just revolve around her.

Chapter 10: Delivery

"Please Mr. Postman, look and see, if there's a letter in your bag for me." The Marvelettes, 1961

In the summer of 1977, Vega completed her final exams. Her enthusiasm for art helped her complete the tests with respectable results. In art she found alternative perceptions of reality without drugs. Art became a non-chemical avenue out of the limited rational mind. Without any fanfare, Vega received her baccalaureate degree and could now enter a university.

But first, she had to make some money. Ironically, she accepted a summer job as mail carrier with the postal service, which had been her father's chosen career for her. She was even assigned to her own home district. She could now deliver letters to herself and even read them in the comfort of her own room, during a break from her postal route. Meanwhile, her full letter cart waited downstairs in the stairway. Most of Vega's letters had been sent by Tom. He wrote with imagination, spinning fantastic stories, just as he had done during long nights when Vega could not sleep. He was able to tell long sequences of fables he made up on the spot.

Dear Vega,
Today my head is spinning. Have been reading Hermann Hesse "Der Steppenwolf" and feel I have entered into the magic theater like Harry Haller in the story. I have found the "Anarchistic Evening Entertainment! Entrance not for Everybody!" Only crazy people have access, people like us, who have traveled far onto the other side of the mind, into the depth of our imagination. I understand exactly how

Harry Haller could not just be content with life in the middle of the road, he had to search for the magical theater with doors into the past and into strange regions of the mind. Like Harry, I too have been in the mirror cabinet. Through a gateway made out of red velvet, decorated with green and yellow silk ribbons, I entered the room, which held mirrors of all sizes and shapes. There were oval ones in golden baroque frames; there were large round ones with beautifully polished mahogany frames; there were full-body-length mirrors with elaborate borders of bronze, and there were small silver mirrors, all clustered together on top and next to each other along the wall. All the mirrors reflected my image. But it was not me as I see myself in the bathroom mirror. In one reflection, I was an old man, bent and gray. In another, I was still a toddler looking back at myself with a round and innocent face. In another one, I was dressed in a monk's robes, my head shaven in the back like the monks in Bebenhausen. Some of the faces stared at me angrily, others looked friendly, and some slept, or screamed, or just stared in silent terror. As I tried to take in all these Toms of the past, present and future, suddenly one of the larger mirrors broke with a loud pang and exploded out of its frame. Hundreds of small shards shattered and scattered around me, and when I looked down, I realized that each one in turn reflected my face. Am I ever going to be able to put all these pieces back together again? What if I miss some and can't find the central puzzle pieces? Will I then remain a fragmented, incomplete person? Then I realized that even the smallest sliver showed my whole face.

Now, the important task is only to find the real me under all these splinters. I know that I will be able to find myself again when I see you. Together we are complete. I'm counting the hours until you come and we begin our journey to the Netherlands. I hope the enclosed powder will make your job a little easier and

make time go faster for both of us.
I love you forever,
Tom

After reading the letter, Vega shook the envelope and a small package fell out. She eagerly opened it and poured the white powder of cocaine it contained onto her glass table in a straight line. From the purse Vega carried for cash deliveries, she selected a 100 Deutsche Mark bill, rolled it up into a small pipe, and snorted the white line. Thus refreshed, she continued her route in fast-forward mode, racing through the industrial park, past Pete's mother's house, and past small squalid barracks where the inhabitants rarely received mail except for their welfare checks. Before any other carrier, Vega finished her route and returned to the post office in record time with energy to spare, which greatly impressed her supervisor.

Vega became tanned, and her legs grew strong from walking all day. Since she had no friends anymore, she spent most evenings alone, reading, writing, or listening to music exhausted from her tour de force performance.

Vega's mother was delighted. Little did Lisa know that Vega was preparing for a journey with Tom. With the money she earned, they planned to drive to Holland: Amsterdam, definitely; maybe Haarlem; and perhaps the beaches of the Northern Sea. This journey was not merely going to be rest and recreation. They had another agenda. After all, Amsterdam represented the European Mecca for hippies. The Dutch tolerance and legalization of hashish and marihuana attracted them like a magnet.

Chapter 11: Shangri-la of the Netherlands

"It was the repository of all the cultural treasures of the planet, and its inhabitants were opposed to all violence and materialism."
James Hilton, about Shangri-la in *Lost Horizon*, 1933

Amsterdam, lush, colorful oasis in the midst of middle-class wasteland. Haven, meeting place of kindred spirits who thought alike, and looked alike, even though they were trying hard to be different. As soon as they arrived, Tom and Vega went to a head shop where they bought scented and tinted rolling paper and for Tom a T-shirt displaying the five-petal hemp leaf. They browsed through a flea market next to the idyllic Leidsegraacht where Vega purchased a black fox stole, complete with a stuffed head, bushy tail, and four dangling paws. The stole complimented her black, Moroccan cape, and worn close to her face, it felt soft and comforting while at the same time providing a kind of shield into which she could bury her face when she preferred to be invisible.

At night, Milky-way beckoned: a four-story playground for European hippies, with a cannabis market in the basement. Tom and Vega snacked on hashish-laced brownies and purchased a small bag of crumbly, green Lebanese hashish for a reasonable price, over the more expensive heavy, moist, black Afghan dope. African merchants robed in the green, yellow, and red colors of Kente cloth tempted them with bags stuffed full of pungent-smelling, dried marihuana leaves. They negotiated calmly, in slow motion, smiling. Smoke and music, by Ravi Shankar and Jefferson Airplane, wafted through the vaults of the old basement and lured them away from the colorful vendors, enticing them to go upstairs, where bands played on several stages.

On the first floor, Tom and Vega lounged on slanted wooden

slats covered with thick oriental carpets and a generous number of
multi-colored pillows. From here, they had a clear view of the stage
and dance floor where guests moved slowly to the music, arms
waving, bodies swaying in dreamlike trances. They smoked their
Lebanese in the scented rolling paper and watched veils of smoke
snake and twist its way through the building in harmony with the
dancers. Vega and Tom looked at each other and smiled. They had
found paradise.

At the snack bar, a taste of sweet halva from the Middle East, dark
chocolate from Belgium, and baklava from Greece satisfied their
cravings. At last, Tom and Vega felt like they had come home to their
own planet.

From the Milky-way, they walked to the Paradiso, a psychedelic
Eden for the followers of Timothy Leary and Carlos Castaneda. On a
giant projection screen behind the dance floor, synchronized to the
music of Pink Floyd, morphing, psychedelic images transformed
multi-colored mandalas into rainbow-colored snowflakes. Tom and
Vega danced in front of cresting wave patterns in aquamarine,
turquoise, and indigo blue. Musicians' silhouettes outlined with
rainbow auras appeared behind the live band on the screen. Planets
traveled through distant galaxies, supernovas exploded. Coded
messages from Timothy Leary, the LSD guru from Harvard,
encouraged dancers to find the key, hidden deep within their DNA,
which would unlock the cosmic, alien origins of the human race.

**

The Cosmos, a hippie day-spa cured any lingering fatigue from the
previous night. A sauna to cleansed their bodies of any chemical
residue. After a dip in the ice-cold pool, they relaxed on wicker
lounge chairs in the topiary filled greenhouse area, under the
octagonal glass roof, next to indoor palms. They held hands and
blinked up at the yellow canaries chirping in ornate wrought-iron
cages, which studded the branches of the trees. The birds' twittering
mingled with the soothing ripple of a fountain in the center of the
space. The water trickled from a pyramid, flowed down its sides in all
four directions, and spread serenity. Before venturing out into the
city, they nurtured themselves with creamy Dutch yogurt and organic
granola served by friendly, long-haired hippies.

"I can't believe how nice everybody is," Vega said to Tom.

"Why shouldn't they be nice? They're happy. This is Shangri-la."

"It's incredible that such a place even exists." Vega remarked as they walked outside into the mild summer day.

Tom blinked into the blue Dutch sky. "Amsterdam is the best." He had been to the Dutch capital before and was less impressed than Vega. "Let's go over to Vondelpark and have a smoke," he suggested.

"Already? It's barely noon."

"Come on, that's why we are here," Tom insisted.

**

At the park, a colorful tribe of hippies and journeymen had congregated under chestnut trees and listened to bits of melodies drifting by. Nearby, someone had brought a guitar and lazily picked out strings of music. After a few hours on the grass in the green heart of Amsterdam, Vega wanted to visit the Rijksmuseum, for a non-chemically induced trip to the Dutch Baroque.

"Several amazing paintings I've only seen in books hang here, and I really want to meet them in person," she said.

Chapter 12: Tripping on Art

"The untalented visionary may perceive an inner reality no
less tremendous, beautiful, and significant than the world
beheld by Blake; but he lacks altogether the ability to express,
in literary or plastic symbols what he has seen."
Aldous Huxley, *Doors of Perception*, 1954

In the hallowed halls of the Rijksmuseum, Vega searched for one of
her favorite paintings. When she had seen the *Portrait of a Young Man*
by Nicolae Maes in her art history book, she immediately felt drawn
to this nameless youth from the 17th century. He looked pale,
vulnerable, gentle, and sad. Of course he had long, wavy hair and
wore the kind of clothes Vega and Tom searched for at the flea
markets: a velvet gray jacket, with puffy sleeves tapering out into
tightly fitting cuffs, with a hint of lace at the wrist. Tom glared at the
youth indignantly. He did not find him attractive in the least. Vega
pulled him along to the next gallery.

"Vermeer," she claimed, "was actually on a trip all the time."

Tom grunted. He was more interested in music than paintings.

"Just look at the way he painted the kitchen maid's blue apron in
contrast to the ultramarine blue napkin on the table. You cannot
even find a blue like that in real life. This blue is pure hallucination.
Nobody in their normal state of mind can see like that!"

"Ultramarine?" Tom asked, attempting to sound interested.

"He had to grind down pure lapis lazuli. It was expensive and
complicated, but he was obsessed with natural ultramarine. Mixed
with lead white, it becomes luminous. The light from the open
window falls on it, but the blue actually glows from within."

"He must have been on something," Tom admitted.

"Maybe he didn't need any chemicals to see colors radiate light and forms create shapes. I don't understand how he could bear to see everything with such intensity: every detail of the crumbling bread crust, the shiny rim of the milk jug, the slightly gray and cream colored plaster of the wall. It must have been overwhelming to constantly take all that in."

"Maybe Vermeer lived in vertical time," ventured Tom. "Maybe with all the visual overload, he couldn't handle anything but paint."

"It's true he didn't travel. He hardly left Delft, or even his house, because all he needed was right there in his studio. He painted it over and over: the same window to the left, the old map in the background, the table covered with a tapestry. He probably didn't want to go out much because the visual onslaught of a busy Dutch city street would blow him away. His simple kitchen table had as much visual and mental stimulation as he could handle. It must have been like being on a trip and getting paralyzed and terrified by the intensity of what he saw."

"I like the maid," remarked Tom, unimpressed. "She is so absorbed in pouring milk, like that's all that matters."

"For centuries, art lovers and scientists have stared at her, scrutinized her, studied her with magnification glasses and x-ray machines."

"I don't think her magic can be explained by science. She looks like she's in some kind of meditative state," Tom said.

"Right. She doesn't seem to think about who she is or where she is or where she'd rather be or who she wants to be. At the moment he captured her, no internal chatter is going through her mind. She doesn't think about gossip from the other maids or what she had for lunch or what to get for her mother's birthday. She just pours milk, and she's not going to spill a drop of it. And that is enough. Just like the bread and the jar and the cracked windowpane and the little nail in the plastered wall and the faint cracks in the surface. They all simply are what they are. They are not fancy symbols. They do not pretend to be anything more or anything less."

They looked at each other, both feeling slightly embarrassed, realizing what Vega had just said. In contrast to Vermeer's maid, ever since they had met, Tom and Vega had tried to be something else, be somewhere else, or in a different state of mind. They had attempted to escape from what and where they were at all costs. Instead of vocalizing these thoughts, however, they wandered on into the next gallery.

"I suppose if you saw the world like Vermeer did, it would be hard to do anything else but paint. Even interacting with other people must have seemed unimportant, distracting, annoying," Vega suggested.

"That's probably why the kitchen maid does not look at us," responded Tom.

"Maybe Vermeer just wanted to be left alone. I don't think Vermeer was a religious man, but to me his paintings are quite spiritual. He created a calm atmosphere in his paintings. They draw me into a state of silence and simplicity. Like a monk, Vermeer isolated himself from the bustle of ordinary life. How he lived was a 17th century alternative to taking LSD."

They stopped in front of Rembrandt's painting of *Titus in a Monk's Habit* from 1660.

"Titus was Rembrandt's son from his first wife Saskia. She died when Titus was only a baby. He was about nineteen at the time of this painting," Vega told Tom, dredging up buried information from the art history class she had taken during her last year of school.

"No, not at all. Rembrandt and his family were Protestants. But he's wearing a Franciscan monk's habit."

"So why the costume?" Tom asked.

"I don't know," Vega said. "Titus looks very introspective, don't you think? He seems lost in his inner world. He is also very pale, and if I remember right, he was a fragile young man, who died a few years after his father painted this portrait of him."

"Are you trying to say," Tom asked, "that Rembrandt knew his son would die when he painted him?"

"Possibly. He could have also used him as a model for a painting of St. Francis. Even though Rembrandt was a Dutch protestant he often painted saints or scenes from the bible. He tried to understand them in his own humanistic way."

"Wasn't St. Francis the guy who talked to the birds?"

"He thought that the birds are like our brothers and sisters. Supposedly he could communicate with animals."

"But I thought you said Titus was a withdrawn and sickly child. He doesn't look like he spent a lot of time outdoors," Tom said, visibly exasperated.

Vega sighed. "I don't have all the answers. Maybe it's just a night scene. It is obviously very dark. With a little imagination you can see a bush in the background."

"A bush," Tom exclaimed. "Now, Vermeer, he could have painted a bush. Or a face, or some fruit that you can recognize! But this, this has no detail, no contours, no real shapes. It's just a rectangle, covered with various shades of brown with a small, blurry face in the middle. I'm not even sure where the light comes from."

"Well, I think Rembrandt didn't care much about the details. To him, they were not interesting and not important. Not even the surface of his son's face mattered to Rembrandt. All he wanted to capture was the expression, the raw emotion underneath the surface. Think of the kitchen maid of Vermeer. Her face completely expressionless, there is no emotion, she is not happy or sad, she is simply doing her job. Look at Titus' face in contrast. There are powerful emotions right here, right in his eyes."

"He does look vulnerable," conceded Tom, "Some things are definitely going through his mind, and I don't think they are happy thoughts."

"Look at the dark circles under his eyes, the heavy eyelids, the unnaturally red lips in an otherwise really pale face. Titus is not sleeping well. He's sick, and he knows it. He is suffering, and his father painting him like this is suffering too. This is a painting of a parent's grief. Rembrandt had already lost his wife, Titus' mother, whom he had loved very much. Then, he had to watch his son fade away, knowing quite well that he would probably lose him too. At this point, details were irrelevant compared to the desperation and love he felt for his only son Titus and his pain."

Tom stopped in his tracks and looked more intently at the pale face gazing out of the canvas into another century, into another space, allowing the observers of a future time a glimpse into his soul.

"With this painting, Rembrandt shattered the isolation of each individual existing in his or her own universe, suffering or enjoying in solitude," said Vega, somewhat embarrassed about her own pathos.

With heroic brushstrokes, he had broken through the surface, through the time barrier and through the emotional armor Tom and Vega carried around with them. He managed to touch them both inside. The dark, shielded eyes of young Titus moved them, and the compassion of the father who had painted them came across so raw and unprotected that Tom and Vega just stood in silence for a while, forgetting about the murmur of the Rijksmuseum galleries around them, forgetting about visitors milling about, forgetting about the other masterpieces on the wall. They were literally drawn into the painting, into a different time and place. A silent exchange had taken place three centuries ago not far from Amsterdam, between a father and a son, painter and model. That bond revealed itself to be so powerful and pure, that Vega and Tom had to fight back tears.

"Titus is not engaged in any task. He's engaged with himself and with his father. Both are still reaching out to us, centuries later, unashamed and unafraid to share their intimate moment," Vega concluded.

"Maybe Rembrandt was no better than Vermeer in handling everyday life," Tom finally remarked, taking some solace from this fact that corresponded so well with his own inability to take care of himself and to function reasonably in society.

"Probably," Vega replied, "but I think it was for different reasons. Here is a self-portrait Rembrandt painted, when he was fifty-five years old. That was one year after the portrait of Titus. This man did not lead a reclusive life; he was not trying to avoid contact with his fellow humans or with us for that matter. On the contrary, he looks directly at us. Rembrandt made dozens of self-portraits in his life, but Vermeer not a single one."

"Rembrandt must have been pretty vain, if he loved his own face so much," said Tom, standing his ground defiantly right in front of the priceless painting, in spite of the suspicious glances from a female security guard near the doorway.

"I don't think he was vain. His self-portraits aren't flattering. Look at the bloated, red face and the messy clothes. They show a man who lived life to its fullest, when he could afford to. He enjoyed every pleasure, did not restrain himself, and lived with considerable passion. It is said that he felt life's blows and gifts deeply and let them mark his face. In this self-portrait he shows, without mercy and almost proudly, the scars, and traces the years have left. He seems to say: My face is the canvas on which life painted this image. This is what it looks like, and I have felt it all. Every line and wrinkle I have earned. I know who I am now, and I know what made me look this way."

Vega paused, feeling she had been carried away by her own feelings, but then she continued. "Rembrandt painted himself as the apostle Paul, that's why he holds letters in his hands. Paul had something to say. So does Rembrandt, and I think he is saying: Don't be afraid to feel; don't be afraid to suffer; don't be afraid to expose your feelings; don't be afraid to let life leave its marks on you."

"Wow," Tom exhaled with a huff. "That's heavy stuff."

Again they had reached a moment where art pointed a finger back at them. They did exactly the opposite of Rembrandt, insolating themselves with an ever-expanding padded armor of drugs from their own feelings, from the world around them, from other people and their suffering or their joy.

"Let's go have some ice cream," Vega said. She didn't want to relate Rembrandt's message to their own lives.

**

They stepped out of the shadowy museum into the bright sunlight of the Leidseplein, which buzzed with trams, people of different nationalities, shades of skin color, and exotic dress. Fragments of conversations in Dutch, German, English, and French floated around and reached their ears in an audio-collage. Young people, with long hair and tie-dye shirts, rode by on white bicycles. Vega soaked in the metropolitan flair of Amsterdam, so different from the small, provincial German towns Tom and Vega came from.

Strolling along slowly, Tom with a chocolate and Vega with a lemon sherbet ice-cream cone, Tom asked in a pondering tone, "So why did Rembrandt paint everything in brown?"

Vega thought for a moment. "I don't think color mattered that much to him. Many of his paintings are almost all brown surrounding a white face. Deepest darkness to extreme brightness and all the shades in between interested him. Rembrandt was not content with the visual world around him. Seeing nature and objects in such clarity, as Vermeer does, can be very satisfying. If you can see like that, then probably painting is all you'd ever want to do. Other people would feel in the way, distractions. It must be like being on a trip and not wanting to communicate with others because you are so absorbed in what is happening. I don't think Rembrandt was like that. He was as intense as Vermeer, just in a different way. Vermeer withdrew into his own, private, protected, and orderly space of his studio. Even the light was filtered and enters indirectly. Rembrandt wanted to reach out to others at all cost."

"So what does all that have to do with the picture of his sickly son in a monk's habit?" Tom asked between licks of strawberry ice cream.

"Do you remember the color of Titus' robe?" Vega asked back. "Of course. It was all brown, like the rest of the picture."

"The Franciscan monks wore brown habits. I think Rembrandt chose this color and this order on purpose. St. Francis founded the Franciscan order in Assisi, in Italy. The monks did not live in monasteries. St. Francis wanted his monks to go out to the people and not hide behind abbey walls. He wanted them to reach out, give away personal possessions to those in need, and practice compassion. The Franciscans committed themselves to lives of poverty, humility, and care for the less fortunate. Rembrandt could identify with these values. That's why he chose the brown habit for Titus."

"Do you remember the monks in the Cloister of Bebenhausen?" Tom asked suddenly.

"How could I forget?" Vega answered.

"I am trying to remember the color of their habits. They were not brown. They were white or gray, or some sort of beige."

"You're right. I had forgotten about that. Those monks were Cistercians and wore white habits of un-dyed wool. The Cistercian monks wanted to lead lives of simplicity and contemplation. They withdrew from ordinary life and spent their time in silent meditation, undisturbed by the needs and sufferings of regular people. They felt they could only find God through silence and prayer."

"Kind of like Vermeer," said Tom putting the finishing licks on his ice cream.

"I guess, you could say that Vermeer was more like a Cistercian monk and Rembrandt more like a Franciscan. One preferred mediation and the other interaction. *Vita active* and *vita contemplative.*"

"Well, this is definitely getting too deep for me. I am not much of a theologian, but Jesus, I know I need a hit really bad," Tom said, concluding the conversation and suddenly breaking out into a cold sweat.

**

Tom and Vega had not come to Amsterdam just to soak in the

sites and the culture. They had come for business. Tom wanted to buy an ounce of heroin for trade and personal use. They wandered over to Amsterdam's old Chinatown close to the Central Train Station. Tom knew that junkies and dealers from Hong Kong and Singapore met here, and heroin was cheap and plentiful.

Chinese shops and restaurant, decorated with small pagodas and red lanterns lined the narrow street, populated with tourists. Vega knew Amsterdam had the oldest Chinese quarter in Europe. She thought about all the immigrants who had come through here with high hopes for a better life. She wanted to soak in the atmosphere, but Tom had intentions of a different kind. He pulled her into a narrow side lane where laundry hung in front of windows, and the facades were dark and grimy.

An Asian youth in a black leather jacket leaned in a doorway, and as Tom and Vega passed by, he asked quietly, "Smack?" Tom looked at him and nodded, so the dealer motioned them into a shady courtyard where another Asian man with greasy long hair waited. Vega noticed his pockmarked face, his darting eyes, and a scar on his left cheek. She wanted to run. Her heart raced. What was she doing here? The two dealers completely ignored Vega. They only dealt with Tom.

The second man produced a Ziploc bag full of white powder, and Tom tasted a sample of it by placing a fingertip of the powder on his tongue. He nodded again. Then the second dealer pulled a knife from his back pocket.

Vega gasped. She saw herself with a cut throat lying on the cobble stones, the dealers leaving with all her money. Blood drained form her face and she felt dizzy, so she pressed herself against the soot-covered wall of a building, hoping she wouldn't faint. Tom shot her an angry glance. Wasn't he aware of the danger?

But the dealer used the knife to cut a small amount of the powder on a pocket mirror into two lines. He held it up to Tom and let him snort the lines through a straw. Relieved, embarrassed, and nervous, Vega watched the transaction from the shadows.

Satisfied, Tom nodded his approval and weighed the bag with a letter scale he had brought. He handed over Vega's entire wages, earned from a long summer of mail deliveries. He didn't even bargain. Vega saw the envelope disappear into the coat of the dealer. After pocketing the baggie with heroin, Tom grabbed Vega's hand

and pulled her out of the courtyard before anybody could change their mind. The dealers melted into the alley.

They walked out of Chinatown as fast as they could, realizing that they had spent all their money. For anybody watching, Tom and Vega looked like a harmless couple of hippies on a Dutch vacation, but they could not even afford another night at their modest hostel. The only solution was to leave Amsterdam and drive north toward the ocean to spend a few days on the beach of Haarlem.

Chapter 13: The Lowlands

"Netherlands: Country below sea level on land claimed from the sea." Merriam-Webster Dictionary

Approached the shore of Haarlem in Little Feet, a landscape painting by Jacob van Ruisdael Vega had seen at the Rijksmuseum came to her mind. Ruisdael's *View of Haarlem*, showed the land seen from the dunes as a flat, green plain. Two thirds of the painting consisted of sky, just like the land in front of Vega's windshield where only four small church spires and two tiny windmills ruptured the straight horizon line. The buildings represented the Dutch accomplishment of establishing a tentative foothold on land they had claimed from the sea. Ruisdael captured a short period of balance in the tumultuous history of humanity's relationship with nature in the seventeenth century..

During that window in time, Dutch people stopped living in constant fear of natural disasters. They also had not yet started to exploit and pollute their land's resources. The pragmatic Dutch burghers had tamed the powerful forces of the water with dykes, and they utilized the power of the winds with windmills. Landscape paintings emerged, because for the first time, the Dutch were able to depict and enjoy nature. Before the Renaissance, nature in art was shown in walled gardens or confined spaces as an element that had to be feared and controlled, just like human nature.

In Ruisdael's painting, as well as in Vega's sweeping view, a few tiny farmers dotted the land as small as a scattered flock of birds dotted the sky. The painting's main attraction was the sky, depicted without fear of storms, but with respect and awe for its grandeur and beautiful cloud patterns. The church spires pointed toward heaven as a reminder of God, but the buildings themselves were insignificant in the grand scheme of the composition. Worship not only took place inside the churches, but also outside in the landscape, which gave eloquent testimony to God's greatness. Ruisdael, like his contemporary Rembrandt, was a Protestant and did not paint angels or saints. He saw God in the high and cloudy skies, barely illuminated by a hidden sun.

**

As they approached the beach of Haarlem in the late afternoon under a cloudy sky, Vega was not aware that their visit to the lowlands would turn out to be a low of a different kind.

While Vega compared the landscape outside her window to Ruisdael's painting, Tom slumped in the seat beside her, his eyelids drooping and his pupils tiny as needle pricks. He had sampled a large portion of their purchase from Chinatown, which left him barely conscious. He was dead to the world, to Vega, and to the views of the sea and the sky.

The brief balance between fear and domination of nature in the seventeenth century did not last long before it tipped, and the land became exploited, polluted, overcrowded, and stripped of its dignity. That was how Vega found it when they arrived at the beach that summer of 1977. The dunes at Overveen were littered with candy wrappers and soda cans. Condoms and plastic bags floated like deflated jellyfish in the incoming tide. She felt dwarfed by the mighty sky, which had not changed much since Ruisdael's time apart from the frequent airplanes and jets flying overhead. She had imagined a sunny, empty, and pristine beach, but in reality, all three assumptions turned out to be wrong. Nevertheless, she parked Little Feet and carried their meager belongings to a spot in the dunes, close enough to the ocean to hear the lapping of the waves, but out of sight of families and beach walkers.

Vega brought a blanket from the car along with her black cape. Her bag doubled as a pillow. Tom, rallying enough to help, brought a belt, syringes, a spoon, a lighter, and the bag with white powder they had purchased in Amsterdam. He had no eyes for the ocean, the dune grass swaying in the sea breeze, nor the sky, though it dramatically exhibited shifting masses of gray clouds piled up high. A few feeble rays of filtered light from a pale, setting sun streaked through.

Tom got down to the business of setting himself a shot, cursing as the wind extinguished the lighter flame he needed to cook the potion.

Vega looked at him with resignation. She had been looking forward to this trip all summer; had worked for it, delivering letters six days a week, getting up at 4:30 each morning to sort the mail. She had anticipated this journey for months, their reunion, and their time together at the ocean, alone, with time and the great sky above. Tom did not even look at her, much less talk to her. He just ordered her to create a windshield with her body, so he could keep his flame going. Vega obliged, and then they sat silently next to each other.

"I am cold," she said after several minutes, hoping for some acknowledgement, an arm around her shoulder, some body warmth.

"I can set you a shot," Tom offered with a drawl.

Vega did not want a shot. She wanted contact, not isolation, but she saw no other way to get through the night. She nodded slightly. Immediately, Tom made the preparations with focus and concentration then pushed the tincture into her bloodstream with the same needle he had used earlier. Vega briefly wondered about using the same needle again, before the familiar kick and the warmth spreading through her body erased all thoughts.

"Feeling warmer?" he asked and sank back onto the sand.

Vega nodded again and stared out at the ocean. She should have known better. A shot could not bring them closer together, but she had conveniently chosen to forget that fact. Taking a deep breath, she smelled the salty ocean air trying not to sink into oblivion. Growing up in a land-locked city, nine hours away from the nearest beach, she always yearned for the spacious openness of the sea. By the water she could relax and let her thoughts stretch further. Tom had grown up in an equally land-locked location, but he showed no awareness of his surroundings. He floated in that particular state of heroin limbo. When Vega asked him what he liked so much about this feeling, he answered, "I don't feel my body at all; I don't feel anything, no pain, no emotion."

This was, Vega concluded, as close to obliteration as one could get while still being alive.

The problem was that once Tom left that state, every sensory and emotional perception became so intense and magnified that, apart from the real pain of withdrawal symptoms, he wanted to return as quickly as possible into the dullness and isolation of non-existence, which was provided by the drug.

That night, Vega lay wrapped in her cloak in a depression of sand behind a dune next to Tom. The chill and dampness of the ocean air returned after the effects of the shot wore off. Tom laid on the blanket with his back to her, his leather jacket the only protection from the cold. He slept deeply, or was simply unconscious. For all Vega could tell, he was lost to the world. She tried to cuddle closer, to share some body warmth. But he was as far gone as if he was on the other side of a glass partition in a quarantine ward.

Vega felt cold and small and very alone under that overcast Haarlem night sky. The pale sliver of a crescent moon did not have enough strength to provide comfort and her star Vega did not make an appearance. She wondered what gender the Dutch moon had. It did not look any warmer than its German version.

**

"We are leaving," Vega told Tom the next morning. "We are driving back."

"Okay," he said indifferently. "I'll just have a hit before we go."

As Vega packed up their few belongings, she watched him go through the ritual again, inwardly fuming. How easy it had been for him to abandon their first vacation together. How little he cared about how this sad, aborted journey ended. He asked no questions, not, "Why do you want to leave?" nor even a simple, "How are you doing?"

Despite Vega's somber mood, the sun broke through the cloud barrier with a vengeance. A clean-swept sky arched overhead in brilliant Prussian blue, with only a wisp of a cloud directly above the distant church spire, as if the cosmic sweeper forgot a speck of dust from the messy gray sky of yesterday. Dune grass shimmered in polished silver green, and the sand gleamed golden yellow on the rolling dunes extending toward the water. Waves of the morning's incoming tide sprayed fresh aquamarine mist onto the beach. Droplets from the surf sparkled in the sunlight like pearls breaking off a necklace. The shifting water looked so inviting that Vega almost changed her mind about leaving. It would be a long time before she could smell ocean air again, or feel the prickling, invigorating sensation of cold saltwater on her naked legs. But the memories of the damp night, aching bones from restless sleep, and a grumbling stomach brought her back to her senses.

As they clambered up to the street where Little Feet was parked, a young Dutch family passed them on their way to the beach. The husband had blond-streaked hair and carried a newspaper and a beach blanket. The mother followed, holding a small girl by her chubby hand resting trustingly in her mother's. The mom, a handsome woman, her own long blond hair twirled up in a casual bun, strode on strong, tanned legs. Her well-toned arms carried a basket containing breakfast buns, a thermos, and fruit.

Maybe it was just the food combined with her crumbling stomach, but for a moment Vega would have given anything to go with this healthy family, to change places with this woman who seemed so content and so sure where she was heading. Vega imagined the smell of freshly brewed coffee being poured from her thermos, and the strong, kind grip of her hand. She thought of her own mother, and how much she had wanted to get away from Lisa's sad life. Vega yearned to be like this family: normal, middleclass, healthy, boring yet self-contained, heading to the beach for a relaxing, uneventful day.

Instead, she scrambled up the path, wrapped in her soggy black cloak, hungry, pale, with knots in her hair. She wondered how she and Tom appeared to this family. What did they see in the ragged couple trudging up the dunes? Did they feel pity or contempt? Or did they just see another couple of strung-out hippies littering their beautiful country?

**

Climbing into Little Feet, Vega tried hard to control her disappointment, her rage, and her hunger. Tom drifted in a space where no one could follow. They drove south toward the German border, using country roads leading to one of the barely controlled border checkpoints. She pulled over and got out the baggie with heroin noticing how much their supply had shrunk already. By now, it consisted of little more than a small snack bag. At this rate, the purchase would be used up in a few days, a whole summer's earnings gone without a trace, except for the needle markings on Tom's arms.

She hid the bag under Little Feet's back upholstery inside an old sock. If the border patrol officers took the little Volkswagen's backseat apart, they would still only see a long-lost sock, which had gotten stuck between the seat and the backrest.

"Put on your sunglasses!" Vega hissed, pulling up to the checkpoint. "Hide your eyes!"

Tom's pupils were as tiny as needle points, and no change in light intensity could dilate them. Nothing could penetrate through these eyes into his mind and his soul that had dissolved into a white fog. Vega knew border officers were trained to recognize this sign of a person under the influence of hard drugs. The bouncers and admission personnel at the Paradiso or Milky-way clubs in Amsterdam also knew and refused admission to heroin junkies. They could identify them immediately by their tiny pupils, in contrast to the large, dilated pupils of a pot smoker.

**

The officer at the sleepy border crossing near Arnhem leaned casually against the wall of his guard shack. When he saw the VW approaching, he looked up and pushed his sunglasses onto his forehead.

"Passports, please. Do you have anything to declare?" he asked Vega through the open window on the driver's side.

"Here are the passports, and we have nothing to declare, officer," Vega said with a pretty smile.

He checked the passports with a bored expression then glanced at Tom, slumped in his seat.

"Sir, can you take off your sunglasses, please?" he asked.

Vega's heart skipped a beat, heat rose in her cheeks. She felt dizzy as she looked at Tom.

"Sir, I would like to oblige, but my eyes suffer from extreme light sensitivity. I could endanger my cornea if I exposed them to sunlight," Tom drawled.

"Too much partying last night?" the guard officer asked with a wink.

"Yes sir," Vega said with a laugh of relief. "The nightclubs in Amsterdam are too great."

"I know. I go myself, when I'm off duty." The guard waved them through.

**

Safely on the German side, Tom and Vega exchanged a smile of relief, the first friendly interaction they had had in days. Now, they could enter the Autobahn, heading south. With the tension of the border crossing behind them, Vega felt hungry and exhausted.

"I need to eat something," she told Tom.

"We have no money," he answered. He had a point. All their financial assets were invested in white powder inside an old sock.

We are also running low on gas," Vega said, which got his attention.

"Let's stop and sell something," he suggested, checking the blue highway signs overhead. "Darmstadt is coming up. I know where to go there to sell some dope."

"Okay," she consented, glad for this modest sign of initiative. Time to get a return on her investment. They took the exit into Darmstadt and maneuvered *Little Feet* close to the city center. Vega parked next to the central park called Schlossgarten, because Tom said he knew a place at the Herrengarten pond where the junkies hung out. They packed up some individual portions of powder into small amounts, called "letters" and containing just enough for one shot.

"No need for you to come along. Why don't you wait here?" suggested Tom, motioning toward a shady spot of grass. "I'll be right back."

**

The park looked peaceful and calm. Gently swaying beech trees surrounded a small stretch of grass and protected it from the street. At the sight of the shaded lawn, Vega felt her exhaustion. The lack of sleep and the lack of food crashed in on her. She left the car and lay down on her cloak in the speckled sunshine. She fell asleep immediately, and when she woke up, the shadows had deepened and crept across the entire grassy expanse. Tom sat next to her, smoking a cigarette. Vega sat up.

"How did it go?" she asked.

His expression was blank. "Not good," he said, looking straight ahead, not at her.

"Meaning what?" she asked still groggy from sleep.

"Meaning, they took all the smack from me."

"That's good, isn't it?"

"Yeah, but they took it without paying for it."

"What?"

Tom turned toward her now. She noticed how pale and saggy his face looked. It had acquired a spongy and pasty appearance and his eyes still had minuscule pupils. An expression of failure and defeat clung to his features. His shoulders sagged, his body slumped, his mouth twisted into an apologetic, helpless grimace. "They took it at knifepoint. But at least they didn't take everyhting," he finally said.

"Where? How?"

"We went into a pedestrian tunnel for the exchange, and two other guys waited there. They pushed me into a corner and held a knife to my throat. I had no choice. I had to give it to them."

Vega stared at Tom, realizing that she didn't believe him. She should have been glad and relieved that he was unhurt, but instead she felt suspicious. Was this the truth? Had they reached such a low in their relationship that she doubted his loyalty and suspected him of ripping her off for a couple of grams of dope? They stared at each other, unable to communicate. The rift had become too wide to bridge with words. She was disappointed and angry at this latest example of his failure, wasting more of her money. She despised him for leaving her once again in charge of finding a solution to increasingly difficult situations.

He sensed her contempt but did nothing to counteract it. He had given up long ago.

When he had tried to kill himself, Vega should have seen the signs, but chose to deny them. Now, she was forced to confront the fact that he had no fighting spirit left in him, no will at all. "Now what?" she asked sarcastically, expecting no answer and receiving none.

She drank water from a fountain and hoped the gas would last until they reached her hometown. It was a straight shot on the Autobahn. Like a wet dog, Tom followed. Wordlessly, they got back into Little Feet. Vega chewed some stale pretzels she found on the backseat and started the engine. In silence, she navigated out of the city, following the blue Autobahn signs.

As soon as they reached the freeway and entered the stream of southward flowing cars, Tom relaxed in his seat. Driving in the car together had always been their favorite pastime. While the landscape flitted past outside, they sat inside their safe cocoon and could spin their tales of wonder and imagination, grown in their own realm of fantasy.

That realm was shattered now, and Vega did not relax. She drove on with a grim determination, knowing exactly what to do, but dreading it. How would he react to what she was planning? Would he be as passive as she expected, or would he put up a fight? At the first rest stop after Darmstadt, she exited. There was a service station right off the freeway with a cafeteria-style restaurant, a gas station, a convenience store, parking for trucks, toilets, and picnic benches.

"What are you doing?" Tom asked, confused. "I thought we had no money!"

"We are not buying anything," Vega answered.

"Then why are we stopping?"

"You're getting out," she said quietly.

"I'm what?"

"I'm throwing you out of my car," Vega said slowly and deliberately and brought Little Feet to a full stop past the restroom, on a stretch of grass and shrubs, which lead back to the Autobahn's onramp. She reached across him and opened the passenger door.

"We are in the middle of nowhere. You can't just throw me out," Tom protested.

"Watch me," she answered. "You can always hitch a ride with a truck, sell some of those, or use them for comfort," she added nastily and threw a few little letters with heroin out of the car.

Tom scrambled after the letters and picked them up quickly, before the wind could blow them away, behaving just as Vega had expected. After he had pocketed all of them, he turned around.

"What am I supposed to do?" he pleaded.

"I really don't care what you do," she said and threw his bag and leather jacket onto the shoulder of the road.

"Hey, you can't do this to me," he shouted

"Yes I can. Good luck with the rest of your life," she said, or maybe she just thought it.

Tom lunged for the car, trying to grab her, struggling to get back inside. Vega's heart beat so fast that she thought it would break her ribcage. She felt Tom's hands on her shoulder, the same hands she had longed for on the cold beach of Haarlem. Now they did not provide comfort, instead threatened to break her arm.

"Let me go," she screamed, and with a great effort, she twisted toward him in the driver's seat and kicked him in the side as hard as she could. He was an emaciated junkie, but he was still stronger than her. She put all her rage and frustration into this kick. It catapulted him back onto the curb. Caught by surprise, Tom's reactions were slow and he fell backward. His head hit the curb with a sickening cracking sound. Vega watched his body go limp as a puddle of blood pooled beneath his head.

Instinctively, she stepped onto the gas pedal and darted off. The open passenger door slammed into the lock but didn't latch. A hundred feet away, she stopped to close the door and looked back at Tom lying motionless at the curb. He's dead. He's dead. I know he's dead.

She glanced around. Had anybody seen them? Plenty of distance existed between Little Feet and the bathrooms and snack shack. Nobody was paying attention to her, but the police could easily connect her and Tom.

She had to make it look like an accident, an overdose, like Pete's. Tom had been going down that road, anyway. Vega scrambled back to his body. A part of her was relieved to be rid of him. But not like this. The blood still pooled behind his head. She took three paper packages of heroin out of his pocket and found his syringe and a spoon. With shaking hands, she cooked the concoction with water and inserted it in his vein, letting the needle stay in his arm. Anybody finding him would believe he died from an overdose. Just like Pete. It would have happened eventually anyway, she tried to convince herself.

Back in her car, she was out of gas, out of water, out of heroin, and free of Tom but burdened by the terribly load of what she had done.

Chapter 14: The Black Madonna

"We come from and are contained by darkness".
Meinhard Craighead, Austrian artist and nun, about the Black
Madonna,1970

After Vega left Tom at the Autobahn rest stop in September 1977, she expected to end the drug period of her life then and there. Little Feet ran out of gas twenty miles from her hometown. With her last coins, Vega called her friend Klaus. He came, and Vega told him as little as possible about the ill-fated Holland trip. She gave him the rest of the heroin for a can of gas. Vega knew he could sell it and make a good profit. She did not want to see, smell, or deal with dope ever again.

At first, Vega felt great relief as if she had cast off a heavy stone tied to her neck. She realized how naïve she had been, believing that she could save Tom with her love and loyalty when, in fact, she had simply joined him on his ride down a dark tunnel. The episode in Darmstadt had finally triggered a self-preservation mechanism that caused Vega to pull the emergency brake and to kick everything Tom represented out of her life. She was horrified about what had happened and did not tell anybody why he was suddenly out of the picture. Nobody asked. Vega felt ashamed of her relief, but she was not ashamed of getting rid of Tom.

Her own withdrawal symptoms were once again minor since she had just snorted the occasional line and only once injected heroin on the beach of Haarlem. A cough, a scratchy throat, aching bones she could handle. She had shaken off the curse of the white powder.

**

Vega found a summer job in a department store which hosted a traveling sales exhibition of Russian icons. She helped customers understand the images, explain their origin and purpose, and entice them to buy an icon or two. This job was much more interesting than delivering letters. Vega's favorite icon was a sophisticated nineteenth century reproduction of the *Black Vladimir Madonna* also known as *Theotokos from city of Vladimir*. Vega reacted to her serene, gentle face with a feeling of calm and peace.

A Russian art courier named Irina Tankova had accompanied the icons from a Moscow gallery to the third floor of the German Kaufhalle department store. Irina was a dynamic woman with short dark hair she constantly brushed out of her face. Before returning to Russia, Irina answered Vega's questions and explained to her in heavily accented English that the original Vladimir Madonna, from the twelfth century, hung in the State Historical Museum in Moscow.

"Nobody knows which Byzantine artist painted *Vladimir Madonna,* but soon become obvious this Madonna has enormous powers."

"What did she do?" Vega asked.

"Well, in beginning, she did obvious miracles, healings and such. She was transferred to central Russian city of Vladimir by Grand Prince, Yuri Dolgouky. Here she saved people from Mongol invasion. In sixteenth century, city of Moscow was under attack from Tartars. So, people of Moscow, they need Black Madonna to protect them, and they bring her to Moscow. People very afraid. Then Saint Vasily have vision. People of Moscow should pray and repent sins for intersession of Madonna and their sincere prayers to save city."

Vega tried to memorize the Russian names, so she could repeat them to future customers, but even though she found the story fascinating, she had a hard time concentrating. Her belly ached and she felt weak. Irina continued.

"Even Tartar leader, Kahn Makhmet, have vision of the Madonna. He sees her surrounded by powerful army sweeping down on Tartar troops. Tartars flee in fear, and Russian Capital saved. So, on third June, Russian people celebrate in honor of Vladimir Madonna and saving of their city."

"Wow, what a powerful story. But why is she black?" Vega asked as she fingered the metal cover of the icon, which only left the dark face of the Madonna visible.

"That is good question. Are many theories. Some say, is just soot from centuries of candle smoke right in front of face."

"Just like the face of the Christ child she is holding, even though he is a little lighter."

"Both exposed to same amount of candle smoke. Some scholars think they descendants of Egyptian goddess, Isis, and son Horus. That explain dark skin, and images of Isis with young Horus on knees, these popular in Egypt."

"But how did an Egyptian subject get to medieval Byzantium?"

"If look at icon of virgin with child in Monastery St. Catherine by Mount Sinai, you find same face and features. Without expression. Same three-quarter profile and long, narrow nose. That is link between Egypt and Vladimir Madonna."

Vega had heard of the famous St. Catherine monastery in the middle of the Sinai desert. Built in the 6th century, its high walls fortified it against raiders in the hostile desert and protected invaluable Byzantine art. It also contained the burning bush Moses saw in his encounter on Mount Sinai before he received the Ten Commandments. One day, Vega dreamed, she would visit this mythical place. With her attention back on the icon in front of her, she asked, "Why is she covered with a metal armor, which only leaves her face and hands free?"

"This metal covering is called *riza*. Is customary in 17th century. Original Vladimir Madonna did not have."

"What is its purpose?" Vega felt puzzled.

"Several reasons to use *riza*. First, open up and see under. Always open icons with riza to see if fully painted, not incomplete. Look here, what do you see?" Irina folded back the elaborately decorated and molded riza, heavy from the multi-colored semi-precious stones imbedded in it, and revealed the image underneath.

"Oh, I didn't expect it to look like that!" Vega exclaimed.

The elderly security guard, who was charged of protecting the icons, walked over to see what was underneath the metal armor. He offered to get stools for them, and Vega gratefully accepted. She really wanted to learn, wanted to keep this job, but she felt dizzy, weak, in pain, and afraid she could not continue standing next to Irina much longer.

Sitting down, she observed that the Madonna and child's hands and faces revealed through the riza had been carefully rendered. They varied in hue and shading, depicting three-dimensional and realistic, though slightly elongated, hands and faces. The tiny face of the Christ child touched his mother's cheek, a sign of tenderness and affection. But the rest of the icon, underneath the riza, consisted of robes and a gold-leaf background, which had been rendered completely flat, without any color variations or spatial illusion. The folds of little Jesus' garments were stylized and geometric to the point of abstraction.

"Now, I understand what you mean," Vega had to admit. "It was not a big step from this stylized gold background to the metal cover."

"Exactly. Plus riza give icon protection. Enable artist to give valuable jewels and stress precious nature of virgin. At same time, patron shows his wealth and devotion. This way, he think Madonna would put in good word for him, in this life or life after."

"The icons are fascinating. I will enjoy spending time with these saints and heavenly beings." Vega said.

Irina smiled and responded, "Good. This makes me feel better, to leaving them here."

Together they looked at the icon of the Vladimir Madonna in front of them. Without the riza, it looked exposed and vulnerable, like a knight without his armor or a turtle without its shell. The Black Madonna is not afraid of her vulnerability, Vega thought.

As if reading her thoughts, Irina said, "This type of icon called, loving kindness. Stresses deep bond between mother and son and focuses on human nature. At same time, detach look in Madonna's eyes. She does not look at little Jesus, just into distance, or what do you say? Inward? Virgin knows precious son will die young and make sacrifice of his life. Her love shadowed over by this." Irina paused.

Vega was struck by the Madonna's dignity and poise in accepting her son's future. She clearly was enjoying the tender moment and calmly contemplated that it would not last. The Madonna does not complain or rebel about this injustice. As trivial as it might sound, just looking at her calm face made Vega feel calmer. The Madonna simply dealt with her destiny with quiet composure. The subtle message to the followers of the orthodox Christian church was this: You deal with your destiny too. Whatever has been allotted to you, bear it. The Virgin Mary and her son had much worse to deal with, and they bore it with great dignity, even with joy in the case of the Christ child. He is the one who actually comforts his mother. I probably don't deserve it, I have done something unforgivable. But maybe he could comfort me too, Vega thought.

**

Two days later, a well-dressed middle-aged lady strolled into the small icon display area. Her steps and pace communicated that she was in no hurry and did not have to follow a schedule. Glancing around aimlessly, she shook her head slightly to toss aside chin-long hair, which was carefully styled with a perm and highlighted with chestnut-colored accents. Her carefully made up face, well-toned body, camelhair slacks, cream-colored silk blouse, Versace scarf, and two large shopping bags with designer names indicated that she took good care of herself. Moderately interested, she pointed toward the Vladimir Madonna and asked Vega, "Is this an original? It looks slightly familiar."

"In a way, this is an original, madam. This reproduction was painted by an anonymous 19th century Russian icon painter, in the style of the famous 12th century Vladimir Madonna. I am not surprised she looks familiar to you. This Madonna is one of the most popular images in Eastern Europe, which just reflects how much hope and affection people place in this Virgin Mary."

"Tell me a little more about her? Why is she black?"

By now, Vega had greatly expanded on Irina's interpretation. "The famous Black Madonna from Vladimir is one of the most powerful images in art. Not only did she drive out the Mongols and the Tartars from Russia, but she is also a descendant of the mighty Egyptian goddess, Isis. Isis had the power to bring the dead back to life, as she did with her husband Osiris. Isis was the mother to the Horus child, and she was the nurturing goddess, compassionate and always willing to hear the pleas of her worshippers. But her black color also points to another more mysterious aspect of her nature. Going back to prehistory, she is nothing less than a personification of the all- powerful earth goddess. She is black like the most fertile soil. She is black like the Indian goddess, Kali, mistress over life and death. She is one of the last links to an ancient time, when matriarchy ruled, and women were the dominating gender." Vega concluded triumphantly.

The lady smiled slightly. "I'll take it," she announced with authority. After Vega wrapped it up for her, the woman walked off with a little spring in her step.

Vega should have felt good after her first sale, but she didn't. In fact, she felt outright horrible. She was always tired, and her belly hurt so badly that she could barely stand.

Finally, the elderly security guard took a long look at her and said, "Vega, you better go see a doctor, you look terrible. Your face is outright yellow."

"I don't feel so well, but I'll be fine. I like this job. I don't want to go home sick after only three days," she protested, but after work she went to see her doctor. He took one look at her eyes, now completely yellow, and diagnosed acute Hepatitis B.

"But how?" she wanted to know.

The doctor shook his head slightly. "Exchange of bodily fluids, a dirty needle…"

Vega lowered her head. Wanting to get warm at the beach of Haarlem had done her in. She thought she had gotten away, but Tom had caught up with her.

"Now what?" she asked.

"You are going directly to the hospital and into quarantine."

"But I have a job."

"You are highly infectious. You cannot interact with anybody for the next few weeks."

"Weeks?"

"I called the hospital and an ambulance. They are expecting you," the doctor insisted.

"But I can drive myself."

"No, you cannot. Do you have anybody who can pick up your car?"

Vega thought about Klaus. He owed her. He'd take care of her car. The time had come to face her problems, to face herself.

"Can you call anybody to bring you some clothes and toiletries?"

Vega nodded. From the doctor's office she called Lisa and asked her to meet her at the hospital.

**

Lisa met her at the hospital with a small suitcase and a pained expression.

Just like the Vladimir Madonna, Vega thought. She did not have the strength to explain herself.

"I will be back tomorrow, dear," Lisa said through the glass barrier, separating patient and visitors. "Do you want anything?"

"Please bring me the Max Ernst print from my room," Vega said and turned toward the wall. She felt bad knowing Lisa had to take a long tram ride home, and for causing her mother more suffering.

Chapter 15: Diamonds in the Sky

"Look for the girl with the sun in her eyes and she's gone—Lucy in the Sky with Diamonds . . ." John Lennon and Paul McCartney, 1966

In the quarantine ward, a glass panel separated Vega from the rest of the world. The sterile isolation room became her bubble where her body could heal its jaundice and for her mind might regain its sanity. The impression of that room would stay in her memory and reemerge years later. In this room, for five weeks, twenty-four hours a day Vega was alone with her thoughts, memories, nightmares, and guilt.

At first her mother visited every day, then every second day, and finally once a week. Vega was glad the visits diminished. She knew how hard it was for Lisa to travel the long way to the hospital after work. They felt uncomfortable around each other. Vega because she felt guilty for adding to Lisa's burden, and Lisa because her daughter was a drug addict, a disappointment, and had damaged her liver at a young age.

Klaus came once. He did not have good news. Little Feet had caught fire in Klaus' workshop and was now in the junkyard, the graveyard for cars. Like so much else from her recent past, Vega mourned it briefly then let it go.

Besides these few visits, Vega's only anchor to the outside world was the print of Max Ernst's painting *Die Ganze Stadt,* the entire city. Despite its title, the painting did not look like a city but like a coiled snake. The picture became the gate through which Vega could enter the agitated regions of her mind. It became a tool, helping her to pry strands of her recent experiences, still undigested, and forge them into words.

She began to realize that words could give substance and form to the fears and feelings she did not understand. Words made those difficult feelings manageable and allowed her to deal with them. Giving shape to the unexplainable was what artists did every day.

**

"She saw the city lying in front of her on a hill. Like a sleeping snake, she lay curled around the summit," she wrote as the first sentence of a story unfolding inside Max Ernst's city. Once Vega had entered the painting, the story seemed to write itself.

To gain access, however, she had to traverse a layer of menacing looking plants sprouting eyes and small jaws in unexpected places, which populated the foreground of the painting. The creatures of darkness seemed like fugitives from a Hieronymus Bosch painting of hell. Gaping mouths, spiked heads, claws shaped like tentacles. Curious mixtures of carnivorous plants and malevolent imps, ready to gnaw her approaching legs, ready to enter her nightmare and lodge themselves into the crevices of her mind. This micro-jungle had to be conquered just to reach the outer walls of the city or the thickest part of the snake's body.

In the dark-green sky above the city hung a lemon-yellow full moon. The moon, like the glowing night sky in which it traveled, had a green tint, giving its light less warmth and more menace. Like the cold moon on Vega's first date with Tom, this was a German, male moon. Like a middle-aged gentleman, he disapproved and illuminated the creatures of the night that should have stayed hidden in darkness. Inadvertently, he might have drawn them out with his pale light. Unlike Ernst's painting of the *Great Forest*, the moon in *The Entire City* did not offer an escape hole. She could only save herself by reaching the center, following the snake to its inner core.

Vega sat in her hospital bed, typing feverishly. Once inside the painting, she could follow the coils of the giant, brown cobra rolled up into a spiral, ascending toward the middle in ever-tighter loops. At the very center, a fortress loomed, or maybe it was just the distorted head of the snake above the brown layers of its body. That center was her destination. There she would encounter herself and turn her experiences into art.

**

Her doctor came to check on her blood values, but she barely responded to his questions.

"You're making good progress," he told Vega.

"I am glad."

"Fortunately your acute Hepatitis B will go away by itself eventually with plenty of rest, good nutrition, and fluids. Our main goal is to keep you from infecting others, and to prevent the disease from progressing into chronic hepatitis, which won't go away."

Once in a while, the young doctor allowed Vega to smoke a cigarette with him, which was obviously strictly forbidden but tasted even better because of it. He wanted to gain her confidence in order to assess her drug abuse and mental state. He asked her what she was writing.

"It's just a story about the city in this picture," Vega responded evasively.

"I don't even see a city," he said. "It looks more like a huge, brown snake to me."

"Exactly."

"What's the story about?"

"All the strange creatures I meet inside."

"Inside the picture?"

"Inside the painting and inside the city."

"Hmm," he pondered. "Who painted it?"

"Max Ernst. He was a German Dadaist and Surrealist, from the early twentieth century."

"The more I look at it, the more interesting stuff I see, like those creatures in the foreground and that green moon. So, you spend all day with this snake?"

Vega nodded.

"Can I read it?"

"I don't think so."

Vega had no intention of inviting this doctor into her fever dream. She couldn't let anybody know what she had done. Getting back to writing was her only salvation. Her pent-up emotions wanted to pour onto the waiting paper. Writing had become part of her inner healing process running parallel to her body getting better, stronger, and cleansed of toxins. By naming the images and metaphors that flooded the empty pages in her typewriter, she began to digest what had happened and to make it less disturbing. Her sanity depended on entering this city and on following the upward spiral toward the summit. She knew she had to unravel the knots that kept her off balance and separated from the center of her own being.

In her nightmares, she finally conquered the little monsters by giving them names and petting their ruffled feathers. She silenced their shrill twitters by feeding them berries and bark. Now she could approach the city and find an entrance between the folds of the outer layers.

In eerie silence, she walked up the ramp between the windowless walls of snake skin. As she reached the first turn on the empty path, she heard a warning rattle. At the curve leading to the spiral's next level a rattlesnake kept guard. Like an Indian Kundalini snake curled up at the bottom of one of the Chakras, the eight power points along the spine, this coiled snake threatened to leap into action and take over her life. Only writing kept it under control.

Along the path, she encountered eight small snakes, each one with the face of Tom surrounded by a halo of his blood. Unleashed without precaution, the ancient serpents could become lethal. To tame them, she coaxed and befriended them by telling them soothing tales of the ocean and of the wide open sky. If she could handle and awaken them correctly, their dangerous power might become a source of insight and wisdom. But Vega was still a long way from that goal.

Where did all these snakes come from? Why did she have to confront them? Their raw energy remained dormant in most people. It dawned on Vega that piercing the reality of the world around her had uncoiled the Kundalini snakes and set them free. The unraveling had begun the moment Vega had stepped through the gates of perception, when she took her first trip with Tom.

**

During the long, quiet days in the hospital, she hammered out her story. At night she sat in the empty, white room and gazed over the balcony banister. She saw the city spread out in front of her; saw the golden fingers of dusk set the windows of skyscrapers on fire. The city lights twinkled and glimmered at twilight. To Vega they looked like multi-colored diamonds displayed on black velvet. Sparkling, glittering and desirable, yet out of reach. The city lights shone like a glamorous mirror-image of the starry sky above. Both made her feel small and unimportant. She found comfort in the thought that it didn't matter whether she traveled among the stars or the lights of the city. Neither cared. They remained cold, indifferent, and unaffected.

Yet, as small and insignificant as she felt on a cosmic scale, Vega knew that like everybody else, she carried her own private universe.

Part II

Macrocosmic Traveler

Chapter 16: Vega in Lyra

"Memory is selective at best and deceptive at worst. Not much use in a court of law, but maybe sufficient for a story like this, because it preserves what impressed itself upon the mind most urgently and shaped it into what it is." Vega Stern, 2001

Vega lay on her back inside a pink sleeping bag on the cool sand of the Dead Sea's beach. She looked up at the night sky, searching for the far outstretched wings of the constellation Swan. When she found it, she let her eyes wander slightly in a southeastern direction until her glance fell onto the fifth brightest star in the sky: Vega.

Looking for the great summer triangle was another way to find her star. Vega, in Lyra, formed one of its corners next to Altair and Deneb, but it easily outshone the other two stars in brightness. No wonder, Vega mused. It was located only twenty-five light years away, one of earth's closest neighbors. The same kind of star as our sun, only three times larger and fifty times brighter, Vega in Lyra is surrounded by a stellar cloud-disc. Like our sun, it possesses planets like the ones in our own solar system. As she focused on the sparkling speck of light far away, she pictured small planets circling her star, even though none had been discovered, yet. Planets with tiny creatures, who could be looking in her direction, to the small and dim solar system in the insignificant galaxy called the Milky Way.

That name triggered a memory about a nightclub called Milky Way in Amsterdam, where she had not so long ago danced to the dreamy tunes of Lynnard Skynnard surrounded by smoky wafts of marihuana and hashish clouds. It felt like a memory from another life, a pleasant idea, but one that was connected with unpleasant thoughts. Those thoughts continued to pop up at inconvenient times, no matter how often she pushed them away. Resolutely, Vega focused back onto the night sky, letting the images from Amsterdam drift and fade into the dark desert around her.

Vega's star was named after the Arabic word for a swooping eagle. That thought led her in a direction she was not sure she wanted to pursue. Just today she had seen two majestic eagles riding the warm air currents in the canyon, below the two-thousand-year-old fortress Masada. They barely flapped their wings, content to simply glide, circling between the red and ochre cliffs of the desert fortress. Vega had sat on the crumbling wall surrounding the plateau, actually looking down onto the great birds. This unusual perspective had given her an idea of what the eagles saw during their flight.

With their super-sharp eyes she imagined them focusing on minute movements in the rocks, movements she could not possibly detect. Vega spent an hour of great clarity and stillness, sitting on the stone wall with the remnants of the Masada fortress behind her and the empty expanse of the Negev desert stretching out in front of her. Nobody else was there, making the silence almost audible.

The colors of the rock formations in their limited palette of yellow, red, beige, and brown repeated themselves in infinite variations. Combined with the razor sharp shadows of boulders and canyons, they created an abstract pattern. The impression etched itself into her mind. She felt very much alive in this deadest of all landscapes, where even the life-less Dead Sea gave no relief.

That thought brought her back to the eagles, the only creatures that had shared the afternoon with her. Eventually one of them had abruptly terminated its lazy glide and dove down with deadly precision to pick up a lizard for lunch. She hoped the swooping eagle had been rewarded with a tasty prey.

Not surprisingly the ruins of Masada inspired morbid thoughts. After all, two- thousand years ago, during the Jewish revolt against the Romans, almost one thousand Jewish rebels had chosen to commit mass suicide, rather than surrender to the Roman army when it stormed their fortress after a three-year siege.

Vega shuddered at such uncompromising fanaticism, but the stark landscape seemed to encourage it. There were no shades of gray to be found in this desert—there was only survival or death, beauty or terror. Those eagles circling beside the bizarre jagged edges of Masada had reminded her of a phoenix, rising out of the flaming heat of the desert. She hoped she could be like them and not fall again.

She wanted to stuff the past into some drawers of her mind, start over, and rise above the wreckage. The Dead Sea beach seemed as good a place as any to change. It held no memories, no references to her former life, nobody she knew, no familiar language. It contained only a stark and empty landscape. In fact, she wanted to be nowhere else than right there, right now. She wriggled more deeply into her sleeping bag. The soft sand of the beach molded itself according to the contours of her body. Lying there like a shiny pink mummy, she felt strangely safe and protected.

While her heavy eyelids started to droop, her mind conjured up the image of a painting by Salvador Dali entitled *The Burning Giraffe*. Vega remembered the painting with an orange burning giraffe galloping through a desert in front of a dark-blue twilight sky. In fact, despite the painting's name, the burning giraffe was only a small feature. Instead, a very tall and skeletal body of a woman took up the entire foreground. She barely fit into the picture frame, and part of her faceless head was cut off at the upper edge. Crutches propped up her body, and her arms were outstretched in front of her as if she was attempting an unsure step ahead. Her left leg and chest were studded with partially open drawers. It was impossible to look inside and see whether they were empty or contain any objects.

On her right, the woman was flanked by another female figure also held upright by crutches. She extended her right arm holding aloft a flaming cloth. That Vega vividly remembered the burning giraffe, which is just a small detail in the painting's background, and not the towering women, was an example of the imprecise nature of human memory. The mind processes only those bits and pieces it deems important and worthy based on an unknown priority system.

Vega's mind, on the edge between sleep and wakefulness, wandered vaguely, drifting through the image. She floated over the empty desert landscape to the small, untidy drawers, gliding like the eagles she had observed that afternoon, without effort or self-control. Within her mind's journey, Vega opened one of the drawers and found four broken mirror pieces inside. When she looked into them, she saw the same face staring back at her from each shard. It was not her own. It was Tom's, pale and lifeless; behind him dirty, wet asphalt and a pool of his blood.

Vega quickly shut that drawer and moved to the next. Here, she found a picture of her mother looking sad and timid. Lisa's limp, brown hair framed her kind face with its shy, brown eyes anxiously smiling. Vega quickly slid this drawer back into its slot.

A midsized drawer toward the middle of the figure's thigh opened to reveal a small, shiny shape of a pyramid: the promised pyramid, a phantom, or a figment of her overactive imagination. This pyramid was the engine of her quest, the driving force behind her journey. Vega's world view, her personal universe hinged on its existence. She had no idea what shape it would take and where she would find it, if she ever found it at all. Therefore, she had to be open to all possibilities.

She sighed and moved on to another, slightly larger drawer, which contained an image of a different nighttime beach, where she had slept not long ago, and not too comfortably either. Unlike the quiet, empty stretch of sand where she lay now, on that beach she had been surrounded by the sounds of a harbor and by lights piercing the darkness. The sounds of cargo ships being unloaded during the early morning hours had kept her awake. She did not want to be reminded of that night either.

Her curiosity about the contents of the drawers stilled, she moved her attention to the smaller figure on the right. Suddenly it turned toward her, and Vega recognized the outlines of the Statue of Liberty with her flaming torch reduced to a burning rag. Her formerly stately body, now thin and feeble, was supported by a system of crutches. She was as unstable as the large central figure. Vega saw her sway and feared the woman would fall. She meant to warn her, but as Vega looked for her face, she realized there was no mouth, eyes, or ears to perceive a message, only a red and brittle surface that now cracked and broke into pieces. The crackling face reminded Vega of an old painting whose varnish consisted of a web of minute cracks created by centuries of exposure to heat and cold.

Deciding to open one more drawer before going to sleep, Vega's mind drifted to the largest drawer on the woman's chest. It opened onto a white and sterile hospital room. In the bed, right in the center of the room, she saw a thinner, paler version of herself wearing a light-blue hospital gown. In the nearly empty room, only an old-fashioned typewriter sat on the small bedside table. With this image, Vega drifted off to sleep.

**

When she woke up, the sun glared onto her face, and her mouth felt dry and sandy. Time to drive south to Eilat at the entrance to the Sinai desert. Vega stopped briefly in the Ein Gedi snack bar for some coffee and a muffin. Few tourists were out at this time of day. She had the small coffee stand to herself as well as the view of the eerily still Dead Sea in front of her. Crystallized salt pieces floated like chunks of ice.

She liked early mornings, before the crowds came out, and was grateful for the silence of the young attendant who listened to the radio and ignored her. He filled all the coffee pots and set up for the rush of the day. After breakfast, Vega walked to the bus stop and waited in the shade for the bus. She did not mind the wait, the temperature was pleasant, and the glistening Dead Sea in front of her looked like a surreal foreground for the bright yellow mountains of Jordan, on the other side of the small inland water.

She let her thoughts wander back to the beginning of her journey. She had come a long way from the sterile hospital room in Germany, and she had not gotten to this desert in a straight line.

Chapter 17: Departure

"I'm free, I'm free – and freedom tastes of reality."
The Who, *Tommy*, 1969

Vega stepped outside the hospital door, released from quarantine, and presumably cured. She felt free, very free, even a little too free. She didn't know where to go or what to do next. Klaus had totaled Little Feet while she was in the hospital, leaving her unencumbered by any possessions. She had no attachments, emotionally or chemically, and the pains and pleasures of her past seemed meaningless. She thought she had freed herself from Tom, but his ghost haunted her every night. His pale face surrounded by red blood appeared in her nightmares.

During the day, avoiding emotions became her goal for fear they would swallow her up. Maybe her life was over; she had ruined it. She simply walked through a state of limbo until disaster struck, as it was bound to. However, after pursuing death for so long, she had decided to live. She had to do something. Since art remained the only thing that appeared meaningful, the only thing that made sense and lifted her mind out limbo, she wanted to spend more time understanding its power. She decided to study art history at the University of Tübingen.

**

May 1977: Tübingen
But an unbridgeable gap separated her from the other students. Vega felt disconnected and alienated. She had killed a man. How could she trust anybody? How could she be trusted? They could not know what it was like inside her mind. They seemed only worried about grades

and dates and lunch. Vega worried about prison and death and eternal damnation.

Unlike Nietzsche she was not beyond good and evil. Philosophy and art couldn't help her, couldn't keep the nightmares at bay. Deep-rooted fears for her mortal soul fought with her reasoning that she had acted in self-defense.

After another sleepless night interrupted by dreams of Tom's lifeless face, she crept through her classes. Her own face was deathly pale and with dark circles under her eyes. As soon as the lights went out in her art history classes to show slides, she nodded off, only to startle awake after seeing Tom's face.

**

After a few weeks at university her mother Lisa called with an urgent message.

"Vega? How are you?"

"I am okay, Mom. What's up with you?"

"The police were here looking for you."

Vega's heart skipped a beat, and she felt fear rising up to her throat. She could barely talk. "What did they want?" she croaked."

"They wanted to talk to you. Something about Tom."

"Oh god, is he in trouble again?" Vega improvised.

"I don't know; they weren't too specific. I gave them your address, but I wanted you to know, so you are not surprised."

"Okay Mom, thanks."

Vega hung up and her first instinct was to flee immediately. She ran to her room and with shaking hands, threw some clothes into a bag. Fortunately, she hardly owned anything. How much time did she have before the police showed up? Where could she go?

Klaus owed her. She could stay at his house in the country for a few days until she figured out what to do. She grabbed her bag and went to the cafeteria to get something to eat before catching a bus leaving town.

There, as so often at significant points in her life, a coincidence occurred. Maybe it was serendipity or an intervention of fate, but it might as well just have been dumb luck. At the cafeteria, Heidi stood in line next to Vega. A former schoolmate, Heidi was one of the girls who had treated Vega like an outcast when she got involved with drugs. They both held dishes of mashed potatoes and meat smothered in gravy, with limp lettuce, served in cardboard bowls and non-recyclable Styrofoam plates.

Heidi mentioned casually that she had been offered a summer job as a stewardess on a cruise ship, which crossed the Mediterranean Sea. "The ship is part of an Italian line, but unfortunately the season starts before the end of the semester, so I had to turn the job down," she explained.

A job on a cruise ship might be just the escape hatch Vega needed. Pictures of the port of Venice popped up in her mind; whitecaps on the open sea, a passage across the Mediterranean with no land in sight until the emerald green of a Greek island emerged in the distance. Far away from the German police and their inquiries about Tom's demise, she would be unreachable on a ship at sea.

"Heidi, how can I contact the cruise ship company? I am interested in the job."

"The ship leaves in a week," Heidi answered sullenly. "The semester won't be out until three weeks after that."

"I know, I know, but can you just give me the number? I'm considering finding out more about it."

"Well, suit yourself," Heidi responded dismissively. She still did not like Vega and resented the idea of helping her. "They only speak Italian."

With this threat, she gave Vega a name and a very long number, which Vega wrote down in her notebook next to her class notes about the Italian Renaissance.

"Thank you, Heidi, thank you very much." Vega walked away before her schoolmate could hurl more obstacles in her direction.

Cornelia Feye

Chapter 18: Mountaintop Encounter

"Come up to me on the mountain, and wait there…" *Exodus*, 24:12

For the first time since leaving the hospital, Vega felt emotions: fear, excitement, a morsel of hope. Maybe her life was not over; maybe, once she crossed beyond Europe's border, fear of discovery would lift from her shoulders and she could breathe easier.

The cruise ship, *Anaeas Lauro*, sailed from Italy to Greece, Egypt, and Israel. Vega had never been outside of Europe. She had only been to Switzerland and Austria as a child. Lisa, Vega and her brother used to visit their Swiss aunt Mary, an artist who lived in an ivy-covered old house in a part of Locarno called Minusio, directly across the road from the Lago Maggiore. Now she pictured the pyramids in Egypt, the walls of Jerusalem, and narrow ancient streets peopled by men wearing long robes, conversing in languages undecipherable by German, English, French, and Spanish language skills.

In broken English, an operator for Lauro Lines answered the phone. Vega had to use creative communication skills to explain that she wanted to work on the cruise ship for the summer. Apparently the message got through because within two days Vega received the first telegram of her life. It read: "Anaeas Lauro leaves Genoa on May 13 Pier 53 stop…be on board before 1 PM stop…room, board, and salary provided stop"

"I guess I am packing," she said to herself.

**

Fortunately, her art history professor agreed to let her complete an assignment during the semester break, using her access to Renaissance art in Venice, and her Anthropology professor was outright delighted that she was "planning fieldwork" in the Middle East as she had put it. Vega intended to visit the Bedouins in the Sinai desert and write about their culture. Thankfully, Vega didn't have to deal with engineers and scientists like Heidi, who studied Architecture.

**

For a few days, Vega stayed with Klaus and blended in with his country commune of assorted hippies and drop-outs. Klaus was emotionally stable and did not use heroin. He enjoyed smoking pot and taking acid, which he considered harmless and conducive to increased creativity. When she told him she was going to sea for a few months, Klaus offered to drive her to the ship in Genoa. Their friendship was pleasantly non-committal, and Klaus still felt bad for totaling Vega's car while she was in the hospital. The trip would be his payback.

They left on a Friday afternoon and drove south to Switzerland toward the Gotthard tunnel into Northern Italy.

To spice up the long drive, they took some acid at nightfall. As they entered the seventeen-kilometer-long tunnel, digging its way through the Alps, the chemicals started to take effect. The empty tube of freeway running underneath the massive mountains became a portal into a different dimension. Time seemed to slow down, and the *Alan Parson Project*, provided appropriate space-age background music. When they popped out on the other side of the tunnel, a complete change in climate and scenery greeted them. Palm trees and warm breezes delighted their senses. Enchanted, they felt like entering a magic realm.

**

The warm air and glittering lake reminded Vega of her childhood and family vacations at the Lago Maggiore. Her aunt Mary, old but still with a sparkle in her ice-blue eyes, had one day announced that they needed to take a day trip to a tiny mountain village of Indemini. Mary, Vega, her mother Lisa, and her young brother had taken the mail bus on a hair-raising journey up narrow switchbacks. The bus driver had honked his horn at every turn of the road to warn oncoming vehicles. Once in a while, they had to drive backwards to a turnout place to let the downward-bound traffic pass as they were caught between the abyss on one side and the steep mountain ascending on the other.

Why had Vega's aunt, an artist, insisted on this trip? She usually was quite content to paint or throw pottery in the shady courtyard of her Ticino house, where overgrown vines covered the entire facade of the old buildings, including balconies and outside stairways.

Mary wanted them to see Indemini for a reason. Something about the place was really important to her. It used to be a smuggler's paradise, remote, and midway between Switzerland and Italy. Vega wondered if that could have been the reason for her invitation. What was her attraction to this tiny place?

Once they had arrived in the miniscule mountain village, which hung on the rocks like a swallow's nests attached by mud and straw, Vega walked away from her family to sit on top of the rocks and look down over the vast valley below. She had been twelve at the time, starting to create her own inner life, and she already cherished time spent by herself. The wind up there felt cooler, the small purple flowers looked scrawnier than down in the lush, tropical valley, and the view seemed endless.

Sitting on a rock, Vega decided to return in the future. She couldn't define what attracted her. Was it the sparse and ascetic beauty, or its hidden and mysterious location? Was it Mary's high esteem for Indemini? Vega admired her aunt and trusted her judgment of the village as important and special. She knew her aunt had brought them there for a reason. The villagers' mud and stone walls concealed a secret, she suspected.

Her family finally called her back to the bus for the arduous descent back down to the lake. There was no time for further exploration, but in her diary that night, Vega had meticulously recorded the way to Indemini including names of small villages they passed along the road, and turn-offs to take.

**

Seven years later, Vega found herself in similar surroundings.

Names on directional signs sounded familiar.

"We have to go to Indemini," she announced to her driving companion.

"What is Indemini?" Klaus asked.

"It's a small village. I visited there as a child, and I need to go back," Vega tried to explain. "It's just off to the left, up the mountain past Locarno." She remembered her diary notes written in childish handwriting, which she had tried to adjust to make it look more grown up.

"We have to turn off here," she announced with authority as they passed the quaint town of Magadino, then the dark, smooth surface of the Lake to their left, and the gently swaying palm trees on their right, their patterned bark eerily illuminated by the orange glow of the street lights.

"It's getting pretty dark, and I really would prefer to stay on the well-lit roads along the lake," Klaus answered patiently.

"I know, but we have to go to Indemini. This is very important. This is why my aunt took us there many years ago. The whole purpose of this trip might be to come to Indemini. Maybe the whole purpose of my life is to go there now."

"Well, in that case," Klaus said, with a trace of irony, which was completely lost on Vega. Resigned, he turned into a narrow road to their right, climbing up the mountains. They attacked the hair-raising ascent, on slippery switchbacks, in complete darkness.

The road seemed to go on forever, between the steep abyss to their left and the rocky boulders interrupted by pine trees on their right. Fortunately no other cars were foolish enough to attempt either the climb in or out of the mountain range at night. The time stretched as they drove, silently concentrating on one switchback, one curve at a time.

**

Helped by acid, a film unraveled in Vega's mind, showing scenes from her life up to this moment. However short in years, it appeared to be full of significant events. She felt determined that it had been a quest, a search for purpose and for the divine.

She saw herself as a small girl at church with her mother on Sundays, kneeling on a wooden bench, shifting uncomfortably.

Automatically, she answered to the Latin phrases of the priest *Domino, Filio et Spirito Sancto.* Not knowing what she was saying, she still thought it sounded good and hoped it was some kind of spell that would magically establish a connection between her and God, or Jesus, or Mary. She was not quite sure to whom she was supposed to pray. Every Sunday, she had stared at the stiff, bronze sculpture of the risen Christ hanging behind the altar, as she listened to the organ blasting in her ears. She enjoyed smelling the incense, fanned over the congregation by the priest with the help of an interesting swinging pendulum contraption. She imagined that the wafting smoke helped to open the doors to another world. She admired the priest's gold and purple robe as he sprinkled holy water over his flock with a flask that looked similar to the bottlebrush by her sink at home.

**

Vega's thoughts snapped back to the present, during a switchback on the glistening road winding itself tightly around a hair-raising bend. As the car made a slippery turn, tall pine trees appeared like ghosts in the darkness, like guardians barring the way to the top.

"How much farther do we have to go?" Klaus asked in a strained voice.

"It can't be much longer. It has been a long time since I was here, and that was during daylight. It's hard to tell," Vega answered a little doubtful.

"I wish it was daylight now," Klaus said tersely.

"Do you want me to drive?" Vega offered.

"Yeah, that would be nice. I'm getting really tired."

They stopped at a narrow turnout, and as Vega walked around the car to the driver's side, she smelled the moist mountain air, sprinkled with the scent of pine. She noticed the outlines of the trees in rainbow colors. They have a rainbow aura, Vega thought astonished.

She sat down and took the wheel, determined to see this trip through to the end. But as she continued the slow and precarious climb, her thoughts soon strayed again, this time ten years back, when she was nine years old.

**

On the holiday of Corpus Christi, flags had lined the pews. The altar boys had worn their best red and white outfits lined with lace around the collars, and their hair was combed back with sugar water. They had stood like an honor guard on the stairs leading toward the altar, each holding a candle. The priest walked by in slow and measured steps underneath a baldachin, carrying the monstrance with the sacred body of Christ. The procession wandered through the streets and stopped at the Stations of the Cross, which had been laid out as flower carpets by pious women. The congregation sang hymns. Vega looked enviously at the girls, all dressed in white, who marched together in the front of the procession, immediately following the baldachin. They proudly displayed their fancy, new communion dresses. During this time of innocence, Vega still believed that the church could open the doors to heaven. It was before she had her own communion and her first disappointment in the powers of the church.

**

All these images went through Vega's mind as she curved up the Swiss mountainside toward Indemini: the flower carpets in the streets at the Corpus Christi procession, her own cream-colored dress and pearl-covered tiara, and the shame of failing to live up to her elaborate expectations of First Communion. She remembered her Aunt Mary dressed all in white, taking her to Indemini. Vega's experiments with drugs now seemed like an extension of the quest for reaching the divine. All those experiences had led her to this moment, this night in May, this Swiss mountainside.

The car reached a plateau. The road evened out. Snow piled up high at this altitude in the Alps. There were no more trees, no more boulders, and Vega could not remember crossing a field of this kind on her first visit to Indemini.

"This is it," her companion said. "I am not going any farther. It is two o'clock in the morning, and I've had enough."

Fortunately, Vega was still reasonable enough to recognize he was right, especially since they were driving his car. They stopped at a parking platform surrounded by piles of snow. No stars penetrated the cloud cover, no Vega in the constellation Lyra served as a guiding light. Reclining the seats and pulling out blankets, they decided to stay here until morning.

**

Much too high for sleep, Vega lay quietly in her seat, peering out of the windshield at a sign in front of the car. She could make out strange fields of bright color that began to move and become liquid. They swam into each other, constantly reshaping themselves and forming new patterns, like oil and water, only more complex. The colors seemed to possess a life of their own, like jellyfish, or amoeba in a fertile swamp. She did not dare to make a sound, but suddenly she heard voices. Vega knew that these voices were in her head because her companion, who had fallen into an exhausted sleep beside her, did not seem to hear them. The voices came through something like a narrow, long pipe directly into her mind. Vega panicked.

Her heart raced madly. Fear took hold of her, fear of a heart attack, fear of losing her mind. The communication in her head continued in a language she could not determine, but it felt like thoughts being directly transmitted into her brain. She was certain there were several entities interacting with her mind.

"Who are you?" she thought.

Her question was greeted with laughter from the other side of the portal. "Who do you think we are? Who have you been trying to reach so desperately?"

"I suppose, I've been trying to contact the gods," Vega conceded, feeling foolish.

Again laughter.

"Are you real? How do I know this is not just an illusion or a hallucination? Can you give me a sign, proof that I am not just imagining this? Am I really communicating with you?"

"Aren't you demanding?" was their amused response. "What kind of proof did you have in mind?"

Vega thought feverishly. Not an easy task to define a fitting proof for divine existence. "A pyramid?" she ventured. After all, she was going to Egypt. To her, the shape of the pyramids had always represented cosmic and divine proportions.

"If that is what you want, a pyramid it shall be," came the

answer directly into her head.

"Wait, don't go away! Now that I finally have you on the line, so to speak, I need to ask you some questions. What is the purpose of my life? Will I ever be forgiven for what I have done? Will I be caught and punished? Can you tell me what I am supposed to do?"

These requests seemed to greatly amuse them as their laughter grew. "You ask things you already know. Be yourself. Live truly and honestly in the moment. Forgive yourself if you want to be forgiven. Practice wisdom and compassion. But you know all of this."

With these pronouncements, the connection was severed, and Vega suddenly slumped down in her seat, like a deflated balloon. The strain of driving all night caught up with her, and she felt utterly exhausted and drained.

Typical, I should have known, she thought. Of course they would throw me back onto my own devices. They couldn't tell me something more specific like the purpose of my life is to save orphans, or to save the rainforest, or something like that. They could not tell me what I should do for penance, only that I had to forgive myself. Instead: Just live in the moment.

Exhaustion rose through her body and into her head. The chemicals and the adrenaline fueling the encounter and the search for Indemini slowly subsided. It is the story of my life, she thought. I have unlimited freedom to make my own choices and my own mistakes. She had certainly made choices and some huge mistakes. Now she had to live with that.

**

As teenagers, Vega's friends had envied her for her tolerant mother who let her go where she wanted, do what she wanted, and come home whenever she wanted. Without limits, Vega had pushed ahead exploring borderline situations; those bordering on death, on madness, on the criminal. She had explored the dark side of freedom. How could her mother and now these supernatural entities have so much confidence in her, assuming that she could handle so much freedom? Hadn't she demonstrated sufficiently that she was floundering, that she did not have good judgment, that she needed guidance? Guidance was apparently not what she was going to get.

**

As she drifted off into a light sleep, Vega felt grateful and confused at the same time. She had experienced a form of communication completely unknown to her until now: a communication that did not depend on language, words, or sound but somehow arrived with complete clarity directly inside her head. It had even expressed emotions like humor and amusement. Amusement, she realized, at her expense; however, wasn't it flattering to be a cosmic laughing stock? There also had been a promise, a pyramid to soothe her doubts, give her something to hold onto, something to look for on her journey.

**

Waking up in the morning, feeling stiff and freezing cold, Vega realized she and Klaus were less than five-hundred meters away from Indemini.

They arrived in the village and over café au lait served in big white mugs and sweet buns at the small bakery, Klaus asked casually, "So, this is it, the place of your destiny?"

"Actually, I had a very strange encounter last night," Vega began, reluctantly. Now, in the pale light of morning, her sacred conversation seemed a lot less significant than the night before. Maybe it had just been an acid dream. She decided she was done with LSD. It had taken her as far as it could, and she had not forgotten her fear of a near heart attack. If she got her proof, then she could be content, and if not, that would be an answer as well. "I communicated with several beings that were more than human."

"What did they say?" What had they told her? Not much.

"I asked them about the purpose of my life."

"Always a good question to ask. Did they tell you?"

"Well, they told me I already knew the answer. And that I had to live authentically, moment to moment." She omitted her question about forgiveness.

"I could have told you that. Are you sure there were several?"

"Definitely several. And I asked them for proof of their existence."

"That's a little more interesting. What did they say to that?"

"They promised me a pyramid."

"Why a pyramid?"

"It seemed like a fitting symbol."

"Well, you are going to Egypt. Maybe you'll find one," Klaus said without much enthusiasm.

"Yes, maybe."

They concluded their conversation and breakfast to complete the rest of the journey to Genoa uneventfully. Klaus dropped Vega off at the pier in front of the gigantic cruise ship Anaeas Lauro. They said goodbye without much hope for a future reunion. Klaus seemed relieved to end this adventure.

**

He drove back to Germany after depositing Vega. It was going to be a long drive because he had not slept well the night before in his car on the freezing mountaintop. He had better ways to spend his weekend than driving halfway across Europe, without rest, without proper food, following the weird whims of Vega. He shook his head thinking about the wild-goose chase up the mountain along the dark, treacherous roads. They could have killed themselves. And why had he put himself and his car in all that danger? So she could have breakfast at a godforsaken little village and fulfill some sentimental memory from a childhood vacation. He was glad it was all over. He just wanted to go home and have a bath. He had performed beyond the call of duty. He had dropped her off at the ship, and now, frankly, he hoped that he would never hear from her again. Communications with divine entities? Right. She'd gone off the deep end, over the edge, taken one too many acid trips. Klaus shuddered.

Chapter 19: Floating World

During the Edo Period (1615-1868), a uniquely Japanese art form, was known as *ukiyo-e*, or "pictures of the floating world." The Buddhist concept, *ukiyo* originally suggested the sadness, or ephemeral nature (*uki*) of life (*yo*).

The Anaeas Lauro transported twelve-hundred passengers with the help of six-hundred staff. Upon entering this floating city, Vega was assigned a berth on the C deck, three stories below sea level, a stewardess uniform, and a duty schedule.

Right away, Vega felt ridiculously happy and free on this ship. Every morning at seven, she reported for her first shift upstairs on the pool deck, six stories above the water. She was usually still groggy from her night shift in the cocktail lounge, part of her eleven-hour workday. But when the warm breeze hit her from the South, and the Mediterranean Sea spread brilliantly blue all around her, there was no other place in the world she would rather be. She had left Tom, Klaus, and her small German town far behind, and she was out of reach of the German authorities, too far from shore even for seagulls. From the pool deck, Vega could see the gentle spray from the prow wave forming sparkling drops in the air. The haunting face of Tom dissolved into mist.

Every morning, the Italian boys staffing the outdoor bar got a large café latte ready for her without prompting. They knew she first had to have a strong coffee before they could venture into any sort of conversation, which was limited at best, because their Neapolitan accents posed a formidable obstacle to her heroic efforts at communicating in Italian.

"*Tutto a posta?*"

"*Si, tutto a posta?*" Yes, all was well.

Fueled by authentic Italian café latte, Vega began her shift. As the sun traveled higher toward its zenith, the boys supplied her with an elaborately decorated piña colada, topped with a small turquoise umbrella and a bright-red maraschino cherry. Vega paraded around the pool with the drink on her tray even though nobody had ordered it. After the tropical cocktail caught their eye, Vega solicited three orders from passengers sunning themselves in the deckchairs.

"What is that? It looks good. Bring me one of those as well, will you?"

"*Natürlich*, certainly," she answered. The grinning bartenders prepared her orders and in exchange she got to drink the initial bait piña colada.

Most of the travelers on the Anaeas Lauro were Germans, and as the only German crewmember, Vega had a language advantage over her colleagues. This resulted in above average tips. Vega got to know the guests who came to the pool in the mornings, to afternoon tea in the salon at five o'clock, and to the cocktail lounge at night. They told her about their lives and their children, and she told them nothing at all, but responded to their stories with apparent interest. In exchange they tipped her generously.

After the night shift at one in the morning, the crew demolished what was left of the elaborate midnight buffet. Each night the ship's chefs created complex ice sculptures, cream desserts, fresh seafood, and fruit. Normally the crew had their own dining room for lunch and dinner. They cherished the late-night passenger food when they got to talk to each other and unwind.

Vega shared her small cabin with five other girls. Triple bunks hugged each side with a narrow walkway in between. It was tight and dark, but the swaying of the ship and the humming of the engine put her to sleep each night like a baby in a cradle. Her roommates were an international crew: Charlene from Boston, Tara from Pittsburg, Madeleine from Australia, and Carmen from Naples. Madeleine had been traveling for two years by the time Vega met her. She justified her lengthy journey with the fact that Australia was so far away, and it was not worthwhile taking a shorter trip. She decided to keep touring until she had seen Europe, Asia, and the Americas. At the rate she was going, that would take her at least another five years.

Carmen hardly interacted with anyone. She spoke limited English and had been on the ship for two years. The Anaeas Lauro was her home, and she resented these foreigners who dropped in and out. She particularly disliked Vega who was so popular with the passengers and usurped her tips. To Carmen, Vega was an unwelcome intruder.

Charlene, a nurse by profession, had trouble coping with the cramped quarters and long hours. She always complained that she needed to talk to someone.

"So talk to us," they prompted. But she would only repeat her need.

"You are talking right now," Madeleine objected.

"Aren't we 'someone?'" asked Tara, who had an analytical mind.

"Don't we count?" Vega wanted to know.

Charlene did not admit it, but apparently they did not count. They were just hippies and drifters in her mind, while she was a professional.

**

The Anaeas Lauro was not a bad place to drift. Even if they had to work long hours, the work was not backbreaking. For a while, Vega felt like a teenager again, discovering life without the burden of her past.

During night and morning shifts, Vega noticed a handsome officer lingering around the pool and cocktail bar. In the morning, he lounged by the pool reading in his bathing trunks, revealing tanned, muscular shoulders and legs. He had wavy brown hair and the proud profile of a member of a patrician Venetian family. His warm hazel eyes often twinkled with amusement, but without any arrogance. In contrast to ordinary crewmembers and mere stewardesses, the officers were allowed, and even encouraged, to mingle with the passengers in their off-duty time. The rest of the crew had a separate deck for rest and recreation, not accessible to the passengers. But the crew worked such long hours that leisure time was practically not existent.

At night, Vega saw the handsome officer more and more frequently in the cocktail lounge, dressed in an attractive white uniform with elaborate gold tassel, which only an Italian man could wear without looking gaudy. He stood at the bar, and every time Vega walked by carrying drinks on a tray his eyes followed her. The name on his uniform read Giulio de Maria, a name that rolled off her tongue when she tried to say it. Fraternization between crewmembers was strictly forbidden but she figured that was only regarding the Italian boys from Naples manning the bars and coffee machines. Certainly she would never allow her interactions with them to go beyond a friendly teasing in broken Italian. But Giulio de Maria must be exempt from all rules.

By the poolside he read books on philosophy and spoke beautiful English with a charming accent. She could not let the opportunity pass to strike up conversations about Nietzsche, which he countered skillfully. As Vega inquired on his reading, leaning down to his lounge chair, she could not help notice his perfectly toned and bronzed shoulder muscles flexing as he changed position. His eyes might have strayed to her bare legs below her uniform a bit longer than necessary.

Giulio's nightly visits to the cocktail lounge seemed to coincide with the end of Vega's duty shift. She felt a jump in her heart rate as they happened to exit the lounge together one night. They causally wandered to the deserted aft deck of the ship. A mild breeze caressed their faces as they looked at the reflection of the moon on the ocean. Vega noticed a golden wedding band on Giulio's ring finger. Good, she thought. No danger of attachment here. The full moon created a shimmering band of golden light in the wake of the mighty Anaeas Lauro.

When their hands and mouths touched for the first time, Vega felt little electric sparks exploding between them. The air was traced with salt and the scent of Africa. They floated between continents, between night and day, between sky and sea, so surely all rules were suspended here. Vega hoped Giulio's wife and children would forgive them because it did not take much seduction skill on either side, before they ended in Giulio's ocean-view cabin on the second deck. Instead of the hum of the engine, they heard the gentle lapping of the waves. And instead of her narrow, dark bunk, Vega stretched in a wide bed bathed in moonbeams. Before the first light of dawn, she had to sneak down five stories into the bowels of the ship to the C deck, only to see Giulio a few hours later poolside, smiling innocently.

**

Twilight coincided with Vega's off-duty hours, as the Anaeas Lauro approached the harbor of Port Said, Egypt. A fading sun streaked the sky and Vega sat cross-legged in her jeans on the crew deck, in the bow of the ship. She felt like sitting on the tip of an arrow flying towards its goal.

Charlene and Carmen sat close by, staring at the sunset. They had noticed Vega's nightly absences and made snippy remarks.

"Been working all night again, Vega?" Charlene quipped.

"Feeding the dolphins all night?" Carmen followed up.

Vega ignored them. The harbor of Port Said opened up before her like a giant book. The huge cruise ship entered silently, gliding into the harbor on both sides. The crimson sun setting over the desert tinted the walls of the whitewashed houses blood red. Muezzins called the faithful to evening prayer from elegant, slender minarets, using their sophisticated loudspeaker systems. Women wearing long *abayas* hushed and gathered children inside. Men settled down on the cooling ground, unrolling prayer rugs, setting their shoes to the side in an orderly manner. Camels stalked by on wobbly legs, swaying gently from side to side like long-legged fashion models.

Chapter 20: Wanderlust

"One's destination is never a place, but a new way of seeing things."
Henry Miller

Vega wasn't the first in her family with wanderlust. Her grandfather had gone to China in the early years of the century, where he'd established himself with an import-export business. In Manchuria, he had married Vega's grandmother, and his oldest daughter, Vega's aunt had been born there. The same grandmother ran a milliner's shop together with her cousin Mary in Port Said. This was the same Aunt Mary, who later lived in Locarno and showed Vega the village of Indemini.

The adventure-genes had skipped a generation and now resurfaced with force in Vega. How could she have thought her life was over, when she hadn't had any idea what was out there? How could she have limited herself to Europe? The world's giant book of wonders and mysteries began to reveal its marvels, and the harbor of Port Said was only the beginning.

**

As they docked at the pier, Port Said's floating market came alive with shimmering, flickering lights. A labyrinth of bobbing boardwalks extended, swaying on the calm waters of the protected harbor. Covered boats lined the wobbly walkways in every direction, loaded with all kinds of goods: sandalwood statues; copper trays decorated with chiseled ornamentations; round, foldable tea tables; spices in open sacks; papyrus scrolls; elaborately inlaid chess sets, with alternating mother-of-pearl and ebony wood patterns.

The passengers disembarked to enter buses bound for Cairo and the pyramids in Giza, while the crew members had a few hours of shore leave and could wander around the floating market. Vega proudly displayed her crew identification, making sure the merchants understood she was not a tourist.

"Crew, crew," they acknowledged and brought out more merchandise from the back of their boats. Vega had her eye on a chess set, glistening with a black-and-white, geometric star pattern. It folded up into a neat box with the carved chessboard inside.

"How much for this chess set?" she asked, trying to sound indifferent.

"Ah," the Egyptian merchant answered, cradling the chess set in his arms like a precious, fragile baby. "This is very special. Made by our most skilled craftsmen in the desert, using an ancient method of inlay. Only using the finest ebony wood and flawless mother of pearl."

"In that case, it is clearly too special for me. I'm just a crew member on the mighty Anaeas Lauro. I will be back in two weeks and have time to look at other chess sets," Vega said and turned away.

"So sorry. I did not realize you crew. Of course, we are all crew. I work on this little boat, you work on big one. We are in the same boat, as they say. Of course, I have a very special price for you."

"How special?" Vega asked, mildly interested.

"Half price, for you. But do not tell anybody," the merchant pleaded.

Vega pondered, and after a lengthy negotiation, agreed on a price.

She ran her fingers over the surface of the board, feeling the texture of the mother-of-pearl star pattern. She carried it back to the ship, the most precious object she had ever owned. She had bought it with her own money, and she had found it in a market in Northern Africa where her ancestor had lived.

Although she felt a connection to Port Said, no pyramid crossed her path. While the passengers visited the plateau at Giza, the crew members on the Anaeas Lauro sailed to Alexandria to pick them up again. From there they continued to Haifa, Israel and Kalamanta, Greece, and then back to Venice, bypassing the great pyramids altogether.

Chapter 21: Sacred Conversation

Sacra conversazione (Italian), Sacred conversation

At the completion of the first two-week cruise, the Anaeas Lauro docked in Venice to embark new passengers. Vega would have liked nothing better than to sit with Giulio de Maria in the Café Florian on the Piazza San Marco, sip cappuccino, talk a little about philosophy, and watch *tutto il mondo* saunter by. However, she had to fulfill her art history assignment by inspecting Bellini's *Madonna Enthroned* in the church of San Zaccaria.

Giulio, after a short consideration, realized that the chance of being seen by one of his Venetian acquaintances with a long-legged blonde who clearly was not his wife, were a lot slimmer in the dimly lit church of San Zaccaria, than at the Café Florian in the middle of San Mark's Square.

They wandered over to the 15th century church whose architecture combined Gothic and Renaissance elements. Inside, the usual buzz of the faithful greeted them. Italian matrons in black dresses lit candles in front of their favorite saints or straightened up brocade altar cloths in side chapels, all the while rattling off Hail Mary at record speed. Few tourists stood around in the aisles, looking out of place in inappropriate shorts and tennis shoes. An elegant, middle-aged woman, dressed in a magenta Armani suit, kneeled on a foot bench toward the back of the church. A silk Versace scarf covered her head. Possibly she repented her sins after completing confession, or maybe she intended to embark on a new one, judging from the furtive glances she cast from under her scarf.

Giulio and Vega positioned themselves in front of the large Bellini painting of the *Madonna Enthroned* from 1505. It was completely surrounded by other religious paintings of similar scale, if lesser quality. Its location high on the wall, plus the dim lighting, made it difficult to see its beauty and details.

Mirroring the pilasters of the church, the Virgin in Bellini's masterpiece sat on a marble throne inside a two-dimensional shrine with spatial perspective. Easily recognizable in her red dress covered by a blue drape, Bellini's Mary held a small, but sturdy Christ child on her lap. Mother and child were flanked by Saint Peter, identified by his keys, Saint Catherine holding the palm frond of martyrdom, and Saint Jerome carrying his Latin translation of the Bible. At the foot of Mary's throne, an angel played the viol. A dome-shaped cupola, inlaid with gold mosaic interspersed with green vines, composed the upper third of painting. The figures sat calmly in the soft shadow of the space. Golden hues of the dome reflected in the skin and drapes of Saint Peter. Bellini's figures were bathed in deep, warm magenta reds reflecting the soft light of the Venice lagoon. The figures didn't look at each other, existing in their separate spaces; serene, and seemingly lost in thought.

"Meet Bellini's *sacra conversazione*. Of course, the saints and the Virgin lived at different times and in different places," Vega mused.

"Then how," Giulio wondered, "are they having a conversation?"

"They must have other means of communication besides words," it dawned on her. Their sacred conversation transcended time and space.

"What do you mean?" asked Giulio.

Vega decided not to share the details of her encounter in Indemini with him.

"Maybe they share the same thoughts?" she said vaguely.

"About what?" asked the scientific mind of the ship's first engineer.

"Obviously, the Christ child in their midst connects them all. Maybe they think about how he has changed their lives, or even how he will change the world."

"That is possible except they do not even look at *il bambino*," countered Giulio, a good catholic.

"But they all share the same space," Vega insisted.

"It's an odd space," Giulio noticed. "There is an egg hanging right in the center of the dome—"

"Yes," Vega interrupted, excited, "a dome in the shape of a shell. Botticelli's Venus rode on a shell, and an egg is connected with Easter and fertility," she pondered further.

"But what does that all have to do with Bellini's Madonna?"

"Botticelli's Venus was known to Bellini. Venus rode to shore on a shell, and this Madonna sits under one. Both women have the same mysterious smile, and both are associated with purity and fertility."

"Are you trying to say the Virgin and the Venus are the same?"

"Maybe not identical but connected. Bellini used classical symbols of Venus and attributed them to the Virgin. This made her more appealing to the people of his era, the Renaissance."

"I always thought that Venus, the goddess of love, and Mary, the mother of Jesus were opposites," Giulio protested.

"They had more similarities than differences especially to a Renaissance mind. Venus may have been purer than we give her credit for, and the Virgin was a more sensual beauty in art than the bible let on. The artist had some wiggle room for his own interpretation according to the time and place he lived."

"Considering Bellini lived in Venice, it is not surprising that his Virgin is a beautiful and sensual woman," admitted Giulio, being a true Venetian at heart with a great appreciation for beauty.

Vega and Giulio both noticed that the woman with the Versace scarf had been joined by a well-dressed, middle-aged man who kneeled beside her in the pew. They whispered to each other, then got up and left the dim interior of the church together. Giulio and

Vega acknowledged their departure with a smile.

"The Saints Catherine and Lucy lived in different countries and different centuries. But they communicated with the Virgin without words," she said.

Giulio accepted her interpretation. He had discussed enough art for the day.

Vega was convinced that Bellini's sacred conversation was similar to what she had experienced two weeks earlier on the mountaintop. To her, the painting confirmed the possibility of a communication between mortals and divinities. Across space and time, Bellini had proved its existence.

**

Months later, after she had written the report for her art history professor, he handed it back to her with his comments written in red ink underneath:

"Courageous in the way you include unconfirmed and imaginative interpretations. Should be more solid on technique and historical background." He gave her a C. What could she expect? He probably never had a single sacred conversation in his entire life.

Chapter 22: The Great Wave

"Ride the wave, dude." Southern California surfer, 2001

To Vega, the Anaeas Lauro felt less like a ship and more like a floating city. Slowly, Vega became acquainted with its nooks and crannies. She discovered a huge laundry facility buried right in the center of the ship, where no daylight ever reached. In the middle of giant piles of bed sheets, towels and tablecloths, sat Italian workers from Naples processing an enormous amount of fabric, washing, starching, and ironing. Their colorful pet parrots accompanied them, sitting close by on rods in the middle of the undivided room, chatting away inconsequentially. Like seafarers must have done for centuries, the crewmembers had taught the birds phrases in Neapolitan dialect that even to Vega's untrained ear sounded like the sounds of a drunken sailor.

Despite the absence of any pyramids on her path, Vega was energized and happy on the voyage through the Mediterranean Sea. Maybe it was her conversation on the mountaintop or because she had managed to break away from Tom and her past, but she felt she could go wherever she wanted and explore as far as she dared. The momentum of a giant wave carried her. She felt like being inside the woodblock print *The Great Wave,* by Katsushika Hokusai, from his series of *36 Views of Mt. Fuji.* In this print a giant wave crests and frames, within an elegant S-curve, the tiny snow-covered peak of Mt. Fuji in the distance. At first the sacred mountain looks like another wave, dwarfed by the great one. Two small boats with even smaller fishermen rowing inside are also completely dwarfed by the huge surge. The wave looks both powerful as well as destructive. It might crush those poor little rowers in the boat, who humbly crouch on the bottom of their vessels, rowing for their life, or the wave may lift them up and carry them higher and farther than they had ever dreamed.

Vega thought she knew what they felt, and she was willing to stake the tips of her Saturday evening at the cocktail lounge on their survival. No, not just their survival, they were going to soar. A wave like that has power, but not malice. A wave like that is elegant in its curve and sway. A wave like that, with colors of deepest indigo reflecting the depth of the waters, and foam of white and turquoise blue, shows crispness and clarity. A wave like that comes along only once in a lifetime as every surfer knows. A wave like that also needs to be ridden properly. You can't fight it, or it will crush you, as the people in Hokusai's boats well knew. They hugged its valley humbly and went with its flow. You have to go with its upturn and ride it unafraid. The wave kept the mountain in focus, the central point of the whole composition, despite its diminutive size.

According to the Japanese Shinto belief, the sacred Mount Fuji is the home of the gods. It is also the entrance to the Buddhist Paradise of the West, where followers trust Amida Buddha will welcome them. Life revolves around that peak, but the mountain remains eternal, a solid basis that can provide orientation during the confusing, ever-changing course of life. Mt. Fuji is the perfect connecting point between heaven and earth, gods and mortals, permanence and impermanence.

One evening as the Anaeas Lauro negotiated a particularly rough and stormy passage through the Aegean sea, Vega swayed with the movement of the waves, and lost not a single cocktail glass off her tray, in contrast to her fellow cocktail waitresses.

Chapter 23: Eloquent Stones

"The name Jerusalem is derived from the same root as the word "shalom", meaning peace, so that the common interpretation of the name is now "The City of Peace" or "Abode of Peace". Biblical Hebrew Dictionary

Vega's twenty-first birthday coincided with the date the Anaeas Lauro docked in Haifa. From there, most passengers chose to go on a land excursion through the Holy Land for three days.

"I want to go to Jerusalem on my birthday," Vega told Giulio.

"It's possible. You can take a co-op taxi for up to six people. If you share a ride, it won't be very expensive. Israel is small enough for you to be back the same evening."

On the morning of her birthday, Vega found herself in an oversized yellow-and-blue Mercedes taxicab, shaped like a limousine but shabbier. It had enough seats to accommodate six passengers. They drove east from Haifa toward the ancient city of Jerusalem. Sharing the cabin, were two silent Palestinian women clad in elaborately embroidered dresses and white headscarves; a Palestinian man ate pistachio nuts out of a bag and conversed in Arabic with his small son; he never talked to the women. Next to the small boy sat a skinny American student in blue jeans and curly brown hair. For the first hour or so, nobody spoke. They just stared out the window and sometimes cast quick, shy glances at each other. But the ride lasted two-and-a-half hours, and eventually they settled into their seats more comfortably. The Palestinian women started to chat with each other. The presumed father pointed out details to his son, and the American student struck up a conversation with Vega.

"Israel is amazing," he remarked. "It is just like America. It has deserts, cities, and mountains, and all that, just like at home. Only it is a lot smaller here. It is kind of like a miniature America."

"I didn't know America had ancient ruins, temples, mosques, and cities over 2000 years old," she remarked acidly. Her irony was completely lost on the young lad.

"Oh that," he laughed. "Sure, they have lots of history here. But basically, the landscape is very similar. I'm staying at a kibbutz near Haifa. They're cultivating orange groves and grapefruits. It's just like Orange County, California."

"Is that where you are from?" she asked politely, marveling at his ability to appropriate every feature of his host country and assuring himself that America was the same, just better.

"Yes, Orange County. Have you been there?" his eyes shone brightly.

"No, I have never been to America. So I would not know whether it is anything like this."
"Oh, but it is."

Before he could launch into an enthusiastic monologue about his homeland, Vega quickly cut him off. "What do you do at the kibbutz? Why did you go there?"

"Well, I am Jewish. I mean my parents are, and they thought I should know what it's like here. Find my roots, experience life in Israel."

"Do you like it?"

"Yeah, it is really interesting. I pick grapefruits, and that is definitely an experience. I have never worked so hard before. And the people you meet, amazing. At my kibbutz, we have thirty volunteers from twelve countries. One even comes from South Africa."

"Can anybody volunteer at the kibbutz?"

"Sure, you just go to the central distribution center in Tel Aviv, and they assign you."

"Is that how you ended up in your kibbutz? Did you know anybody there?"

"No, I just wanted to be somewhere close to the coast because of the heat and all. My kibbutz is one of the biggest in Israel. It has several swimming pools and over 500 members."

Vega made a mental note to look for the smallest kibbutz possible, if she ever wanted to pursue volunteering in one. By now they had reached the outskirts of Jerusalem, and the two women sat up straight and stared out of the window. The father-son conversation stopped except for the occasional hushed explanation pointing out a feature of the landscape or the approaching city sites. Awed, Vega looked at the hills covered with olive trees and concrete housing developments, imagining Jesus walking beneath those trees on his way to the Garden of Gethsemane.

"The temple, where is the temple of Solomon?" she whispered.

"Oh, that's long gone, but you can still visit the Wailing Wall. That's a lot of fun," said the American.

Maybe not for the people who are wailing, she thought. Apparently his idea of fun differed significantly from other people's concept of amusement. At that moment, Vega saw an apparition, a golden, sparkling dome rising from behind a hill. The reflection of sunlight from the gilded surface radiated into the aquamarine sky. She gasped.

"The Dome of the Rock," the boy said bitterly.

The taxi deposited them at Herod's Gate, the entrance to the Muslim quarter of Old Jerusalem's walled city. The Palestinian family disappeared quickly and quietly into the dark and narrow streets of the old bazaar. Vega stretched her legs and collected her belongings.

"Where are you heading?" asked the boy.

"Maybe get something to eat," Vega said evasively. She had missed her usual cappuccino and breakfast pastry onboard the Anaeas Lauro that morning.

"I know an old Arab bakery, not far from here. It is very authentic. You want to go?" the boy offered enthusiastically. She wanted to get rid of him, but maybe she'd wait until after breakfast. It was her birthday, after all. Why eat alone?

Diving into the maze of Jerusalem's old town, she felt like entering a time warp or a set for *1001 Arabian Nights*. Dark and proud-faced men wearing long *thobes*, women in the most elaborately decorated and embroidered *abaya* dresses, covered from arms to toes, milled about in the narrow cobblestone lanes. They argued and negotiated, pushing in and out of small shops and stalls lining the street. This was by far the most exotic place she had ever seen.

Spice shops displayed sacks piled high with cinnamon, curry, and turmeric in hues of orange and yellow, their pungent smells wafting by. An olive merchant displayed his wares in huge, wooden barrels filled to the brim with green, black, and brown olives. There were olives of a wrinkled variety, and plump, juicy ones filled with a slice of red pepper. There were also small, hard, and green ones and fruity, brown ones as big as plums. Voices speaking in guttural languages bargaining back and forth filled the air around her. Owners and customers accompanied their vocal offers with expansive gestures. Pedestrians barely avoided their flailing arms in the narrow lanes. Vega and her guide passed shops with fabrics, carpets, and metal wares from *menorahs* to tin and copper vessels. They brushed by buildings seemingly built in the time of Jesus Christ. If only the stones could tell their stories, she thought.

When they reached the unassuming bakery set in a small recess in the wall, Vega's head was spinning. Intoxicated by all the visual and sensual impressions, she sank onto a simple wooden bench in the front of a shop. Inside a wood-burning oven and racks to cool the flat and crisp pita breads completed the furnishings. Two Palestinian women with shy smiles brought glass cups of tea with sprigs of fresh mint and two oven-warm flat breads with honey. They smelled like heaven.

"Happy birthday to me," Vega said as she sunk her teeth into the crisp crust.

"It is your birthday?" the boy asked eagerly.

Vega cursed herself for giving him this insight but was too happy to really care.

"My twenty first," she answered, chewing with a full mouth.

"Want to go to the Wailing Wall, now?" he suggested in his chipper manner.

"I think I'll pass. I don't feel much like wailing. I am going to the Dome of the Rock, instead."

The reply stopped him in his tracks, good Jewish boy he was.

"Well, suit yourself," he said as they parted in front of the bakery, "and happy birthday."

**

She dove back into the maze of narrow lanes. If she followed the small icons engraved into the stones of old Jerusalem, she could find her way out of the labyrinth to the dome. It was like a scavenger hunt. Because of the myriads of languages spoken in Jerusalem, the directional signs used visual symbols. The Dome of the Rock's simple, symmetrical, and geometrical icon was easy to recognize but hard to find. As Vega stood at another fork in the path, searching the walls for the tiny symbol, a young boy in a white *thobe* and black vest tugged on her sleeve. His huge brown eyes under long lashes looked up at her. He could not be more than twelve years old. Vega's hand quickly moved to her backpack to confirm that her wallet was still there.

"You are lost?" the boy asked.

"No, no thank you. I am fine." Vega straightened from searching the lowers parts of the stone wall and pretended that she knew exactly where she was going.

"You want guide?" he insisted. He nodded his head eagerly and held up a plastic-covered badge. "See? I am very good guide. I know history and every place in Jerusalem."

Vega looked at his badge. It was covered in Arabic calligraphy and had a somewhat official looking red stamp in one corner. She had no way of knowing what it said or to whom this badge actually belonged. But it also showed a little picture of the Dome of the Rock.

"Which direction is the Dome of the Rock?" she finally asked.

"Ah, Dome of the Rock, I show you! I am expert. I know everything about Dome of the Rock." His eyes shone with enthusiasm as he pulled her down one of the lanes.

Vega allowed herself to be led in what she hoped was the right direction. After a few minutes, shops ceased to line the streets, and the narrow passageways turned eerily empty. These stones had seen in succession Jews, Egyptians, Babylonians, Greeks, Romans, Byzantine Christians, Persians, Arabs, Turks, Central European crusaders, Palestinians and Israelis all marching through and claiming ownership of this holy site.

"Three thousand years ago King David named Jerusalem in Hebrew the City of Peace," her young guide announced proudly. By now Vega had found out that his name was Abid, and that he was actually fourteen years old. As they climbed Mount Moriah to reach the golden dome, Abid told Vega about this fiercely contested piece of Jerusalem real estate.

"On this hill, King David Solomon built his temple. But soon, Nebuchadnezzar II of Babylon destroyed it and forced the Jews into exile. Fifty years later, Cyrus of Persia conquered Babylon and allowed the Jews to return to Jerusalem. The second temple was finished in the 5th century BC," Abid continued like a wind-up toy.

"How do you know so much about it?" Vega asked, impressed by his knowledge.

"I told you. I am Jerusalem city guide," Abid repeated proudly.

"Yes, but you are only a kid," Vega exclaimed.

"I study English and history," he proclaimed

Sheepishly, Abid pulled a piece of paper out of his wide trouser pockets. It was crumpled and looked worn. Words and sentences were underlined. Vega looked at it and realized it was an outline of Jerusalem's history.

"You memorized all that?" she asked.

"It is my job. I help my family," Abid declared with dignity.

"How many brothers and sisters do you have?"

"I have five brothers and two sisters. My older brother is also city guide. He teach me."

"Well, alright, carry on then." Vega settled in step beside him as they slowly proceeded up the Temple Mount.

"In the 1st century BC the Romans took control of Jerusalem. After Jesus' death, the Jews staged two revolts against the Romans, and the second temple was destroyed. The hill was empty until Emperor Hadrian built a temple to the Roman God Jupiter. But Jupiter did not last, because of Emperor Constantine. He was Christian and quickly destroyed the Jupiter temple when he ruled Jerusalem. For two hundred years, Christians came for worship and pilgrimage to Jerusalem. Then the Muslim Caliph, Umar, took over after the death of Muhammad in 7th century. He built a small mosque on Mount Moriah. But a small mosque was not enough because an important event in the Prophet Muhammad's life happened here."

"What important event?" Vega asked, with her interest piqued.

"*The Night Journey* happened here," Abid declared proudly.

"What is *The Night Journey*?" Vega was clueless.

"Ah, it is a beautiful story, and it makes Jerusalem the most important site of Islam after Mecca and Medina." Abid was now starting to enjoy himself. He did not have to repeat his memorized information, anymore, but could instead tell the famous story.

"In the ninth year of the prophet's mission, the angel Gabriel came to him and awoke him from his sleep near the Ka'aba in Mecca. The angel brought Al-Buraq, a white winged beast, whose name means lightning. It is smaller than a mule but bigger than a donkey.

Al-Buraq's strides stretch as far as the eye can see, and riding on its back, Gabriel and Muhammad reached the Al-Aqsa mosque in Jerusalem on Mount Moriah in no time. The prophet got off Al-Buraq and prayed near the rock. Abraham, Moses, Jesus, and other prophets gathered and prayed behind him. Muhammad was given a vessel of wine and a vessel of milk by the angel. The prophet chose the milk and Gabriel said, 'You have chosen the true religion.' A ladder of golden light emerged. Muhammad climbed along its glittering shaft through the seven heavens into the presence of Allah. There he received instructions for himself and his followers. Allah's instructions included the command to pray five times a day and this message. 'The messenger believes what was sent down to him from his Lord,'" Abid ended dramatically.

Another sacred conversation between a god and his messenger took place on this site, Vega thought. However, this god did not communicate an ambivalent message. He proclaimed loud and clear: We are the new religion, which supersedes the previous ones, and Mohammed is the true prophet because he is the latest one. No major interpretation was necessary. Believers were just to follow the instructions given directly by Allah. He would regulate all aspects of life.

"The next morning, Muhammad returned to Mount Moriah with this message. He was exhausted from speaking to god. His message and his Night Journey were so important that Caliph Abd al-Malik in he 7th century, built a great mosque here, the Dome of the Rock. It was modeled after the nearby Christian church of the Sepulchre to show how Islam is built on the foundations of Judaism and Christianity."

"Abid, this is really interesting," Vega admitted. "If this is all true, then you are a little wunderkind," she added.

"It is all true," Abid protested"

"Thank you Abid. You have been very helpful." Vega gave the boy some money. He accepted it grinning from ear to ear. "You have earned it. I'll go along by myself now." They had reached the gardens surrounding the magnificent dome.

Abid bowed deeply and murmured, "*Shukran, Salam Aleikum.*" Then, the maze of the old town swallowed him.

Vega thought she heard the whispers of ancient prophets and self-righteous crusaders as she approached the mosque. Incredible sacrifices had been made by so many for so many years just to get here. And here she was, walking right in. The Dome of the Rock was not a regular mosque, but a *Mashhad*, a shrine for pilgrimage. Its octagonal base was divided into a horizontal sandstone band, with columns and niches, crowned by a vertical layer of arches covered with magnificent blue and turquoise tiles and mosaics. The geometric mosaic designs, the simplicity of the shape and colors, the striking contrast between the golden monochrome of the dome and the blue tiles of the octagonal base created an architectural masterpiece. After emerging from the chaos of the narrow lanes, with their confusion and bustle of the bazaar, arriving at the dignity and majesty of this building, Vega felt calm. Rising above the city, it made a statement, expressed in elegant Arabic calligraphy running along the upper rim of the building. "Allah is great". Abstract and simple, without pictorial or symbolic depictions, the building's exquisite proportions had a profound effect on Vega.

The architects of this building had been sure in their faith. Not like her, doubting, wondering, and looking for proof. Here, the sacred conversation that had taken place was immortalized in stone and gold. The argument the building made about the event was convincing.

It is part of the power of art, Vega thought. Art can back up any claims made by religious or political rulers with beauty and grandeur. Art entices us to believe that whatever inspired such magnificence must be true. Whatever could evoke such strong emotions must have a divine origin.

Entering the interior space Vega stepped from the blinding brightness of the Mediterranean sun into the shady gloom of the sacred site. Before her lay the naked rock. In stark contrast to the glorious exterior, it was really just a rocky platform. The rock looked ordinary, brown and crumbling; an anticlimax after the expectations built up by the building's grandiose exterior. The façade would have been more powerful without admitting anyone inside the dim and disappointing interior.

Just like the pyramids, Vega pondered. The pyramids' shape was powerful and impressive from the outside, but people were not allowed to enter while they were alive.

The Dome of the Rocks was one of the most sacred spots on earth. Sacred conversations had taken place here. Did she need more proof that communication between gods and mortals was possible?

Wandering back down the hill toward Herod's Gate, Vega tried to take in as much as possible of the city around her. It was confusing and exhilarating. She saw The Wailing Wall, populated by pious Hasidic Jews, in black-rimmed hats and long locks curling in front of their ears, praying with concentration and intensity while rocking back and forth. Armenian patriarchs in flowing black robes and majestic beards swept down the streets toward their quarter in the southern part of the old city. Christian nuns, with expressions bordering on ecstasy, followed the fourteen stations of the Via Dolorosa, the Way of Sorrows.

Vega reached Herod's Gate in the soft light of the waning day. She still had to drive three hours to get back to Haifa. So many impressions filled her mind, she could not take in any more. But she was not ready to leave yet. Right outside the Herod's gate stood an ancient well, now mostly used as a meeting place. Vega threw a penny into its depth, wishing that she could soon return to Jerusalem and get another chance at deciphering and unraveling its many mysteries.

During the uneventful drive back to Haifa she sat in the taxicab, dozing. Image of the golden dome loomed in her mind.

**

By the time the taxi returned to the harbor in Haifa, it was dark. Vega gathered up her backpack and ran to the docks. The drive had taken longer than anticipated due to traffic and checkpoints along the way. When she reached the Pier 57 where she had left the Anaeas Lauro in the morning, it was empty. Vega first cursed, then almost cried, then remembered that she had just turned twenty one, and with the self-assurance of her new adulthood, she pulled herself together and yelled to some dockworkers, "Anaeas Lauro, where is the Anaeas Lauro?"

They laughed at her, a small, blond girl in jeans with a bulging shoulder bag looking for a seven-hundred-foot ship. "You lost her?" they teased.

"Where is she?" Tears stung in her eyes. One of the dockworkers pointed out to the open ocean.

"No, she can't have left. The passengers aren't due back until tomorrow." She felt desperate now.

"They moved her to dock 48, I think," one of the workers conceded.

"Thank you," she called back to him and ran along the empty piers. They seemed to stretch on endlessly. At least, she would never forget this birthday. From afar, she saw a cruise ship looming, all sparkling lights in the dark. The ship's bright, busy interior held the promise of home after the dark and damp emptiness of the pier. Vega jumped over the gangplank, just as it was about to be closed for the night. She dropped off her bag on her bunk and changed back into uniform. She still had to work the nightshift at the cocktail bar for the few remaining passengers.

"What happened?" Giulio asked quietly, leaning on the bar while she walked by carrying a tray loaded with drinks.

"I nearly missed the boat," she whispered back.

As usual, the crew raided the midnight buffet leftovers at the end of their shift. On the night of Vega's birthday, the buffet had been reduced because most passengers were on the land excursion. But it was still a feast: fried zucchini flowers; baked peppers with ricotta and basil; pizza with onion comfit and sausage; semolina gnocchi with sauce of porcini; cold garlic soup and red peppers melted in balsamic vinegar. For desert, or *dolci*, hazelnut gelato; cherries steeped in red wine; folded peach tart with mascarpone. All were served around an ice sculpture in the shape of a swan.

For someone who was raised on frozen spinach, ravioli out of the can, and spaghetti, the selection on offer was a dream. Food could be more than a necessary evil, an inconvenience to deal with three times a day, as her mother had viewed it. Food could be enjoyed and savored. After stuffing herself to the brim Vega told Giulio about her adventures in Jerusalem, and he gave her a gorgeous, dark-maroon silk sari with silver embroidered borders as a birthday gift.

"From India," he said.

India, she thought, might be worth a journey. Now, that she had gotten a taste of traveling, she did not intend on stopping any time soon.

"Giulio, tell me everything about India!"

**

The next morning, Vega sneaked out of Giulio's cabin, as usual, shoes in hand, on her way to tiptoed down to her own bunk. But as she closed the cabin door behind her, First Officer of Human Resources and Administration, Franco Castiglione, blocked her way. Startled, Vega dropped her shoes.

"Where are you coming from, Signorina Vega?" he asked, dripping with sarcasm.

"I couldn't sleep, so I took a walk," Vega answered.

"You did not take a walk; you came out of Officer De Maria's cabin.

"What are you doing here?" Vega went on the offensive.

"Waiting for you," he answered. "Come with me to my office." He turned around and marched off.

"I have to get ready for duty," Vega stammered.

"No you don't. Your duty is over."

"What do you mean?" Vega asked, scrambling after him barefoot.

"You will find out."

In his office, Castiglione placed a paper on his desk. She recognized the employment contract she had signed when first embarking the Anaeas Lauro.

"You agreed to the rules on board when you signed here. We are a respectable ship, and your behavior is unacceptable."

"I am sorry. I promise it won't happen again."

"It certainly won't, I'll make sure of it."

"What are you going to do? Kick me out?"

"Your employment will be terminated at the next harbor, which happens to be Piraeus."

"I respectfully ask for another chance. I am a good stewardess."

"I disagree."

"How did you know where to wait for me?" she asked. A strong suspicion entered her mind.

"I don't owe you any explanation."

"Carmen? Charlene?"

"Some crew members take their responsibilities more seriously than others."

"What happens until our next stop in Piraeus?"

"You are suspended from duty. You are to remain in your cabin or on the crew deck. And don't even think about contacting Officer de Maria. That would only make it worse for both of you." He got up and pointed to the door.

"I really enjoyed working on this ship," Vega said in parting.

.   "I am sure you did."

The door closed behind her.

**

After the passengers had left for shore leave in Piraeus to see the Acropolis, Vega was escorted to the ship's ramp in her jeans with a travel bag slung over her shoulder.

Everybody had assembled to watch her leave in disgrace: Officer Castiglione, stern and triumphant; Carmen, avoiding her gaze; Giulio, brown eyes looking wounded, and perhaps scared. He couldn't allow this scandal to become public.

"I am sorry," he whispered as she walked by. She nodded slightly. She hadn't expected anything else from him. Tara had tears in her eyes, and Madeline mouthed something like "Fuck them," while motioning toward the officers and giving them a covert middle finger.

Vega paused. "Gentlemen, ladies it has been a pleasure serving aboard the Anaeas Lauro." she said and stepped onto the gangplank, sounding braver and prouder than she felt.

**

Vega knew she would never see Giulio again, and that was fine. They both had things to do. He had to go home to his family. Vega had to go back to university, back to Jerusalem, and maybe to a kibbutz. Their paths had intercepted for a while. They had not exchanged addresses or promises to stay in touch. It would have been a lie. Despite his cowardice following her dismissal, Vega had fond memories: nights in the back of the ship, looking at the path of the moonlight on the water's surface. She had the pomegranate-red sari, igniting her imagination about places to go, places farther and more exotic than anything she had seen so far. It was easy to move on, easier than to stay in place. After the painful experience with Tom, she felt grateful for a relationship without emotional strings attached.

Chapter 24: Arcadia

A mountainous district in the Peloponnese of southern Greece. In poetic fantasy it represents a pastoral paradise, and in Greek mythology it is the home of Pan.
Oxford Dictionary

Vega stepped onto the firm ground of Piraeus, feeling free. Free to find her pyramid and free to return to Jerusalem where the penny in the well outside of the old city kept calling her. Europe's boundaries suddenly seemed too tight for her, and she decided to keep going. She planned to return to Israel through Greece and then via ship to Haifa. Nothing awaited her back in Germany, except guilt, fear, and the demons of her past.

She was in love. Not with a man—but with the adventure of exploration and discovery. Vega was hooked as intensely as she had been addicted to drugs, but this time she felt alive and far from the banks of the river Styx. She wanted to keep riding the wave, feeling the excitement of discovering places she had never seen, and to not knowing what to expect the next minute. She wanted to feel the rush of being completely in the moment, constantly encountering a new world. This feeling resembled being in love with a man. It included the accelerated heartbeat and the heightened perception, which comes with a new affair. Vega was more in love with this feeling than with any person. Therefore, she let Giulio go easily.

She traveled light: a pink sleeping bag strapped by a golden belt to a large canvas shoulder bag containing all her possessions. With contempt, she glanced sideways at the ugly green and blue nylon backpacks of her fellow travelers and at their padded, sleeveless nylon vests, which bulged underneath their wide shoulder straps. In her breast pouch, Vega carried the combined wages and tips she had earned on the Anaeas Lauro. She hoped her money would last through most of the winter. She had no intention of returning to Germany and its gray and wet weather and heavy mood before Christmas. In the meantime, she was in no rush to get to Israel. It's the journey, not just the destination that counts, Vega told herself. First she had to pay homage to the birthplace of Dionysus, god of wine and oblivion. He was Nietzsche's favorite god next to Apollo, the god of art, music, beauty, and the sun.

Ascending the steps to the National Archeological Museum, in Athens, a young woman in front of Vega made a sudden movement and jabbed Vega in the ribs. The woman did not notice. She waved to someone, and as Vega looked up, she saw a young man running toward her. He was tall and dark, the young woman petite and blond. There was a spring in his step and a sparkle in his eyes as he approached.

"I brought you your jacket," he said as he handed her a flannel cloak. The woman's eyes lit up as she reached out toward him. Their hands touched. They were oblivious to anyone around them, and Vega carefully sidestepped them. That short encounter brought back the recognition of that spark that only comes with a new romance: the surge of blood in the ears; the quickening of the pulse; the amazed realization that this is really happening. Lovers can see the world with totally new eyes. Vega recognized the condition and instantly perceived the world like the young lovers. She noticed the orange of the heavy flowers on the African tulip tree; the fragrance of the early evening air; the reflection of the twilight in the fountain; the freshness of the breeze from the eucalyptus trees, all suddenly became deeper and more intense. She was grateful for this precious emotion, glad that she could still feel it, that she was alive and mature enough to recognize it. She felt young and willing to chase this feeling around the world as if it were a beautiful and elusive butterfly.

**

Upon entering the museum, Vega promptly found an object for her infatuation; a gorgeous Greek youth with a perfect body, divine proportions, a classical Greek profile, and an enigmatic smile. Unfortunately he was made of marble and had been dead for over 2500 years. In her eyes that barely diminished his appeal. She worshipped his beauty and lamented his short earthly life, which he had lost in a heroic battle around 530 BC. Through this tragedy the Kroisos from Ananvysos had gained immortality in the prime of his youth, and his image was admired as a classic example of archaic sculpture.

'Stay and mourn at the tomb of dead Kroisos, whom raging Ares destroyed one day as he fought in the foremost ranks" said the inscription. Kroisos was not in a cemetery, and his bones were not next to his image. Instead, his home became the National Archaeological Museum, in Athens, where thousands listened and obeyed the words of this dedication. Pilgrims from all corners of the world paid homage to his beauty and were captivated by his mysterious expression. He smiled knowingly, as if two-and-one-half millennia ago he knew his memory would endure. He was poised and calm, yet muscular and ready to spring into action, waiting patiently for the admirers to unveil his secret. Not that he was hiding anything. His body was bare, nude not naked, and proud—without shame or self-doubt.

Vega wanted so much to be like him, self-confident and contained, calm and poised, yet strong and prepared. She wanted to touch his cool marble skin, now devoid of the paint that used to cover him. But the museum guards kept an eagle eye on the statue, so she could caress him only with her glances. As soon as she felt unobserved, she recklessly stretched out a hand to reach a small patch of marble on the right thigh of the Kroisos. Immediately, a vigilant guard, scolded her noisily and escorted her from the museum under a staccato of Greek expletives.

Chapter 25: Butterfly of the Heart

"Stay near me-do not take thy flight! A little longer stay in sight!"
Butterfly, poem by William Wordsworth

From Athens Vega boarded boats to the Greek islands of Samos, Paros, and Tinos. Then serendipity intervened once again, this time on the unsteady planks of a ferryboat bound for the island of Rhodes en route to Haifa. Vega sat among a huddle of green-faced and seasick travelers. A late October storm churned the Aegean Sea into an obstacle course of lead-gray spikes. The boat rolled and thumped from side to side and up and down. With each new descent into a valley of ashen water, the contents of many travelers' stomachs heaved in unison. All available spots along the railings had long been taken up by miserable passengers hoping for relief from the wet sea breeze blowing onto their faces. Others lay moaning on deck, curled up in fetal positions, rocking gently back and forth, or staring white-faced at the overcast sky.

Vega sat in the lotus position on top of her folded, pink sleeping bag in the center of the deck, practicing Pranayama breathing exercises, focusing her gaze onto a spot just above the horizon. She had had enough opportunities to learn how to deal with choppy seas on the Anaeas Lauro, even though the large ocean liner, unlike this fragile ferryboat, had absorbed most of the waves. She also possessed a sturdier stomach than most of her fellow passengers. Instead of suffering, she actually enjoyed the dramatic sky and sea.

"Would you mind if I sat next to you?" asked a voice in cultured English. "Unfortunately my previous position has become unsuitable for occupation due to the unfortunate food retrieval of a fellow passenger."

Vega peered sideways, not wanting to break her concentration.

She saw an Italian-looking man with brown, slightly curly hair reaching half-way down to his shoulders. He squatted next to her on deck. She blinked. "Of course I would not mind. There is no reserved seating on this boat. This spot is as good as any. Because of its central location, the impact from the rocking waves is less noticeable here."

"You seem to handle it well enough," the intruder remarked with a small smile as he sat down.

"It's just a matter of practice and luck. I have the stomach of an ox, and I know a few Yoga breathing exercises that help," she responded lightly.

"You know Yoga? Have you been to India?" Even though his accent was Mediterranean, he pronounced his English words carefully and deliberately.

"Oh, no, I have never been to Asia. I'd like to go one day. Have you been there?"

"Yes, many times. It is one of my favorite places to spend the winter."

A particularly high wave broke at the prow of the ship and sent a spray of cold saltwater over the assembled travelers. A little moan went through the crowd, and even Vega felt her stomach lurch in an unpleasant way.

"You don't mind the storm?" she asked, trying to get the rhythm of her breathing back, focusing on the horizon in front of her.

"I am quite used to it, and like you, I try to breathe through it."

"Well, if you don't mind, I'm just going to get back to breathing then," she replied a bit tersely.

He smiled again. "Is your final destination Rhodes, or are you planning to continue from there?" he asked unperturbed.

"I'm going to Israel," she sighed.

"Rhodes is a very beautiful island and so are many of the other Dodecanese."

"I know. I visited a few of them, but now I am moving on."

"Visiting the islands was not an entirely rewarding experience, I gather?" he continued to probe.

"It was fine. Some islands are beautiful and striking. The colors of the white houses in front of the dark blue sea and sky are stunning, but—"

"They are getting crowded and touristy?" he interrupted. "Is that what you wanted to say?"

"I am a tourist, too, I guess. It was hard for me to communicate, I don't speak Greek," she admitted.

"I don't either," he conceded, "but the island, where I am traveling, used to have a large Italian population, and many inhabitants still speak the language."

"You are Italian then," she concluded.

"Yes. I am sorry. I have not introduced myself. My name is Lorenzo Rizzoli from Milano, and I am on my way to Kastellorizo the smallest and most enchanting island of the Dodecanese," he said.

Vega had to smile despite herself. His well-mannered tone and demeanor seemed so contrary to the rather casual and messy circumstances in which they found themselves.

"Nice to meet you, Lorenzo," she answered trying to sound proper as well. "I am Vega, from the constellation Lyra in the swan."

He laughed. "Vega, I am delighted to make your cosmic acquaintance. I did not expect to meet a star when I woke up this morning."

"I did not expect to be caught in a storm, on a nutshell of a boat, when I woke up this morning."

"Vega, if you would let me show you my small island of Kastellorizo, you could actually experience the true spirit and magic of Greece. It is an island without the pollution of cars and crowds. Instead, wild pine and olive groves flourish, and the aromas of thyme and rosemary still hang in the air."

"You sound like a poet, Lorenzo."

"I apologize. I must sound pompous to you. I am not a poet, just a photographer, and I love my little island, that's why I get carried away."

"Why is it 'your' island?" Vega asked in a reserved tone, feeling a little overwhelmed by his suggestion.

"Again, I apologize. I am afraid it is a figure of speech. Of course, the island is not mine, but I own a small piece of it. I bought a house there on top of a hill. It overlooks the coastline and the narrow passageway to Turkey. That's where I am going now."

"What do you do on your island?" Vega asked feeling slightly intrigued.

"I fix up my house. I meditate. I swim. I dive. I read. I talk to my friends. I work." Vega noted that work was not at the top of

Lorenzo's list of things to do.

"You should come and see the last place in Greece that is still calm, serene and untouched by time, before it is gone. Then you can continue to Israel or wherever else you want to travel," he said.

His passion about his island was appealing, but Vega said, "I don't know. I only met you ten minutes ago. Maybe I have things to do, appointments to keep, places to go."

"Maybe you do have appointments to keep. But I think that you, Vega of Lyra, operate on a higher level. Just look at this as a cosmic intervention. Maybe this is the real reason why you came to Greece."

"If this is a cosmic intervention, I better consult my guide to the galaxy," Vega answered and opened the side pocket of her canvas bag to pull out her dog-eared copy of the Chinese oracle book of the I Ching.

Lorenzo laughed again. "I had a feeling you would be prepared for every eventuality in the universe, and I agree that the I Ching is the right oracle to ask the question whether to go to Kastellorizo."

Vega saw that he had a twinkle in his eye. She grinned and he grinned back. She rummaged in her bag for a small pouch. "Regular coins will have to do," she explained. "I hope the ship stays level long enough for me to toss them and to read their value."

As if in response, the boat gave a violent lurch to the left, and Vega quickly grabbed her bag before it slid all the way toward the ferryboat's edge. She selected three identical Greek coins from her purse and tossed them six times onto the surface of her sleeping bag. From the combination of heads and tails, she constructed a hexagram of six lines.

"The answer of the I Ching reads, Chin, Progress," she reported. "Above Li, the fire and below K'un, the earth," added Lorenzo, looking over her shoulder.

"The sun rises over the earth, the image of progress," Vega read from her book. "The light of the sun as it rises over the earth is by nature clear. The higher the sun rises, the more it emerges from the dark mists, spreading the pristine purity of its rays over an ever widening area."

"That sounds just like the sunrise over the hills of Kastellorizo," Lorenzo said.

Vega sternly looked at him over the rim of the book. "A convenient interpretation," she said and continued to read. "The real nature of man is likewise originally good, but it becomes clouded by contact with earthly things and therefore needs purification before it can shine forth in its native clarity."

"Look at the final judgment," said Lorenzo: "Perseverance brings humiliation. To continue on as planned is not recommended, it is better to interrupt the journey," he offered as an interpretation.

"Let me think about this for a bit," Vega said and sat down again on her sleeping bag. As any answer of the I Ching, its advice was enigmatic. She could interpret it many different ways.

What intrigued her was the second part of the I Ching's answer: "the real nature of man is originally good, (like the sun) but it becomes clouded by contact with earthly things and therefore needs purification." Unlike the I Ching, Vega had her doubts about the good nature of humans. She liked the idea but could not quite believe it. The prospect of getting in touch with her true nature, without earthly contamination held great appeal for her.

Vega felt a need for purification. She had committed a terrible crime, subjected her body to poisonous drugs until her liver had collapsed. She had filled her mind with images of death and pain until she had hardly been able to see the beauty of the world anymore. She was recovering, trying to soothe the damage of her body and soul. She pictured this quiet, pristine island and then compared that to the harbor of Tel Aviv, the hustle and bustle of a big, noisy, and aggressive city. She realized that, with or without the I Ching, she was willing to give the Greek Island a chance. It was remote and nobody would find her there. After all, she did not actually have an appointment to keep. Plus, she had a soft spot for Italian men, and Lorenzo was handsome.

"How do you get to your island?" she finally asked.

"We take the Panormitis from Rhodes." His answer came without hesitation and was accompanied by a delighted grin.

**

The Panormitis turned out to be an old, rusty ferryboat. It serviced the island once a week. Kastellorizo means the "red castle," and its red cliffs looked like a fortress from afar. The smallest and most easterly island of the Dodecanese, it was situated halfway between Rhodes and Cyprus, only a stone throw away from Turkey.

Three kilometers in length, without cars or roads, it was home to one small village, half of which was deserted. After making the seven-hour journey from Rhodes, the Panormitis delivered all the goods not native to the island including: cucumbers, salad, matches, nails, orange juice, toothpaste, coffee, sugar, tomatoes, batteries, shoes, and other necessities. Frequently, the only grocery store on the island ran out of supplies as common as flour or milk. On those occasions, the stoic storekeeper simply shrugged her shoulders with the remark. "Maybe we will have it next week after the Panormitis arrived." That hope was not always fulfilled.

Understandably, the arrival of the Panormitis constituted the highlight of the week. Villagers flocked to the landing pier by the boardwalk, awaiting their supplies and inspecting new human arrivals, with whom they would share their island for at least a week. Visitors awaited the ship just as eagerly as their only way off the island. They had been stranded for a week. The number of tourists was further curbed by the lack of artifacts, ruins, or temples, unless one counted as "ruins" empty houses in decaying condition. The islanders pragmatically did not feel it necessary to invest in accommodations for tourists. Visitors were merely assigned a portable cot and directed toward one of the abandoned houses. Once there, they could battle the winds, the lack of windows panes, and running water. On clear days, however, visitors were rewarded with magnificent views of the coast of Turkey and a view of the blue and gray Dodecanese islands receding into the distance.

Like a magical vessel the Panormitis glided into the perfectly semicircular, protected harbor, which had made Kastellorizo a coveted trading port for eons. The lights of twilight began to sparkle on the island, and the first stars appeared in the purple sky. Within minutes of their arrival, the calm of the boat's smooth approach came to an abrupt end. Lorenzo and Vega were immediately surrounded by people. As soon as she set foot onto firm ground, Vega met the most important man of the island, Giorgio, the owner of the only restaurant. Her bags were left, casually resting on the small beach, while Vega and Lorenzo sat at a harbor-side table and looked out at the crescent shaped harbor and rising moon. Observing the unloading of the Panormitis, they were offered tart retsina wine and the promise of the main dish, seafood of the day, soon to follow.

"The menu at Giorgio's is always the Catch of the Day," said

141

Lorenzo. "You don't have to bother reading a menu in Greek." Not that a menu existed. Fresh olives and goat cheese appeared in front of them and mellowed the sharp taste of the wine. The mild evening air carried the promise of a new adventure. Lorenzo was a semi-resident in Kastellorizo, not a tourist, and everybody knew him and treated him with respect.

On top of the hill, his house sat right next to the Greek Orthodox Church. He explained that he planned to fix it up as a vacation rental for tourists. It was a long-term plan because, first, tourists were offered free lodging already on the island and, second, the house needed a lot of fixing up before it was rentable. Fixing up a house on Kastellorizo, where every nail and hammer and piece of wood had to be imported from Rhodes, was painfully slow. The extreme makeover had turned out to be an ambitious and optimistic a project. Furthermore, tourism was not exactly flourishing in Kastellorizo. Looking up the hill toward the black windows of the house Lorenzo pointed out to Vega, she noticed the great number of empty houses the island possessed.

"Let me tell you the story of the former importance of the island as a trading partner with nearby Turkey. Before relations between Greece and its neighbor went sour, many fully loaded ships anchored in this protected harbor," Lorenzo explained.

After dinner, they climbed the hill to his house with views of the island, ocean, and Turkey, but few improvements. There was no running water, so they had to take a shower by throwing buckets of water over each other on the enclosed patio. The windows had no glass panels, and the *sirocco* wind violently rattled the shutters. Still, it was a magical place of gracefulness, freshly white-washed walls, and views to infinity. The second floor of the house faced south, and light flooded the spacious bedroom. A simple table, wooden chair, and a bed were all they needed. It was an old iron frame bed, comfortable but a bit noisy. It didn't matter. Nobody could hear them. Most of the houses around were empty.

**

As promised, Lorenzo turned out to be the perfect guide. He taught Vega to snorkel and to dive deep down to the old shipwrecks scattered along the island's coast. She learned to ride the waves and currents, and to release the underwater pressure in her ears after every five meters of descent. She collected sea urchins and abalone shells. They caught rides on fishing boats to the inaccessible bays on the other side of the island and spent their days swimming, diving, picnicking, and sunbathing until a boat picked them up again.

In the evenings, they ate at Giorgio's, where Giorgio himself, speaking broken Italian, served fresh lobster, shrimp, or fish in no predictable order. After dinner, they usually played backgammon with Paolo, the old fisherman, who came regularly for a glass of retsina wine.

Walking up the hill one night after dinner, Lorenzo said, "Look, your star has put in a double appearance tonight, in the sky and in the water reflection."

"I don't think I've ever seen Vega so clearly before," she admitted, observing the constellation of Lyra in rare splendor.

"It's a good thing Apollo placed the lyre into the sky," mused Lorenzo.

"The lyre was Apollo instruments as god of music," she remembered.

They sat down on the low stone wall running along the path and looked down at the harbor.

"The lyre originally belonged to the poet Orpheus, who took it with him to the underworld." Lorenzo smiled at Vega.

"He wanted to bring back his dead wife Eurydice," Vega exclaimed. "But it didn't work out. Looking back he lost his wife and died of grief. Apollo placed the lyre safely in the sky, so nobody else could cross the river Styx alive."

Vega had been to the river Styx and back. Enveloped by the soft night air, she felt tempted to tell Lorenzo about her travels on the banks of the underworld. But where to start? Those years remained a yawning black hole in her heart. She was not ready to think or talk about it. Once she opened up, she was afraid the memories would swallow her.

"I guess, you can't make that trip to the underworld and return unscathed," Vega finally said quietly. "You have to pay a price."

They walked the rest of the way silently, listening to the sound of cicadas and smelling the wild thyme and rosemary, always more fragrant at night. Until the cries of the crazy woman, who howled on every moonlit night, pierced the nightly peace.

**

Two days later, a Dutch yacht moored in the harbor, and its anchor line got entangled with seaweed and debris on the sea bottom. Lorenzo dove down ten meters, without an oxygen tank, and freed the line. Jan, the Dutch yachtsman, was so grateful he invited Lorenzo and Vega to dinner at Giorgio's. After eating, Jan talked about other islands he had visited on his yacht in the Caribbean and along the Amalfi coast.

Suddenly Vega realized she'd been on the island for weeks. She had seen the Panormitis come and go, and she had lost track of the days, the weeks.

Jan traveled with several companions on the boat. One of them was Maude, a long-haired woman from Australia with brown, tired eyes.

Vega sat next to her and asked, "How long have you been on the boat?"

"I just hitched a ride for the month of October," she replied in her broad Australian accent. "In exchange for my berth, I am first mate and man the sails."

"How did you learn how to sail such a large boat?"

"I've been sailing for going on seven years now, honey. I been on my share of three-mast sailboats," Maud proclaimed.

"Seven years without interruption?"

"Yeah, love. I've come too far to turn back. It's a long way home to Alice Springs."

"Alice Springs? Isn't that right in the middle of Australia, near Ayers Rock?" Vega pictured a large, red, empty desert landscape.

"You know your geography," laughed Maude. "Most people have never heard of Ayers Rock or Alice Springs."

"I only know about it because of its famous aboriginal art."

"Ah, it's a godforsaken desert. Nothing but a few natives hanging about."

"The Aboriginal paintings are beautiful. And powerful," Vega said.

"Maybe one day, I'll return and open an art gallery," Maud laughed. "But seriously, there is no water, no trees, it's just desolate. Before I return, I first will finish traveling all seven seas. I have crossed five already; only two more to go." Maud gave Vega a proud smile.

Maude reminded Vega of Maggie on the Anaeas Lauro. Just a few years older, Maude looked as if she could be Maggie's mother. Maude's leathery face and her stringy brown hair both fascinated and horrified Vega. For years, Maude had been able to keep going, finding ways to keep traveling. Did the wave still carry her? Vega wondered, if it was just habit by now, or a mere avoidance of stopping anywhere? What would Maude do if she ever returned to Central Australia? How would she fit in again in Alice Springs? Did Maud dive deep or just barely skim the surface wherever she went, without any real friends, and without any real experiences? Did Vega want to become like her, someone tossed about by the whims of the currents, living on other people's charity?

Vega had landed in Kastellorizo by chance, barely by choice. The I Ching had been a diversion, not really necessary to convince herself to come here. Even though Kastellorizo was a beautiful island, the time had come to continue to destinations in Israel and to carry on with her half-forgotten quest for a pyramid—the proof of her sacred conversation.

**

Her mind made up to leave, Vega said goodbye to the island by walking up to the central plateau for a visit of an old abandoned monastery. The rugged middle of Kastellorizo sat uninhabited and windswept high above the placid harbor. After a steep climb, she saw the Dodecanese islands, stretching in layers of blue and gray toward the horizon. Vega tried to bottle up this image in her mind as a memory of the happy time she had spent on this island.

When she returned at dusk, Lorenzo asked, "Where have you been all day?" When Vega told him that she had said goodbye to the island, he reacted angrily and upset unlike his usual mellow self. "You decide to leave just like that, and you don't even tell me?" he asked.

"I am sorry, but it is time for me to go. Thank you for showing me the island."

"Showing you the island? You have been living in my house with me for weeks, and now you don't even bother to tell me you are leaving?"

"There is nothing to tell. I loved being on this island, and I am glad I came. It is just time for me to move on," Vega tried to explain. "Just because you are leaving doesn't mean you have to withdraw from me and shut me out," he said angrily. "You are just a butterfly of the heart. You take what you want and then flutter away."

Vega was taken aback, surprised, and sad about his reaction. His accusation confused her. What did he mean with this image of the butterfly? In Rhodes, before their departure for Kastellorizo, they had visited the valley of the butterflies together. Every year, thousands of monarch butterflies descended there like an undulating, fluttering, trembling, orange cloud. The butterflies moved like a wave of golden dust in the sky. Some wings had gently touched Vega's arms, and she had felt light and almost dizzy in the shifting, moving sea of orange. Then, the butterflies had fluttered off and left just the slightest tingle on her skin.

Lorenzo's words caused her heart to twist and pull in a strange way. She decided to simply ignore it. Listening to her heart had led to sickness, pain, lies, ugliness, and death. She was never going to let that happen again. Lorenzo was right. She was just a butterfly of the heart, and she did not want anything more than a lingering tingle. Actually, she was willing to flee from any deeper emotion.

"I have to go on to Israel and work at a kibbutz and return to Jerusalem," she finally managed to say. "Maybe we can meet again in India?"

"Perhaps," he said vaguely.

"I am sorry, if it's not enough, but this is the only way I can be."

The last night they spent together, was the first one they felt uneasy in each other's company.

**

Early the next morning, Vega left. She managed to hitch a ride on the Dutch sailboat back to Rhodes, where she could catch the ship to Tel Aviv. The three-mast boat sailed all day and reached the port of Rhodes exactly as sunset tinted the port blood red.

To catch the boat to Israel before dawn, Vega had to sleep on an ugly beach close to the harbor, surrounded by litter and rats scavenging the debris. After the calm of Kastellorizo, the sounds and smells of the big port overpowered and disturbed her. Searchlights illuminated the port and obscured Vega's star and the constellation swan. She began to regret leaving the idyllic island, not knowing where she was going and what would await her. She couldn't fall asleep.

Suddenly, Lorenzo sat next to her on this industrialized beach, where the spotlights on the piers and cargo ships shone brightly.

"You're here," she said. "I am so glad."

He smiled and cradled her head on his lap. She fell into a deep sleep, feeling safe and protected with him watching over her. He had reached out for her. He had offered to share his private universe. But she was not ready for that yet. After Tom, she was not going to let any man under her skin. In any case, Lorenzo's presence was just a dream.

Chapter 26: Beit Guvrin

Kibbutz: "Hebrew word meaning 'gathering'. A collective farm in Israel, whose members work cooperatively and do not hold private property." Encyclopedia Britannica

The idea of going to a kibbutz had been planted into Vega's mind by the unsuspecting American volunteer during their ride to Jerusalem. Now, only three month later, she was riding toward her destination in the back of a station wagon. The coordination officer in the Administration office in Tel Aviv had assured her that Beit Guvrin was "the smallest kibbutz" in Israel.

"You want to go to a small kibbutz?" he had bellowed. "Jim from Beit Guvrin is here today. He can give you a lift. Beit Guvrin is very small, in the hills of Hebron."

He glanced at her over his glasses and closed a file on his desk, glad to be rid of her so quickly. Muttering her thanks while stumbling downstairs to the car, she was relieved to leave Tel Aviv and hoping to be on her way to a place where she could unpack her bag. Maybe she'd even have access to a bathroom for a while.

The bathrooms at the kibbutz turned out to be functional and the kitchen was well equipped. Vega assessed the situation the next morning as she stood at the sink of Beit Guvrin Kibbutz, washing the dishes of its seventy-six members. She had been assigned the job of dishwasher. Only short stints in the children's house and on the cotton fields interrupted her duty schedule. The kibbutznik didn't like her performance in either job, so Vega landed back in the kitchen with her hands in the dishwater. It was not glamorous, but her mind was free to wander while her hands performed their mindless duty.

Sometimes, her thoughts wandered and she dropped a plate, shattering it on the brown linoleum floor. Vega's mind had a lot of catching up to do. There were Tom, Lorenzo, and the hospital room to think about. There was also the guilt of growing up in post-war Germany. Even though Vega was born many years after the end of World War II, she still felt ashamed of her German origin. The weight of her country's crimes against the Jews never lifted from her shoulders. Coming to Israel and working in the kibbutz was her penance.

The routine of the small community healed and strengthened her body. In the mornings she worked in the kitchen, and in the afternoons she swam in the pool or roamed the hills of Hebron. She became fit and tanned. But her mind remained restless and her soul raw and vulnerable.

Besides trying to earn absolution for the evils of her country's past, Vega also regarded her current adventure as an experiment in an egalitarian lifestyle. The kibbutz was a form of an idealistic socialist community. Everything belonged to everybody, and everybody's needs were taken care of. In exchange, each member had to contribute and work for the community

Were the members living in this utopia happy? Vega was not sure because they did not speak to her. She was only a volunteer staying with them for a short time, and she came from an undesirable country. She understood their behavior, and thought that all things considered they treated her decently. She received her two packets of unfiltered cigarettes per week, as well as all the tomato and cucumber salad she could eat for lunch and dinner. She didn't complain about the monotonous diet to the cook. He was her boss and they shared the kitchen space with each other all day. Her recent past had been filled with too much excitement, and now she craved routine. Thankfully, the kitchen sink sat underneath a window, opening out onto the undulating hills of the West Bank. The view made up for her unglamorous job.

**

Jim, the kind and frail kibbutznik who had given her a ride from Tel Aviv, had emigrated from England. He was in charge of the five international volunteers, and as such, he assigned Vega to guard duty one night. Guard duty began at dusk, when the gates of the kibbutz were locked, and two kibbutzniks with Uzis began to patrol the fence. Vega and Jim sat down in the little guard shed in front of a disassembled Uzi. She felt like a character in a John LeCarre novel. The Israeli secret service could not be far behind, she thought. This, however, was routine duty for the members of the kibbutz. Holding a cold, smooth gun shaft in her hand, it sank into Vega's consciousness that this automatic weapon could cause a huge amount of damage..

"Jim, what are we preparing for?" she asked as she handed him a polished barrel.

"We just want to be prepared, that's all," Jim said reassuringly.

"But prepared for what?"

"You never know."

"You never know what? I mean, who would attack us?" she insisted.

"Well, we are very close to Hebron, and we are pretty far away from any kind of reinforcement, so we just try to be self-reliant."

"You mean some Palestinians could attack us?"

"As I said, you never know," he repeated.

"But why would they attack us at night? They walk in here every day while they are paving the sidewalks, so why go to the trouble of attacking us in the dark?"

"It's just a precaution," he tried to reassure her.

"Have you ever used an Uzi on anybody?" she asked.

"No, thankfully that has not been necessary. You know, I emigrated from England. I did not serve in the Israeli Army. But the guys who were born here, they used their Uzis plenty."

**

Vega remembered an encounter she had had that afternoon. Coming from the kitchen on her way to the swimming pool, she had seen a Palestinian worker sitting in the dirt in the sparse shade of a Eucalyptus tree, eating a grimy piece of pita bread. He had been paving the path leading up to the dining hall all morning.

She had walked up to him and said, "You know, the dining hall is still open. There isn't much selection at this time of day, but there is always tomato and cucumber salad and lemonade. You can sit at a table. It's a lot more comfortable than sitting on the ground."

He had gasped at her in complete bewilderment. "I could not go in there." He pointed toward the dining hall.

"Why not? What would be keeping you out?" she asked.

"They would never let me go inside. You must be new around here if you don't know that."

"I am not that new. I just don't get out much. They pretty much keep me hidden away in the kitchen washing dishes."

He looked at her incredulously.

"That was a joke," she tried to explain. "It's really not that bad. I kind of like it. Those hills are beautiful and it is so peaceful"

"Peaceful? You don't know what you are talking about. This used to be my village. And yes, it is beautiful if you live on this side of the fence. You see this building down there?" He pointed toward the library. "That used to be my family's house. Now they turned it into a library. A home for books! Meanwhile the people who called it home, have to live in shacks."

She heard anger in his voice, but also resignation and bitterness. "I am sorry. I did not know."

"How could you know? That is not something they talk about. Don't worry about me. I am used to sitting here. We would both get into trouble if I went in there."

Finality hung to his words that did not leave any room for a rebuttal.

"Bye then," she had said to the man.

"Salaam Aleikum," he had responded with dignity, as he turned back to his pita bread.

Vega was at a loss and turned away awkwardly and walked toward the small bungalow she shared with another volunteer from England. She had wondered who used to live there and who rightfully should have been living in her building.

**

As the night of guard duty stretched on, she considered telling Jim the story of the encounter but decided against it. They silently patrolled the perimeter of the kibbutz, walking on top of the circular fence's narrow walkway. A biblical landscape stretched in front of them bathed in magical moonlight, softly illuminating gentle hills pitted with caves and dotted with scraggly olive trees. Vega could imagine Jesus walking through this setting with his small retinue of disciples.

"Who dug the caves in these hills?" she decided to start the conversation neutrally.

"Most of them are natural. The limestone is very soft. But some were inhabited by Jews during the time of the Roman occupation of Israel."

"You mean they're 2000 years old?"

"At least.

"Were there Jews or Christians in the caves?"

"Jews. Jews have always been persecuted. Two thousand years ago, they were persecuted. Fifty years ago, they were persecuted by your people in your country. They were nearly eradicated."

Vega sighed. There was no such thing as a neutral conversation in Israel.

"That's why we are here," Jim concluded. "That's why we have a fence around our kibbutz, and that's why we are on guard duty because we are still persecuted in our own country."

It once belonged to Palestinian families, Vega wanted to say, but held her tongue. She was not in any position to make accusations, and besides she did not know what it felt like to be unwanted everywhere you go. Actually she was just getting a taste of it.

"Are you happy here?" she finally asked. Jim looked at her surprised, a little taken aback.   "Happy?" he said. "I made a choice. I live according to my beliefs. I am part of a community, and I am needed here. I contribute. We are changing this country. We are creating something new, where nothing was before."

Except for another culture, Vega thought. Again, she could not say it. She looked at Jim, at his green, second-hand army jacket, and at his thin beard and narrow shoulders. His eyes behind the rimless glasses looked large and defenseless, despite the Uzi he held. He was an idealist, giving his life to an idea: man living for the community.

"But are you happy doing it?" she asked again.

"There are things I miss," he said quietly. "I grew up in England. Not in London, but down south in a suburb of Brighton. I miss the sea. It is not far from here but I rarely get to go. We are only allowed to use the community cars for community business, not for a pleasure ride. I miss going to the pub for a beer with my friends. Here, we just have the dining hall, and we just have wine for Sabbath, sometimes. It is different here because we are all members and share responsibilities. We see each other every day, so we don't get together socially."

Vega nodded and offered him one of her foul tasting kibbutz cigarettes. They both lit up and smoked silently for a while, looking out over the hills, the scraggly olive trees casting fuzzy shadows.

"It is very beautiful here," she finally said.

"Yes, the countryside makes up for a lot. But after a while, you don't really see it anymore. It becomes work. Or just a dangerous place in the dark. I wish I could go and explore it more. Travel around and visit the sites."

"Yeah, Qiryat Gat is not exactly a major tourist destination," Vega commented and they both laughed. Qiryat Gat was the closest town, fifteen kilometers up the road, but was a concrete vision from a nightmare, emerging out of the desert without a tree, a lawn, or even a place to sit down and have a meal.

"Why don't you travel around? Don't they give you any time off?" she asked.

"It's not the time. It's the money. I don't earn any money here. I have everything I need as long as I stay. Once I leave, I need money."

"I forgot about that," she admitted.

"I miss the music most," he said wistfully. "If I only had money to buy a stereo. And records."

They both fell silent. There are still a lot of unfulfilled dreams in utopia, she thought. Her star was out here somewhere. She looked for it, as she always did when she felt confused or disoriented.

At that moment, a soft wing brushed her cheek. A large shadow glided over them, accompanied by the low flapping of wings. Instinctively, they shielded their faces with their arms, but the winged creature had already past and only left a gentle tingling on her cheek. Jim's Uzi shot up, and before he could stop it, he'd fired a salvo into the silence of the night.

"We just had a brush with an owl. The night bird touched us gently," Vega whispered.

Chapter 27: Owls and Eagles

"In ancient Greece the owl became a symbol of wisdom."
James Hall's Dictionary of Subjects and Symbols in Art

The soft tingling of her brush with the owl's wing on her cheek stayed with Vega for days. The entire moment remained encapsulated like an old-fashioned paperweight in a bubble of solid glass: The swish of wings; the gentle moonlight casting shadows of the olive trees onto the ground; the hills stretching into the distance interrupted only by the stark silhouettes of cypress trees; the subtle scent of pine, more fragrant at night than during the hot, dusty days; Vega standing on top of the enclosure of a fortress, armed with a powerful weapon. What did the touch of the owl mean? Was it a message from the darkness of her sub-conscience?

The incident stirred up images and memories in remote creases of her mind. The *Ship of Fools*, painted at the turn to the 16th century by Hieronymus Bosch, emerged in Vega's inner eye.

The painting depicts a small boat loaded full of medieval peasants including a monk, a nun, and a fool. They are drinking, singing, and one man is throwing up over the rim of the boat. The fool, in a jester's costume, sits on a rope tied to the central tree that serves as the mast of the boat. High up in the tree, at the peak of the triangular composition, an owl looks out across the sea.

The image's name, *Ship of Fools*, plural, implies that all the inhabitants of the boat are fools, maybe even more so than the one wearing an actual fool's costume. They eat, drink, flirt, and pursue unattainable goals. None of the passengers see where the boat is going because they are too absorbed in their frivolous pursuits. Only the fool looks ahead. But high above in the dense leaves of the tree the owl has the best view of all. Peering out of the brushwork, the owl's head looks almost human. The owl is the only one who looks directly at the observer. Its small face is barely visible through the foliage of the branches. It sees, but it cannot be seen.

The owl has become the personification of the eyes of the artist, the one who sees and records but does not intervene. Like the owl, Bosch knows that people are drifting without goal or purpose. Like the owl, he understands that humanity is floating on the seas of time in only a small, fragile vessel. Like the owl, he looks at us from across the centuries with wise eyes, asking, if anything has changed. Are we less confused now? Have we taken more control of the course of our lives?

Vega had been drifting like the figures in the *Ship of Fools*, absorbed by frivolous distractions and running from the consequences of her past. She thought about the falling eagles in her star constellation. The owl and the eagle had always been opponents. What had happened to her quest? She was nowhere near any pyramid, and maybe this quest was just a fool's errand anyway. Her encounter on the Italian mountaintop increasingly appeared like a fading dream. At this point, as so often happened in Vega's life, serendipity had intervened, this time in the form of an owl. Call it chance, destiny, synchronicity, or just dumb luck.

**

She was never assigned guard duty after that night. Jim always looked away when they met in the dining hall or on the paths between buildings. Therefore, Vega was shocked when Jim, without warning, suggested that they go out to eat. She could not believe her ears. No restaurant existed within a fifty-mile radius, except in Palestinian-dominated Hebron where no kibbutz member would dare venture. Curious about where they could possibly go, she accepted. Vega arrived behind the kitchen house at six o'clock, wearing her best, if slightly crinkled black skirt with the embroidered red and yellow patterns. Jim waited togehter with three other single males Kibbutzniks wearing secondhand jeans shirts, baggy pants, and clunky work boots. Neither Beit Guvrin nor Qiryat Gat possessed a clothing store. They had gained permission to use the 1970 blue Ford station wagon for the evening, and everybody climbed in carefully. This car usually transported men out to the cotton fields, so Vega had to brush aside pieces of cotton twigs, half a sandwich, and pieces of orange peel.

As they took off into the fading light, Vega asked, "Where are we going?"

The answer was an evasive and mumbled, "Close to Jerusalem."

"We are going all the way to Jerusalem?" She could not believe it.

"Not quite," Jim asserted.

After that, the men started to speak Hebrew, so Vega settled into the very uncomfortable backseat. She opened the windows to let out the smell of manure and got ready for a long ride, feeling like a passenger in the *Ship of Fools*, moving toward some obscure destination in a not very trustworthy vessel. On the other hand, no ride in Israel is too long. In three hours you could cross the entire country. A little music would have helped, or a quieter engine. The old Ford provided neither. A moonless night descended. Outside the windows she only saw blackness and the passing shadows of sparse trees. After an hour, Vega began to wonder if they would ever arrive, but scattered buildings finally appeared outside. They looked like modern, concrete housing blocks. Five minutes later the car stopped at a crossroad, and they climbed out. The road looked deserted in the fluorescent light of the street lamp with no restaurant in sight.

"Here we are," said Jim with an encouraging nod.

As they crossed the street, Vega saw a few people milling around in front of a takeout stand. Their small group headed in the same direction. Somehow, Vega had imagined her return to Jerusalem a little differently.

"Falafel," Jim said, as if that explained everything. It was Vega's first introduction to the crispy, herb-flavored falafel balls, eaten in pita bread pockets, with salad, tomatoes, and yogurt sauce: a delicious meal, but a real mess to eat. The falafel stand provided no tables, so they stood in the middle of the sidewalk, eating and trying to avoid dripping sauce all over themselves. Vega now saw the wisdom of wearing work clothes instead of a nice skirt. The dinner conversation was interrupted by exclamations of dismay, when a falafel ball fell to the ground or yogurt sauce spilled on their shoes.

"I love Falafel," Ike said with a full mouth.

"Me too," said Jim. "First time I ate it was in Eilat."

"What were you doing in Eilat?" asked Haim.

"I traveled around before I joined the kibbutz, and Eilat was a beautiful place to stay for a while."

"Down by the Gulf of Aqaba, isn't it?" Vega asked.

"Yeah. The Red Sea is fantastic," Jim answered dreamily. "It is one of the best spots for diving in the world; you just have to stick your head into the water to see the most incredible underwater gardens you can imagine; it's full of rays, jellyfish, and corals in all colors and shapes." Vega had never heard Jim utter such a long sentence before. "Where did you stay in Eilat?" she managed to ask between unruly bites of falafel.

"There is a hostel, that isn't too bad. And a couple of hotels. The town is really just developing. The best place is the Laromme Hotel. Five stars. I did not stay there, as you can imagine, but I had a job as a groundkeeper for a while. They are desperate for help, because nobody really lives in Eilat, yet."

"Why doesn't anybody live there? It sounds like a nice place," Vega asked.

"The climate is great and the location too. It's just not a real town yet. Eilat is right at the border to Egypt, at least starting next year, when the Sinai goes back to being part of Egypt."

Egypt, desert, coral reefs, jobs at the Laromme Hotel, a pleasant climate, a frontier town named Eilat. The words clicked into place in Vega's mind, and on the silent drive home in the chilly autumn air, she planned her departure for the Egyptian frontier.

Chapter 28: A Mirage in the Desert

"Something (such as a pool of water in the middle of a desert) that is seen and appears to be real but that is not actually there." Merriam-Webster Dictionary

Vega was falling. She fell into a very deep gorge, slowly enough to see every detail of the red sandstone sliding past on either side. She saw the layers of geological eras, passing by as if in a flight backwards in time. Igneous rock changed to sedimentary rock formations as color schemes blended from red, to ochre, to yellow to beige, to orange. The ground rushed toward her, and she was sure she would shatter any minute on the rock bottom. But the closer she came, the slower became the fall. A soft brush on her cheek stopped the fall completely, and as if walking on cotton, Vega gently landed on the floor of the gorge. The sky was just a narrow blue band high above her. As she examined her surroundings, a woman suddenly stepped from behind a rock outcropping into her field of vision.
It was Isabella, her childhood friend. She looked serious and asked, "Why don't you come home?"

Vega was at a loss for an answer, but she pointed toward a gap in the rock walls permitting a view out over the desert that stretched across an enormous plain. The expanse was dotted with multi-hued dunes and stark sandstone buttes in myriad shades of yellow and red.

"That's why I am not coming home yet," she finally answered.

**

A sudden bump in the road shook Vega awake and she blinked. The view outside the window of the bus looked like an extension of her dream. She thought of her friend Isabella and her family in

Germany. Did they miss her? Did they search for her? She hadn't really given them much thought. It was November now, a gray, wet and cold month in Germany. Nothing drew her back there. On the contrary, she was eager to get as far away as possible. The desert beckoned, spacious, empty, soothing, unlike anything to be found in Germany.

The bus approached Beersheba, a central location in the southern Negev and her transit station to Ein Gedi. From there she planned to travel to Eilat and the Sinai, the big brother of the Negev Desert. The bus rattled and huffed into the bus station, an indistinct concrete building, with fifty slots for overland busses going in all directions. She had to find platform 37 for her connection to Ein Gedi.

Gathering her belongings, Vega scrambled out and into the buzz of Beersheba's terminal. After the quiet solitude of Beit Guvrin and the Negev Desert, the noise and chaos of this transit station came as a shock. Groups of young Israeli soldiers of both genders patrolled the bus station, eyeing the Palestinian families suspiciously. The families traveled with bags and boxes, small children, and women wearing long embroidered dresses. A few Bedouins milled around in floor-length *thobes*. Young Israelis in transit to Tel Aviv or Jerusalem wore casual jeans and shouted at the top of their voices. Their volume amazed Vega. It seemed to be the normal mode of communication. The noise level was astonishing, and the concrete building acoustics increased it further.

Vega stood still for a minute, trying to get her bearing, when suddenly, with a gentle *plop*, the bottom of her trusted shoulder bag broke and spilled the entirety of her possessions onto the dirty floor. People cursed and kicked her things to the side. One man stumbled over her sandals and almost fell, but caught himself and hurried on with an expletive, without looking back. Vega saw her socks, her underwear, and her nice skirt all being dragged around and stepped on by dozens of filthy boots.

"Stop!" she screamed shaking herself out of her paralysis and knelt on the ground to gather her belongings. Angry and annoyed eyes turned toward her, but at least people took small detours around her, so she was able to pile up most of her things into a little heap.

Her canvas bag was beyond repair. Vega had to find another carrying device. Searching her immediate surroundings, her eye fell onto a large trashcan next to a concrete pillar. A trash bag would do, she thought, at least until she found something better. Leaving behind her destroyed canvas bag on the floor, she tried to dash over to the garbage container in the hope of finding an extra bag. Suddenly, a shrill whistle sounded, and a loud barking voice ordered, "Freeze!" Vega stopped in her tracks as two burly Israeli soldiers approached, their Uzis pointed right at her. "Hands up where we can see them!" shouted the first soldier.

Her entire surroundings seemed to freeze with her. Time stood still, as if she were suspended in a frame of a movie. This is it, she thought, this is how it ends. Her mind raced frantically while her body remained paralyzed. Tom's face in a pool of blood appeared in her mind. You've caught up with me. I shouldn't be surprised. I killed a man. Why did I think I was safe here? There must be agreements between the German and Israeli police. At least I came this far. At least I experienced Egypt and Greece and Jerusalem before going to prison.

"What is in that bag?" the soldier bellowed.

"You cannot leave baggage unattended!" yelled the other one. People made an even wider berth around her, eying her suspiciously. "That bag broke. There are only clothes inside," Vega answered as calmly as possible. Her hands raised in the air she tried to look too harmless to be a terrorist depositing a bomb at a busy bus station. At the same time her thoughts rattled on in her mind: I wonder what Israeli prisons are like. Surely, they will extradite me to Germany. How many years will I get for murder? At least I don't have to run anymore.

"Open it! Take the things out so we can see them," demanded the first soldier and motioned her toward the bag with his automatic rifle. Vega tried to move as slowly as possible, even though her heart was racing and she felt the sweat of fear trickle down her back. Vega stepped toward her bag, making sure her hands were always visible. Don't shoot me, she thought. The soldier looked too young and too nervous to be carrying an Uzi. When is he going to arrest me?

Slowly, she laid out her pants, her t-shirts, her socks, and finally her underwear in front of the growing audience that had now assembled to watch the spectacle. At the sight of her underpants, the male spectators sniggered, and the soldiers muttered impatiently,

"Okay, okay. Pack it back up!" the soldier bellowed.

"I just explained to you, I can't. The bag is broken. I was trying to get a plastic bag to collect my stuff," she repeated slowly. Maybe they aren't going to arrest me after all, it dawned on her.

The first soldier spoke briefly in Hebrew to his colleague who then left, disappearing into the crowd. "Stay there, don't move!" he demanded, his Uzi still pointed at her.

Obediently, Vega stayed crouched on the floor, thinking, I just have to do exactly what he says. Maybe they won't arrest me. Maybe they don't know about Tom, they are just worried about bombs and terrorists.

After five minutes, the second soldier returned and handed her a large, black garbage bag.

"Thank you." Relief washed over her. A burden lifted from her heart. Once again, she had gotten away with murder. She began stuffing her things inside.

"Where are you going?" demanded the first officer, making it sound like an interrogation.

"Eilat, via Ein Gedi. Is there any place around here, where I could buy a new bag?"

The two soldiers looked at each other, obviously not used to giving advice about shopping opportunities.

"What is today? Wednesday?" the second soldier barked, and after a nod from his mate, he continued, "The Bedouin market is on Wednesdays. It's just over the hill, no more than ten minutes by foot."

"Thank you. Are there lockers here in this terminal where I could leave my things in the meantime?"

"No, no lockers. We don't allow people to leave their bags unattended," the first soldier shouted, suddenly angry and suspicious, again.

"Okay, I am sorry, just asking. Thanks for your help." Vega shouldered her garbage bag, feeling like an out-of-place Santa Claus on summer vacation. She turned toward the exit, when the second soldier behind her bellowed, "What time is your bus leaving?"

Slowly turning her head back over her shoulder, Vega responded, "In three hours."

"Just don't miss it," the first soldier warned with menace in his voice.

Vega kept walking, noticing gratefully how the crowd slowly dispersed after watching the exchange. At least, they make it clear, when you are not welcome, she thought, as she stepped into the intense midday heat of the southern Negev Desert.

**

The walk took longer than ten minutes because the garbage bag turned out to be an awkward load. By the time she approached the dunes separating the few scattered concrete houses of Beersheba from the desert, Vega's hands were sweaty, and her feet blistered by her sandals. Her head seemed to glow in the heat as she climbed the hill without hat or water, but once she reached the summit, a breathtaking view presented itself below.

Like a mirage in all its chaos and splendor, the Bedouin market spread out on carpets and rugs on the dusty desert floor. Between haughty camels and stoic sheep, Bedouin men milled around in floor length *thobes*, shouting and exchanging words and goods. The women sat on woven carpets behind bales of fabric, in dazzlingly embroidered dresses of black and blue velvet. As Vega descended, she noticed trays with dainty tea glasses balanced on the rugs, in dangerous proximity to dirty, snot-nosed children with filthy hair.

They sat next to women, partially veiled, more for convention's sake than to hide their dark and strong faces. Vega navigated between the displays, astonished by the variety of goods, including perfume bottles, silver boxes inlaid with semiprecious stones, dangling bracelets, plastic combs, mirrors, and pillbox hats embellished with small mirrors.

As she scanned the wares for a new bag, a dress caught her eye. Approaching the woman sitting beside it, she caught a glimpse of a black eye under a turquoise veil. The woman cradled a small baby in her arm under the end of her colorful scarf. Vega pointed to the floor-length dress, embroidered with gold brocade bands of tassels on black velvet in intricate and abstract geometric patterns around the neck and along the hem in the back. Though dazzling, the lines of the dress were simple.

"How much?" she asked with a shrug. The woman smiled, flashing white teeth and wrote something on a piece of scrap paper. Vega read, crossed out the amount, and replaced it with a lower number. The woman made soft clicking noises, shook her head from side to side, and wrote another number down. After going back and forth two more times, Vega nodded. They exchanged the money, and the Bedouin woman threw a small silver comb and mirror into the bargain. As Vega un-shouldered her garbage bag, she realized that she had completely forgotten the main objective of her visit to the Bedouin market. She pointed to the pitiful plastic sack, now close to ripping at the seams, and said, "I need a new bag."

The women at a neighboring display laughed. One whispered something into the ear of a young boy, who disappeared. While they waited for his return, the Bedouin women offered Vega a cup of tea in a narrow tulips-shaped glass. Grateful, Vega drank the hot mint tea, and despite the heat, it tasted refreshing. As she took her last sip, the boy came back with a beautiful leather bag, complete with shoulder strap and side pockets for small belongings. Vega pictured herself organizing her things into proper compartments and being able to find immediately whatever she needed.

"I love it," she said. For a reasonable price, she was able to pack up all her clothes into a roomy leather bag that rested comfortably on her shoulder.

Relieved of most of her funds, but enriched by a new dress, a perfect carrying device, and her first encounter with the elusive Bedouins, she returned to the bus station. Time to get a job.

**

On her way from Beer Sheba to Eilat, Vega stopped in Ein Gedi. She spent the afternoon at the ancient fortress of Masada, watching the eagles circle. During a pleasant night at the beach of the Dead Sea, she gazed at our cosmic neighbor, Vega in Lyra, and dreamt about Dali's surrealist painting of the burning giraffe.

When she woke up the next morning, the sun glared on her face, and her mouth felt dry and sandy. Time to move south, to Eilat, and the enormous Sinai desert. Vega stopped briefly in the Ein Gedi snack bar for coffee and a muffin. Few tourists were out at that time of day, and she had the small coffee stand to herself. Crystallized salt pieces swam in the eerily still Dead Sea like chunks of ice.

Contemplating her journey so far, Vega counted her blessings. She had been lucky so far. Eventually she would have to face the consequences of her action at the rest stop in Darmstadt. She would have to pay for Tom's death. But in the meantime, she wanted to run as far as possible, for as long as possible. She was thirsty for adventure and experiences, before she had to face time alone in a prison cell. At least she wanted to experience as much as she could, press out of life what it had to offer. She lived intensely, because she had nothing to lose. Climbing into the bus to Eilat, she was ready to enter unknown territory.

Chapter 29: In Eilat—Chance rules

"A piece of canned chance. It's amusing to put chance in a can."
Marcel Duchamp, artist, 1913-14

Vega arrived at the back entrance of the Laromme Hotel in Eilat, reserved for employees and deliveries. As she entered, a whole new dimension of coincidence unfolded. Navigating through the hallway in search of the human resource office, she bumped into a girl balancing a tray of empty soda bottles, and wearing a white collared blouse with a slightly oversized powder blue skirt.
"Watch out where you're going," the girl's voice said. She sounded familiar.
"Tara?"
"Vega?"
Tara, her friend and co-stewardess from the Anaeas Lauro; Tara, from Pittsburgh; Tara, her analytical friend who had explained the intricacies of the Jewish Seder to her; Tara, who had shared many midnight buffets with her. Tara, peeking at Vega through dirty glasses and dishes, stood in front of her. They both dropped their loads of bottles, glasses, and luggage, and hugged and squealed uncontrollably.
"You! Here? How on earth could this happen? What are the chances?" Tara screamed until the shift supervisor put an end to the commotion.
"Chance can be a beautiful thing."

**

Several hours later, the two friends sat comfortably in Tara's apartment in what was called "downtown Eilat." The apartment complex belonged to the hotel. The Human Resource manager had hired Vega as a breakfast and lunch waitress, and had assigned her living accommodations with her friend Tara.

"After you left the Anaeas Lauro," Tara began, "Things started to get really weird. Do you remember Officer Franco Castiglione?"

"How could I forget? He was the one who threw me out."

"Well, he turned out to be a real jerk. He started making passes at Charlene and some of the other girls. And not just verbal passes, he cornered them in the hallways and started pawing them and slapping their butts. It was disgusting."

"Slimy pig," exclaimed Vega.

"One time, Madeleine rammed her elbows into his ribs so hard that he collapsed gasping for breath. Then she told him crisply, 'Oh, I am so sorry, how clumsy of me, I never know what my bony elbows knock over in these narrow hallways.' After that he left her alone."

"Good for her. Madeleine's been around; she knew how to handle the bastard."

"But Charlene was another story. Remember how spooked she already was? Always wanting to talk to someone, and when we talked to her, she didn't know what to say?"

"We made fun of her. We always asked her, if we were nobody and why she couldn't talk to us."

"She really freaked out about Franco. He would stalk her at night when she came back from waitress duty. He'd wait in a dark corner and practically jump at her."

"That stinking swine," Vega said.

"We tried to organize an escort for her. Either Madeleine or I tried to walk her to her cabin. But our shifts all ended at different times, so we weren't always available. She got seriously paranoid, and there was just no place for her to go."

"Did he ever try anything with you, Tara?" Vega asked.

"Once. He intercepted me and tried to put my hand on his hard dick in his pants. But I asked him very politely, 'Sir, are you trying to rape me?' He said in his slimy way, 'oh no, I am just trying to have a little fun with you.' And I said, 'This is not fun. If you are trying to rape me, tell me right now, so I can take the appropriate actions.' That kind of sobered him up, and he packed up his thing and grumbled something about a frigid bitch, but after that he made a large detour around me. For Charlene, though, it got worse and worse. She became so paranoid that she simply froze and could not defend herself at all. That only seemed to turn him on more."

"That's so disgusting. I can't believe he got away with it."

"That's what I thought. I had to speak up. I had to voice a complaint. But it wasn't easy to talk to anybody. After all it was an Italian ship, run by chauvinist men from Naples. You think they would just listen politely to me? I finally just walked into the Second Commander's office and told him to listen. He did all right, but after I was finished he told me that if the working conditions on board did not suit me, I was perfectly free to disembark at the next harbor."

"In other words, shut up or ship out," Vega said.

"Exactly. Fortunately the next harbor was Haifa. I'd had enough of the Anaeas Lauro by then, so I jumped ship and worked at a kibbutz for a few months. I always wanted to do that anyways. My Hebrew's pretty good now, and my parents are delighted that I finally acknowledged my Jewish background."

"What about Charlene?"

"She left the ship with me, and I put her on a plane back to the States. She was in no shape to keep on traveling. She had to go home."

"What happened to Carmen? I'm pretty sure she told on me to Castiglione. That's why he threw me out."

"Carmen is still there, thriving. People like her will always rise to the top."

"I am glad you got out of there. Which kibbutz did you go to?"

"It was a large one close to Tel Aviv. They had dozens of volunteers and loads of programs for them. It was fun. What about you?"

"I went to a really small kibbutz, Beit Guvrin. It only had five volunteers. I liked it, but it started to get cold. Plus, I was ready to move on, so I came here."

"Good thing you did, or else we would never have met again."

"Stroke of genius or sweet chance," said Vega and smiled. She had found a familiar soul, and even a kind of home.

Vega thought the apartment was beautiful. Its living room window overlooked the Gulf of Aqaba, and the view extending all the way into Jordan. The space was new, clean, airy, and completely empty. Vega stood at the window for hours, smoking one cigarette after another, watching the day fade and the lights along the coastline slowly lighting up. Proud of her new status as jobholder and apartment dweller, she wrote a postcard to her long-suffering family in Germany. At least Lisa had a right to know that her daughter was still alive.

> Dear Mother,
> I have a really nice apartment overlooking the Gulf of Aqaba in Eilat. I also have a job, in a hotel. I even have a friend. Her name is Tara. The food is pretty good, and every afternoon I am off and can go diving in the Red Sea. The colors of the desert and water are outrageously beautiful! Life is good!
> Love and Kisses to brother, Vega
> PS: I'll be home for Christmas, I think.

This should make her mother feel better. Now she knew that her daughter had a place to stay and a job. Those things always made mothers feel better. Vega didn't add a return address, even though for the first time in months, she had one. On second thought, she also wrote a card to her friend, Isabella, telling her to watch the next full moon together, from different angles of the earth.

These correspondences accomplished, Vega spread her sleeping bag on the wall-to-wall carpeting, climbed inside, and slept like a rock.

**

A daily routine structured their days. Tara and Vega took the 5:30 AM shuttle bus to the resort hotel, had a quick cup of espresso in the staff lounge, and then served breakfast until 11:00 AM. They cleaned up the dining room and set the tables for lunch, which was served from noon to 2:30 PM. After lunch cleanup, they had a bite to eat, and then were free to trudge across the road to the beach. Both were proud owners of basic diving gear, snorkels, masks, and water shoes. The shoes were necessary to navigate the rocky descent into the Red Sea.

Once they immersed their heads, an underwater garden of otherworldly colors and shapes unfolded in front of them. The first time Vega saw the Red Sea coral reef, she was so amazed, she gasped and had to raise her head because she had swallowed too much water. Was she really just steps away from her worksite? How could this wonder world have been there all along, without her noticing? How could people walk around completely unaware? How could she have missed the fact that just under the surface, inches away from their regular lives another universe of indescribable beauty existed?

In the silence of the underwater world, Vega and Tara floated in slow motion. Purple, orange, blue, and magenta coral sculptures, many fragile like lace surrounded them. Others were solid, such as the massive brain coral. Vega imagined they belonged to some underwater omnipresent intelligence. Only inches from their faces, psychedelic parrotfish paraded in neon colors of orange, indigo blue, and lime green. Meanwhile, the tiny orange-and-white striped clownfish darted in and out of poisonous sea anemone tentacles. They were their home and didn't harm them. A group of Emperor Angelfish, in royal yellow and blue with upturned snobbish noses, drifted by, barely giving them a second glance. Who needed LSD trips if this was available, free of charge and without risk to your life or sanity?

Their diving adventures were not without risk, however. After a flotilla of poisonous moon jellies and several man-of-war jellyfish floated by, they stayed out of the water for two days. The transparent creatures had melted into the background but reappeared suddenly pulsating their mushroom-shaped bodies, their trailing tentacles waving alluringly. Vega and Tara looked right through them. Like unearthly creatures, the jellyfish did not obey the same laws of physics as the rest of the planet's inhabitants. To Vega and Tara they appeared like visitors from another world. Despite the danger, Vega couldn't stop exploring the fascinating underwater world.

"If we know where to look, we can discover unimagined treasures," she said to Tara, who was just as enthusiastic about the diving, but a little more careful about how far she would swim out on the reef.

They spent their evenings in the apartment talking and telling each other about their lives. At least twice a week, they went out to Rickie's Bar, the only gathering place in this pioneer city. Rickie's collection of records included the Doors, Rolling Stones, The Who, and the Grateful Dead. The coke was cheap, and the clientele was young, adventurous, and from all over the world. They always met Rafael, Pedro, and Jorge from Colombia at the bar. Often, the five of them walked together, since the three Colombians lived in the same apartment complex and worked at the same hotel as pool cleaners and lifeguards.

"In Columbia, the coffee bushes are the chickens' favorite hiding places after the raid of a *finca*," said Rafael one evening while Rickie played the Grateful Dead's *Ship of Fools* in the background. "I hate it when you have to crawl on your stomach in the dirt to pull them out."

Vega and Tara looked at each other, thinking that due to the language barrier something must have been lost in the translation about this chicken-saving occurrence.

"What in the world is a *finca, por favor*?" Vega finally asked.

"Oh, a '*finca*' is a Columbian farm or ranch," Pedro answered chipper, nodding eagerly. "Our *finca* was raided five times last year, and each time the chickens escaped. So did the ground keepers, and you can't blame them for that, but they shouldn't have taken all the silver. At least we got most of the chickens back, but not the silver."

"I just hate it when you have to pull them out by their skinny legs, from under the coffee brushes, and they claw you and try to peck at you," Jorge added. When he saw Vega and Tara's expression of complete incomprehension, he added cheerfully, "You should come and visit Columbia. It is a very interesting country."

"It does not sound overly enticing," said Tara, but her irony was totally lost on the Columbians.

"We have emerald-green mountains and wild orchids and the most beautiful horses in South America," Pedro and Rafael added quickly.

Vega had fallen off enough horses to last her a lifetime and was not tempted by their invitation. Instead, she turned her attention to the Grateful Dead's Jerry Garcia singing, ". . . ship of fools, sail away from me . . ." in the background.

Tara, in contrast, was very interested in the horses and in Columbian culture. "What about Indians? Is there a significant indigenous population?" she asked.

"Nope," Pedro answered flatly. "The Indians have all been killed off by smallpox. The European invaders handed out infected sweaters to get the job done."

"How horrible," Vega exclaimed.

"The missionaries now have been replaced by drug dealers," continued Jorge.

". . . it is later than I thought . . ." Jerry Garcia sang wistfully.

"Drug dealers run the country. They have their own armies, their fleet of airplanes, and technology far superior to anything the government could afford," confirmed Pedro.

"I'm from Medellin where thousands of people, including kids, live on the streets, desperately poor. They'll stick a knife into you just for a sandwich or the ring on your finger," added Rafael.

". . . I cannot share your laughter, ship of fools . . ." sang the Grateful Dead.

"Is that why you came here?" asked Vega. She definitely wanted to change the subject.

"It's much safer here, the work is easy, the money is good, and the sun always shines," the three said almost in unison.

"It's an interesting choice to come to the borderland between Israel and the Sinai for its safety. This region is considered one of the most dangerous places on earth," Vega said, thinking that apparently every choice depends on your point of view and your available options in life.

Jorge, Rafael, and Pedro laughed. "Life is good here. We like our work at the hotel, we like the beach, and we like the people, especially those working with us at the hotel, and living in the same apartment building, and sitting at the same table with us at Rickie's Bar," Jorge said. They flashed white teeth, and their dark eyes sparkled in their handsome faces under unruly curly, black hair. Vega noticed tanned shoulder muscles flexing beneath the short sleeves of tight white T-shirts, and her stomach made a little lurch of the most pleasant kind.

**

Chance had thrown them together at this particular time and place. Vega thought maybe it was really nothing more than coincidence. On the other hand, Nietzsche had warned, *Die Zeit der Zufälle ist vorbei*. The time of coincidences is over. So often, serendipity had intervened in Vega's life. How could she tell the difference between simple chance and destiny?

Marcel Duchamp, the Dadaist artist had said, "Actually, the whole world is founded on chance, or chance is at least one definition for what happens in the world in which we live." Vega was accustomed to seeing signs in everything around her; in owls and eagles, and in domes and pyramids (actually, not in pyramids, yet). Suddenly she had doubts. Her uncertainty only increased with the influence of the rational and practical Tara and with the easygoing indifference of their Colombian friends.

If everything is founded on chance, then how do we make any decisions? She argued in her mind with the dead master, Duchamp.

"We don't make decisions. We allow chance to make them for us," he would have answered calmly.

"As an artist, you constantly have to make decisions. There is nobody to tell you what to do." she objected.

"A real dilemma. And one of the reasons why I finally discarded brushes and explored the mind much more than the hands," Marcel Duchamp had told Pierre Cabanne, in an interview in1968.

Yes, I know, you gave up art for the game of chess around 1925, Vega thought impatiently.

"I am still a victim of chess. It has all the beauty of art—and much more. It cannot be commercialized. Chess is much purer than art." (to Cabanne)

"Chess purer than art? You've got to be kidding," replied Vega, acting as an outraged art historian.

"I am not kidding at all. The chess pieces are the block alphabet which shapes thoughts; and these thoughts, although making a visual design on the chess board, express their beauty abstractly, like a poem." (to Cabanne)

"You mean chess can be a form of communication, with the chess pieces serving as letters, helping to give form to thoughts that are too vague to express directly?" Vega's questions expanded her inner dialog.

"I have come to the personal conclusion that while all artists are not chess players, all chess players are artists." Marcel Duchamp had declared with authority in his interview.

"Maybe I should give it a try. I am not an artist, but I can play chess. Maybe it will help me handle the arbitrariness of chance."

Vega was attracted to the Columbians, but in a general way. She did not even know which of them she preferred. Chance encounters were one thing, but they did not solve the problem of decisions. For instance, should she proceed in forming a relationship with any of the adorable Columbian guards? If yes, how and with which one of them? When Duchamp did not want to make any more decisions in art, he just played chess instead. So that's what she was going to do. She would follow in Duchamp's footsteps.

**

The following Thursday, Tara, Pedro, and Jorge took off for Rickie's Bar while Vega and Rafael stayed behind to play chess. Vega brought out her Egyptian ebony and ivory chess set from the floating market in Port Said. She set the pieces up on the board on top of a card table in the Columbians' flat. Vega played white and Rafael black. Making the first move, Vega realized this was the perfect nonverbal communication for two people who didn't share a common language. Vega began a relatively conventional, strategic attack, which left her queen momentarily exposed. Rafael put her on guard, and Vega felt a faint tickle of excitement in her stomach. But the queen moved easily out of danger, and instead mounted a heavy attack on Rafael's king with the support of her bishop and her knight. Rafael had to sacrifice his rook and finally his queen. Vega won the match in thirty-five moves.

"You are a good player," admitted Rafael.

"Thank you. You are not too bad yourself," Vega said and stretched her arms over her head.

"Not good enough." Rafael's words held a slightly bitter undertone.

"It's not too late to join the others at Rickie's Bar," Vega suggested.

"I'd rather stay here and go to bed." Rafael accompanied his response with a suggestive wink, which Vega purposely ignored.

"Well, good night then," she yawned and got up to leave, packing up her chess pieces.

"You want to stay for a drink?" Rafael made one last desperate attempt.

"I think not. I am rather tired myself." She gave him a little peck on the cheek and left for her own apartment.

**

Three days later, Tara, Pedro, and Rafael went to Rickie's Bar, while this time, Vega and Jorge stayed behind to play chess.

"Rafael said you're a good player," observed Jorge while setting up the chess pieces.

"Not too bad," answered Vega. She watched his shoulder muscles move under the sleeveless shirt as he made his first move. She countered with her black pawn. After that, they did not speak. Both had to concentrate because they were compatible players. Vega looked up after taking Jorge's white bishop. Small beads of sweat glistened on his forehead under his unruly black locks.

She tried to focus on the board again, seeing the design of the black and white pieces on the ivory and ebony surface. She remembered Duchamp's words ". .a block alphabet, which shapes thoughts . . ." and admired the simple abstract carvings of the pawns and bishops. As she noticed the beautiful contrast of her black king on its white square, she realized that the king was under attack by Jorge's queen, knight, and rook. To save herself, she had to sacrifice her queen. It was a real blow. Her heart beat faster with the tension and a pleasant feeling of suspense.

Jorge looked at her with a sly expression of anticipation and expectation.

Vega castled her king to safety, but that move came at a high price. She lost one of her rooks, and now her king was cornered and under attack by Jorge's combined forces. She felt beads of sweat on her upper lip and some trickled down between her breasts.

Jorge tipped over her king slowly. With no way out, her resistance melted like an ice cube in the desert sand.

Here's to you, Marcel Duchamp, she thought and felt a warm sensation spread in a wave throughout her body, originating at her navel.

Jorge stood up very slowly and reached across the card table, knocking the chess pieces over in the process. Vega surrendered. She felt his muscles flex as he bent back her head. He was riding high on his victory. They tumbled onto the floor and she felt his dark curls tickling her cheek and his body against hers.

**

Long before dawn, Vega was back in her own apartment, but by the time she walked downstairs to the morning shuttle bus, word was already out.

"So, Jorge is a pretty good chess player, I guess," Tara said tightlipped.

"Not bad," responded Vega feeling ill-tempered.

At the bus stop, she was greeted as "the fallen queen" and was offered "a queen for a knight" but fortunately most of the comments were in Spanish, so she pretended she didn't understand. At the hotel, the teasing continued relentlessly. When passing Tara in the hallway outside the kitchen, each balancing a tray, Vega hissed, "That one night definitely wasn't worth all this!"

"Well, you made your choice," Tara said tersely and opened the swinging doors with her hip. But Vega really hadn't made a choice. She had allowed chess and chance to decide, and maybe that hadn't been such a good idea after all. Confirmation of this came after the end of their shift when Tara and Vega walked to the beach and passed Paolo, the Italian barkeeper at the beach cabana.

Paolo called out to her, "How about a game of chess? I am ready!"

"You wouldn't stand a chance," Vega called back, and everybody laughed at her expense.

Whenever they saw the Columbians, Jorge displayed a sickly possessive behavior. Pedro was deeply resentful that she hadn't even given him a chance at "playing chess", and Rafael looked at her with hurt and accusing eyes. The outings to Rickie's Bar stopped. Vega avoided the Columbians whenever possible. The attraction to Jorge was completely gone.

"I think I've got to get out of this place," she said to Tara, expecting a sarcastic answer. "Eilat has turned sour for me."

"Let's go farther down the Sinai. It's getting cold here," Tara suggested. "I've heard about a beach called Dahab. All the divers go there. There is a Bedouin village a couple of miles from the bus stop. It's supposed to be beautiful."

"You'd come with me?" Vega asked incredulously.

"I am ready for a change of scenery, above and below the water surface. Plus I've had my share of waitressing for a while," Tara said lightly.

"I'm so glad to have you as a friend." Vega was close to tears.

"It's the privilege of the traveler to move on, when problems arise, instead of dealing with them. Right?" Tara summarized her

philosophy.
    "Exactly."

Chapter 30: Dahab means Gold

"Meaning 'gold' in Arabic – a reference to the area's sandy coastline (despite the main tourist area having no golden sands to speak of) – Dahab is a great base from which to explore some of Egypt's most spectacular diving and snorkeling. Predominantly a Bedouin enclave at its heart". Lonely Planet Travel Guide

It was so much easier to leave than to stay in place. Within a day, Vega and Tara had settled their affairs, collected their due wages, severed their thin ties to the little drifter community of Eilat, and packed up their belongings. The morning of their departure, Vega rolled up her sleeping bag into a pink spiral, like a snail's house, which she tied together with the golden belt, fixed it to her leather bag, and threw it over her shoulder. She sighed with relief to be moving again. To travel lighter in the desert, they deposited most of their money and baggage at the hotel. The Egyptian chess set was one of the items that stayed behind in Eilat.

By the time they sat in the sparsely occupied bus and rolled out of the city into the brightness and openness of the great Sinai desert, both Vega and Tara felt cheerful and thrilled to be on the move again. The Red Sea on their right separated them from the mountains of Jordan on the on the other side. Vega allowed her mind to wander. The desert enabled her thoughts to run freely, without bumping into buildings, people, or manmade structures. The landscape helped unravel her messy mind.

Only three hours later, the bus deposited them at a bus stop that looked like a scene in a Dali painting. It consisted of a tin roof held up by spindly metal poles resembling crutches rather than support beams. The roof hung over four plastic benches and three water faucets. Next to the shelter, three camels were lined up in a row, looking harmless and patient. Beside the camels waited three Bedouins dressed in floor-length, white *thobes*, lightweight, woven garments with long sleeves and open necks. The robes protected their skin and kept the wearer cool at the same time. Tara and Vega watched the bus recede in the distance after dropping them off. No other passengers had gotten off. They filled a couple of water canisters, and climbed onto the obligingly crouching camels. For a dollar they rode to the Bedouin village of Dahab.

Two Bedouins led Vega's and Tara's camels while the third animal ran ahead with its master. After getting used to the sway of their vehicles, the friends enjoyed the ride. As though to justify its name, the Red Sea to their right reflected the evening sun in warm tones of orange, gold, and red. The heat of the day broke, and a gentle breeze blew off the water. The distant Jordanian mountains appeared dipped in gold and purple. Vega and Tara smiled at each other. Dahab, gold in Arabic, gave meaning to its name.

**

An assortment of dwellings in various sizes made up the village. Each hut was covered with palm fronds as a roof. Tara and Vega were assigned two small huts side by side, both opening toward the ocean. They agreed to pay a dollar per day. It was not much of a shelter: just a few palm fronds tied together on top, stuck in the sand, loose enough to let the breeze blow through. But it felt like a palace to Vega. She spread out her sleeping bag on top of her reed mat and sat staring out at the sea, which now looked like a painting by Turner.

There was no time for reverie because two young Bedouin girls approached their huts shouting at the top of their lungs. "Pita, Pita!" they screamed and waved fresh, crisp pita breads in front of their faces.

The mouth-watering smell reminded Vega that she had not eaten all day. She purchased two breads for fifteen cents from one of the girls, Fatma. The bargain enraged the other, Gulbaran, who cursed, shook her fist, and yelled at Vega.

Thankfully, Vega did not understand a word and just smiled sweetly back at the angry girl. Tara bought two of Gulbaran's breads, placating her temper, and the Bedouin girls sat down next to their huts in the sand and ate peacefully. Vega estimated them to be around ten or eleven.

Vega had rarely seen such filthy girls. Their hair was matted and they wore miss-matched layers of a torn assortment of pants and shirts. The girls' faces were streaked with dirt, and their noses ran. Vega handed a tissue to Fatma who sat closest to her. Fatma took it and looked at it dumbfounded. Vega made a little pantomime of blowing her nose. Fatma smiled and imitated her.

Later, Vega found out that Bedouin women intentionally make their children look as dirty and ragged as possible to prevent the evil eye from being cast on them. A big presence in Arabic Bedouin culture, the evil eye is regarded as a bringer of bad luck, sickness, and death. It needs to be avoided at all cost. By making their children look unattractive and dirty Bedouin mothers try to ward off jealousy, unwanted desire, and harm.

Fatma warmed up to the newcomers and shyly stretched out a hand to touch Vega's blond hair. Vega winced, thinking of the snot the same hand had just wiped off its owner's nose, but she tolerated a quick touch. Observing this, Gulbaran started a whole barrage of obviously unkind and unfriendly words, this time directed toward her friend. As a result, both of them jumped up and ran away.

Tara and Vega looked at each other and laughed. This promised to be an interesting visit. They finished their pita breads and quickly realized that the diet in Dahab consisted of canned hummus, pita bread, water, and tea. Wisely, Tara had brought nuts, dried fruit, and a few apples, which she savored in small doses. Unwisely, Vega had brought chocolate, which she ate the first night.

In a slightly larger hut, a few Bedouin men drank tea. Vadid, the youngest of the group had escorted them from the bus stop. He served mint tea in small glass cups on candle-lit tables. He flashed white teeth at them as a sign of recognition. The hut opened toward the now black sea. Only the sound of waves and an occasional reflection of moonlight on the water interrupted the darkness. Two other Bedouins sat on pillows on the floor, sipping their tea. Six foreigners looked at the newcomers curiously.

Within a few minutes of entering the tent, Vega and Tara met everyone: Marie and Claude, from France; Britt and Mat, from Sweden; Marvin, from Detroit, a garbage man in his real life, who lived with his pet tarantula in a palm hut; and Kate from Washington. Kate's burning ambition was to organize a jeep expedition to the St.

Catherine's monastery on Mount Sinai, fifty miles away.

The foreigners occupied six huts on the beach. Few visitors came to Dahab so late in the season, shortly before the Bedouins moved to their mountain camp for the winter.

"In a few weeks, this village will be shut down," Kate explained with urgency. If she could not organize the excursion to Mt. Sinai by then, they miss their chance. Vadid played Pink Floyd on a small battery-powered tape recorder, lit candles in votive glasses, and observed the foreigners thoughtfully. His *kaffeyah*, a black and white headscarf, was held in place by a silk rope, called *mareer*. He chatted with his Bedouin friends, Mustapha and Ali.

Outside, a sky studded with stars so brilliant they seemed to belong to a different and brighter universe, beckoned. "I have never seen such incredible stars," Vega whispered to Tara, thinking that maybe the tea had been laced with something stronger than mint.

"That's because you have never been so deep in the desert and so far away from any electric light source," Tara explained.

"It feels as if the stars are much closer."

"Less smog, dust, and exhaust stands between them and us," Marvin added with a twinkle.

Vega stepped outside, located her star, pointed it out to Tara, and crawled into her hut where she fell asleep to the low rumbling of waves breaking on the beach.

**

Before they had time to explore the village the next morning, the village came to explore them. Fatma and Gulbaran were back. In addition to fresh bread, they brought four of their siblings. Each of them looked equally dirty, and the smallest one, for convenience sake, just wore a little shirt and no bottom. They stared at Vega and Tara and chatted excitedly. Two of the younger sisters, through sign language, gained permission to plait Vega's blond hair into small braids, accompanied by much giggling and smiling.

Dahab's reef dipped down gently from the beach, and on their snorkeling excursions, Tara and Vega discovered a much wider variety of colored corals and fish than in Eilat. The florescent blue Tang appeared in large schools and swam so close to their diving masks that one actually bumped into the glass. Vega's favorite, the colorful Mandarin fish, wiggled their large, green, red, and blue bodies. Each was adorned with dots, spirals, and ovals and swam vainly in front of their faces, as if to say, "Aren't we gorgeous?"

Near the sandy bottom, Vega saw a huge thorny, gray stingray batting its giant wings and gliding through the water as effortlessly as a stealth fighter plane flying through enemy airspace. It moved just as quietly, and its spine looked just as deadly. Vega froze in terror and awe, confronted with this graceful, and dangerous otherworldly being.

Chapter 31: St. Catherine's Monastery

"The Orthodox Monastery of St Catherine stands at the foot of Mount Horeb where, the Old Testament records, Moses received the Tablets of the Law. The entire area is sacred to three world religions: Christianity, Islam, and Judaism. The Monastery, founded in the 6th century, is the oldest Christian monastery still in use for its initial function. Its walls and buildings of great significance to studies of Byzantine architecture and the Monastery houses outstanding collections of early Christian manuscripts and icons."
Unesco Heritage Site Website

After a week, Kate managed to organize a daytrip in a small jeep, to St. Catherine's monastery. Tara and Vega gladly chipped in twenty dollars for the excursion. Each participant filled up all their water bottles at the bus stop, tied down their hats with scarves around their faces, and rode off into the deep desert. Marvin, Britt and Mat, Vega and Tara, and Kate, and of course their Bedouin driver filled every seat in the jeep. The French couple opted to stay at the beach because they were broke. Even without them, the open jeep was crowded.

Silently, the travelers enjoyed the beauty of the open desert, and after four hours, they approached the ancient structure of the monastery. Their faces were pitted from sand and their mouths as dry as an empty well.

Surrounded by a high sandstone wall without windows or door, the monastery was designed as a fortress. It stood at the foot of Mount Sinai, where Moses had received the Ten Commandments. Byzantine Emperor, Justinian, built it in 527 CE after too many monks and pilgrims, drawn to this holy site, had been murdered by desert bandits. So fierce were the attacks by the tribes that all pilgrims and supplies were hauled into the monastery by a basket and pulley system. Fortunately, the small troop from Dahab could enter through a narrow gate bearing the names of the Emperor Justinian; Theodora, his wife; and the architect, Stephanos.

Setting foot inside the courtyard of the oldest Christian monastery on earth, Vega noticed a large green bush in a corner. It stood behind fences and scaffolding. Its green leaves drew her in like a magnetic, color-filled power. Not surprising after so many hours of driving through a monochrome, sandy landscape.

"I wonder how it survives here," Tara said, standing next to her.

"St. Catherine's is an oasis; it has a water source and palm trees. But this is a very special bush," Vega responded.

"You mean it's THE bush?" Tara asked excitedly.

"I guess this bush was important to both of our religions. Jews and Christians alike believe it's sacred."

"After all these years, it's still alive?" Tara wondered.

"Fire did not kill it, so I guess time won't harm it either."

"God spoke to Moses through this bush, on this very spot?"

"So they say," Vega said, staring at it.

"Moses probably stood right here, where we are standing now and—" Tara began.

"And had a sacred conversation," Vega finished.

"Wait. What did you call it?" Tara asked.

"In art history, a conversation between a god and a human is called a sacred conversation."

"This is not art history, Vega. This is real. I think we had better take our shoes off. God told Moses to take off his shoes because he stood on sacred ground." Despite her rational and analytical mind, Tara deeply respected her Jewish roots.

"What else did he tell him? Do you remember?" prompted Vega.

Tara tried to take off her shoes, but as soon as she put one bare foot on the stony ground, she withdrew it with a gasp. "Ouch, Moses feet must have been really calloused. This ground is burning hot."

"I guess it's okay to keep them on. God will understand. So, what else did he say?" Vega insisted.

"He said, 'I am the God of Abraham, Isaac, and Jacob' and that he had seen the suffering of his people and heard their cries. And he would deliver them with Moses' help."

Despite the heat Vega felt goose bumps on her skin.

"You see, at first Moses didn't want to do what God asked of him," Tara continued "He said it was too big a job, and God should choose someone else."

"Understandable."

"Yes, Moses told God that the Israelites in Egypt would not believe him."

"And what did God say?"

"God said, 'Tell them that my name is I AM, the ONE who is always living. Tell them that I AM has sent you to help them.'"

"Was Moses okay with that?"

"He was still hesitant and wanted a sign, a proof, so he'd have a way to show others the reality of their encounter. He was afraid the people would say it was just a dream or a figment of Moses' imagination."

"Yes, they probably would say that. So what was the sign, the proof?" Vega was spellbound. She didn't know the Bible well, but she could definitely relate to this story.

"God gave Moses a rod that turned into a snake, a hand that changed from health to leprosy and water that turned into blood."

"He gave all that to Moses right here?"

"Right here on this spot," Tara said adamantly.

"Those are strange signs. Three transformations of ordinary things into something dangerous and terrible: a snake, a hand infected with leprosy, and blood." Vega thought her little pyramid was a very humble and harmless symbol compared to these powerful objects.

"Remember, this God of the Old Testament was frightening and terrible. He killed all the firstborn sons in Egypt. He sent the flood. He destroyed Sodom and Gomorrah."

"Of course, I forgot about that. I still think of God as this kindly father-figure, but he could also be very cruel. He allowed his own son to be killed."

"Don't jump ahead, Vega. We are deep in the Old Testament here."

"Sorry. What do you think he meant by saying his name was 'I AM'?"

"Vega, I am not a theologian. I don't know. Maybe I AM means that he neither was, nor will be, but always is."

"He is always in the moment?" Vega inquired with excitement.

184

"I suppose. He always creates the moment," Tara said. "Look, I need to get into the shade. Even without this bush actually burning now, I am practically sizzling in the heat."

Cornelia Feye

Chapter 32: Transfiguration

"Jesus took with him Peter and James and his brother John and led them up a high mountain, by themselves. And he was transfigured before them, and his face shone like the sun, and his clothes became dazzling white. Suddenly there appeared to them Moses and Elijah, talking with him. Then Peter said to Jesus, 'Lord, it is good for us to be here; if you wish, I will make three dwellings here, one for you, one for Moses, and one for Elijah.' While he was still speaking, suddenly a bright cloud overshadowed them, and from the cloud a voice said, 'This is my Son, the Beloved; with him I am well pleased; listen to him!' When the disciples heard this, they fell to the ground and were overcome by fear. But Jesus came and touched them, saying, 'Get up and do not be afraid.' And when they looked up, they saw no one except Jesus himself alone."
Matthew, 17:1-8, *New Testament*

Tara moved from the courtyard toward one of the chapels, taking a sip from her water bottle. With a last glance at the bush, Vega followed, and they stepped into the church of Transfiguration. Entering the dim light of this 6th century basilica, after the blazing desert light, their eyes only adjusted slowly to the darkness. They were drawn to the large golden mosaic, dominating the half-dome of the church's apse.

"This Transfiguration of Christ is the earliest Byzantine mosaic known." whispered Vega.

"You got to help me out here. I am out of my depth. What's a transfiguration?" Tara whispered back.

Shafts of light flooded in through small arched windows and reflected back off the gold background of the mosaic in all directions. The mosaic itself seemed to emit rays, and the awe-inspired, hushed

186

atmosphere it created demanded quiet voices.

"It's a favorite theme of Byzantine artists," said Vega. "It illustrates the story when Jesus climbed a mountain with Simon who is called Peter, James, and John. The apostles, as usual, fell asleep near the top while Jesus continued. He transformed into a divine being at the mountaintop. Jesus talked to the prophets Moses and Elijah who came to join him. When the apostles awoke, they saw Jesus' face shining as bright as the sun and his clothing gleaming whiter than anything on earth. That's called transfiguration, and that is what the artist depicted here."

"They had a sacred conversation," said Tara.

"Ah, very good, you catch on fast. This chat was between three heavenly beings: Jesus, Moses, and Elijah, who of course had been dead for a long time at this point. The earthlings Peter, John, and James crawled on the ground, terrified and astonished by the blinding light and the power of the apparition."

"What did they talk about?" Tara wanted to know.

"About Jesus' impending death. But I think it's not so much the conversation, as the fact that Jesus transfigured that's important."

"Why is that? They all look very composed and glorious while they are talking about such a depressing subject as Jesus' death."

"Actually, it was Justinian's and his wife's pet project to promote the 'divine' nature of Christ as much more important than his 'human' nature. So Justinian loved the transfiguration story because Jesus' divine nature came through so clearly. Christ was beyond death, he was on the same level as Moses and Elijah, at a place where suffering and death have become meaningless. On the other side are the three disciples, prime examples of human nature. Look at them. They are confused and gesturing wildly," Vega pointed out.

She looked around and saw their whole group had begun to listen, including an elderly English couple who had joined them. They nodded approvingly.

"See dear, the docent said that too. Christ is just rising to heaven, and he left behind his human body."

Vega was embarrassed by the growing audience, but she could not let this statement pass. "Actually, he is not rising to heaven, yet. That comes much later, after his death and resurrection. Look at Jesus' hands and feet. He has no stigmata; he still has a while to live. The transfiguration happened before his passion."

"Oh," said the British lady. "I must have gotten it mixed up."

"Understandably," said Vega, smiling, "because the transfiguration is not a common theme in art."

"Where are these figures then, if not in heaven? There is no background, just golden mosaic surrounding them."

"Jesus is in a blue *mandorla*, which is sort of like his own almond-shaped bubble. You are right; there is no landscape to tell us what this mountaintop near Caesarea looked like. The figures have labels with their names. The artist wanted to make sure we know who they are. They are suspended in a field of gold where they float in total isolation from each other. Do you see any interaction between them? After all, they are supposed to have a conversation?"

"No, they don't even look at each other," Britt, from Sweden said in astonishment.

"Do they look at us?" asked Vega, now resigned to her unwanted docent role.

"Well, Jesus does. He seems to look straight out of the mosaic," volunteered the British lady. "He sends his rays out to the others figures as well as to us."

"Just think about it," added Vega, "these six holy men have been suspended here in this sacred space for 1500 years. They are embedded in their golden field. Christ's light beams in undiminished intensity. Does the light cast any shadows?"

"There is no shadow, even though the light hits the bodies of the apostles directly," observed Tara.

"What does that tell us about the kind of light we are talking about? And the kind of space they rest in?" asked Vega.

"It is a supernatural light, and it is a space without dimension, time, or motion," Marvin, the American garbage man from Detroit, suddenly said in the silence following Vega's last question.

"That's great, I like that," said Vega. "An eternal, motionless space without substance where the people stand on rainbows. This space is as real now, as it was 1500 years ago, as it was 2000 years ago when it actually happened."

"We get to share the vision," said Britt.

"The mosaic is like a meditation. It makes time stand still, it arrests motion, and it expands or shrinks space into a field of glory," Marvin said. Everybody turned toward him and stared.

"Wow," said Tara. Marvin blushed and twitched uncomfortably.

"It's okay, Marvin," said Kate, "this is a pretty powerful place. It's supposed to inspire and awe you. Right?" Kate looked around for confirmation. Nods all around.

**

Suddenly it struck Vega. Within the golden background of the mosaic, the tall figure of Christ in the center, flanked by the smaller prophets Moses and Elijah on either side formed a pyramid. The composition was based on the shape of a triangle. The head of Christ served as the highest point and the feet of the prophets as the two corners. It turned into a three-dimensional pyramid in the warped space of the apse's semi-dome. The frontal figure of Christ in the center radiated light onto the prophets and the three apostles, lying prostrate at the bottom. It formed a golden pyramid. A pyramid based on the transmittal of light from God, to prophet, to human. The transfiguration was a metaphor for a sacred conversation and the transformation of an ordinary man into a divine being.

I am seeing signs again, Vega thought. No wonder pilgrims had been coming for centuries. At this location an important exchange between God and man had taken place. The sacred conversation still echoed through the millennia.

**

On their drive home, each member of the small expedition sat quietly and exhausted as the red desert landscape streaked by. They sat absorbed and lost in their own thoughts, just like the figures on the transfiguration mosaic. Surrounded and insulated by the golden backdrop of the desert sunset, each person riding in the Jeep thought about a different aspect of their day and of their encounters at the St. Catherine's monastery.

Tara thought about the burning bush that was still alive. Marvin thought about a state beyond space and time. Kate thought about the age and significance of the site and how she was going to tell her friends in Washington about it. Britt thought about people being caught in their own bubbles, carrying around their own private universes, and about how hard it sometimes was to reach another human being. She put her hand on Mat's, and he smiled at her as if he knew what she was thinking.

Vega thought about the golden pyramid and whether she had found what she was looking for.

**

By the time they arrived back in Dahab, the stars were out in their usual brilliance. Vega sat outside her hut, smoking a cigarette. Tara joined her, together with one of the old Bedouin women whom they had finally identified as Fatma's mother. She often joined them and shared a cigarette with the two friends.

"How much longer do you want to stay here?" Tara asked softly.

"I don't know. I like it here. I am very happy," Vega replied. Her eyes were fixed on her special star in the constellation Lyra.

"I like it too, but the Bedouins will move on soon. There will be no one left."

"I know," Vega agreed.

"The winter storms are kicking up. Soon we won't be able to snorkel safely anymore."

"Let's just stay until the full moon. It's in less than a week."

They both stared at the moon throwing a silvery path onto the water to where they sat on the beach.

"Okay," Tara said. "We'll stay until the full moon."

Chapter 33: Desert Moon

"Those summer nights, when we were young, we bragged of things, we'd never done; We were dreamers, only dreamers, and in our haste to grow up too soon, We left our innocence on Desert Moon."
Dennis DeYoung, formerly from the *Styx*, 1984

On the morning of the full moon, Vega awoke with mixed feelings of excitement and sadness. Her last day in Dahab, the place she had come to love, had arrived. The small community of Dahab did not share her melancholy mood. Everybody prepared for a celebration.

"The full moon is a big deal here," explained Marvin, who had been in Dahab long enough to see the last one come and go. He petted his tarantula "The moon puts on a great show, and let's face it, it's the only show in town."

Vega smiled and walked west over a sand dune into the desert. Quickly, she was out of sight of huts and ocean, and out of range of voices and cries of children.

She sat down on the sand and made up a poem.

Desert, I love you
you surround and scare me
a wild love you need,
a strong and powerful will
you are cruel like the great Genghis Khan
weakness has no chance
no pity for the hesitant.
no place for decoration
heat burns all but the essential
nothing can hide in your glare,

mistakes become apparent
each can be lethal
mistral howls and whistles
in eerie concerts of sandstorms
shooting grains of sand like needles
rewards are colors and emptiness
infinite freedom of mind
thoughts can flow far
nothing stands in their way
nothing clutters their path
desert, I already miss you
as I say goodbye
my hand full of sand

On the night of the last full moon of the year, two large fires burned on the beach. Mustapha and Ali contributed a goat, which slowly roasted over glowing coals. Marie and Philippe magically presented a fresh, green avocado, which they shared and savored. Marvin produced some fine weed, which they smoked. Vadid played a tape by the Doors, to which they danced. Vega enjoyed herself, but did not quite feel she was part of the party. She snuck over a dune into the moonlit desert and sat down on top of a sand hill overlooking the plain.

Here's to you Isabella, she thought while looking at the large desert moon. She sent a mental greeting to her friend in Germany, as she had promised in her postcard. Hopefully Isabella watched the same moon tonight, from a different angle. Tomorrow, she would return to Germany. She would never again be so close to the stars or the great pyramids or the gods—if there were any. This was it. The wave had carried her so far. If she was going to find proof of her encounter on the mountaintop, now was the time for it. No better place for a human and divine interaction existed on earth. Vega sat and tried to empty her mind. She closed her eyes and waited. Nothing happened. She opened her eyes, and the silver-coated desert lay before her in the moonlight in all its heart-breaking beauty.

"You always ask for things you already have, Vega," she muttered to herself and walked back to join the others.

**

As she returned, she saw Tara standing next to two strangers.

"Vega, come here. This is Josh and David from the Moshaf. They came to join the party."

"Nice to meet you," Vega said politely.

"This is my friend Vega, I told you about," Tara rattled on. "I am going to drive back to the Moshaf with Josh and Dave, tonight. We're going to Jerusalem for Hanukkah. I've always wanted to experience Hanukkah in the holy land." Tara sounded excited.

"I guess, it's goodbye for us then," Vega concluded.

"Unless you'd like to come along?" Tara asked hopefully. She motioned over at Josh with a subtle wink. There are two guys here, she was signaling.

"I've promised my family to be back for Christmas."

"I understand. It's been great to spend time with you. I will come to visit you in Germany," Tara said. "I promise."

"You will?"

"Yes, I am not done traveling yet. It's a sacred pledge." Tara made an improvised sign of an oath with her fingers.

"In that case, *Auf Wiedersehen.*"

"What does that mean?" The two Israeli guys, Josh and Dave started to shift uncomfortably from one foot to the other. This conversation went on too long for their taste. And now it even included some undecipherable German words?

"It means 'until we meet again'."

"All in one word?"

"Two actually. German is good at scrambling different concepts together and making one huge word out of it."

"Auf Wiedersehen, then," said Tara, noticing the impatience of her companions.

They hugged, and Tara walked off with Josh and David, talking animatedly.

She just stayed for my sake, Vega realized.

Cornelia Feye

Chapter 34: The Wave crashes

"Don't panic!"
Douglas Adams, *The Hitchhiker's Guide to the Galaxy,* 1979

The morning after the full moon, Vega woke up with a dry and sandy mouth. The sun already stood high in the sky. As she looked around the hut crawling out of her sleeping bag, she realized something was wrong. Her clothes were strewn all over the floor. Her bag was wide open. Her toothbrush and socks cluttered the sand floor. Alarmed, Vega reached for her travel bag. She was sure she had not left the hut in such a mess the night before, but it had been too dark to see anything by the time she went to bed. She dug through the jumble of clothes. Where was her wallet? Had someone stolen her money during the full-moon celebration? She dug again, only to realize that not just her money, but also all her treasures were gone. The decorated Bedouin comb and mirror from the market at Beersheba, a silver bracelet and her leather belt were missing as well.

Vega sat thunder struck. Things like this didn't happen in Dahab, she kept thinking. This is a magical place where everybody trusts one another.

She looked around, and suddenly the romantic palm hut looked pitiful and scraggly. She peered outside and noticed the beach looked rough, and for the first time, she noticed garbage lying on the sand: a tin can, a candy wrapper, an empty pack of cigarettes. Ali walked by, and suddenly the handsome, chiseled face of the Bedouin appeared sinister and suspicious.

My passport! Where is my passport? She dug through the bag again, only to find a mess of sandy clothes, but no travel documents, no wallet. At this point it hit her. She was stranded in the middle of the Sinai Desert. No money or passport. The wave that had carried her high and far had just crashed. It deposited her on a rocky and godforsaken speck of sand. Hot and cold sensations rushed through her body. She pulled on an overall and dragged herself out of her hut just as Marvin walked by.

"Marvin, I've been robbed."

"What?" Marvin stopped in his tracks, looking shocked.

"Someone stole all my money and my passport."

"No way, Vega. That's terrible. How can that happen here?" He crouched down next to her and put his arm around her.

"I'm telling you. It's all gone." She was close to tears now.

"Your passport?"

"Everything."

"Shit, how are you going to get out of here?" Marvin scratched his head. He looked hung-over from the previous night.

"I don't know." Vega leaned against her hut, where she had sat so many times watching the sunset and chatting with the Bedouin girls Fatma and Gulbaran. She had felt safe and protected here.

"Who could have done this? Were there any strangers here last night? What about those guys from the Moshaf?"

"Marvin, I don't know if the robber was a stranger."

"You are not thinking it could have been the Bedouins, do you?"

"I don't know what to think. I just know it's all gone." Marvin sat down in the sand next to her. He tried to come up with a solution.

"Look, I'd give you money, I really would, but I am broke."

"It's okay. You don't have to give me money. Somehow, I'll get to Eilat and pick up my stuff at the hotel. I didn't bring all my money, thank god. But I need a passport."

"Damn, that's terrible. What would anyone do with your passport?"

"Sell it, probably."

"Out here? Well, I suppose everything has a price."

"What do you mean?"

"I mean, it's a high price to pay for the freedom to travel and stay wherever you like."

"Oh, Marvin, I am really not in the mood for philosophy."

**

Vega walked through the village, searching, asking, and looking even in the garbage pile behind the dune. Up to that point, she had ignored or blocked out any awareness of the ugly underside of Dahab. But the stinkin heap of trash barely hidden and barely out of sight of the huts, grew and pestered like a sore; food scraps, tins, discarded pieces of furniture, broken glass. Vega picked through the debris, feeling increasingly nauseous. She had drunk too much the previous night, and hadn't eaten. She was stuck in the Sinai, but what made her feel really sick was the thought that one of the people in this village, people she had trusted and considered friends, could be the thief. The timing was perfect. The village prepared for the winter. Bedouins and visitors were packing, and many had already left. Marie and Philippe were gone. She found Kate who said goodbye with tears in her eyes, giving Vega part of the trail mix she had left. The Bedouins loaded their donkeys and herded their goats together. Whoever had robbed her had chosen the optimum moment. It was impossible to trace anything or anybody in the chaos.

Vega realized she had to make use of the remaining daylight hours and walked to the road to hitch a ride to Eilat. Britt and Mat ended up taking her bag to the bus stop, so she did not have to carry it three miles through the desert. Standing by the empty road, she stuck out her thumb, hoping a car would stop and pick her up on its way north.

**

When a vehicle finally pulled up to give Vega a ride, it wasn't a car but a truck. The looming hauler pulled a shiny, silver oil tank on a hanger that swayed dangerously whenever the vehicle came to a stop. It halted right in the middle of the road because there was no shoulder and the traffic flow was sparse. In fact, nobody witnessed a tall, blond hitchhiker disappearing into the shiny silver cab of the huge tanker truck.

Vega swallowed hard as she eyed the steep stepladder. If she wanted this ride, she had to climb into the cabin above the outsized double tires. She had run out of options. The light was fading, and she had to get to Eilat as soon as possible. So she shouldered her bag and swung her leg up the first step of the ladder, and then the next and the third, up the steep climb. As she plopped onto the passenger seat, she glanced at the young driver in a sleeveless muscle shirt. He had dark, curly hair.

"Hi," he greeted her in accented English. "Where are you heading?"

"Eilat," she answered meekly, trying to look as plain as possible.

"I guess you're in luck," he responded, smiling broadly, showing a row of straight, white teeth. "I am on my way to Beersheba, via Eilat." He ground the large stick shift into gear, and the truck started to move with sounds of grinding and straining. "All roads lead through Beersheba," he added.

"So it seems; though, none of them end there." Vega recalled her incident at the Beersheba bus stop and how glad she had been to leave that way station.

"You seem to know this country pretty well," he observed.

"I have spent a little while here," Vega answered. She would have preferred to just sit silently, staring out at the red, glowing desert, but she did not want to be rude. As long as they kept moving, she could put up with making conversation.

"How long have you been in Israel?" he asked.

"It's been over three months now."

"And what's taking you to Eilat?"

She considered telling him that this was none of his business, but remembered that they still had a long way to go, so she said, "I have to pick up some personal items, and then I'm heading home for Christmas."

"Ah yes, Christmas is coming up. I forgot about that. I don't celebrate it myself, but even out here in the desert, you notice when Christmas comes around."

"Of course, it started not too far from here in Bethlehem."

"I was born close to there, in Ramallah. Where are you from?"

"Germany."

"My name is Moncef, what is yours, German girl?"

"Vega."

"Vega, like the star?"

"Yes. You know it?" She was surprised. Most people had never heard of Vega.

"Vega is an Arabic word meaning a fallen Eagle. I've watched her often in the night sky. It is a beautiful name," he said.

"Thank you. It is nice to have my own guiding star."

"A beautiful star for a beautiful girl."

Oh no, thought Vega, not that already. This was going exactly in the wrong direction. She had to steer the conversation onto a different topic. "You are Palestinian?"

"Yes, how could you tell?"

"It's not too difficult because of your accent, your knowledge of the Arabic word, your being born on the West Bank." If she could steer this conversation to politics, he would probably keep talking for hours.

"The 'West Bank'. What does that mean?" He snorted contemptuously.

It's working, rejoiced Vega and nodded encouragingly but said nothing.

"It is an arbitrary name for an arbitrary piece of Israel. The Israelis treat it just like another piece of real estate given to them by their almighty god for exploitation and settlements or whatever else they want. We Palestinians have lived there for millennia, but that is just a small inconvenience in their eyes. The UN and the world think it should be reserved for our use, which makes the Israelis even more determined to claim it for themselves." He rattled on, his voice rising.

"I know," Vega said quietly.

"You do?" He was so surprised that he forgot to keep on shouting and took his eyes off the road for a moment. Immediately, the hanger began to sway.

"Steady now," said Vega, who was more concerned about her safe passage than about discussing the injustices of the Israeli state.

"Do you think all Palestinians are terrorists? Or don't you?" he asked in a tone that made this notion sound completely implausible.

"No, I don't think all Palestinians are terrorists."

"You are not just beautiful, you are also smart."

Ouch, thought Vega, wrong turn. How can I get back to safer waters? Political discussions were riddled with landmines. She needed a bland and time-consuming topic. Vega's stomach began to grumble. She became painfully aware that she had not eaten since morning. Her only meal had been Kate's shared handful of trail mix. Without a penny to her name, she had not been able to buy lunch. She wished Tara were there, sharing her never-ending supply of dried fruit and nuts.

"I like the local food here," she began, "especially the falafel and hummus."

He took the bait. "Ah yes, we have wonderful food. You should try the dolma and baba ghanouj my mother used to make."

Good, thought Vega, let's talk about his mother. "Does your mother still live in Ramallah?"

"My mother is dead," he shot back curtly, and Vega winced at the bitterness in his tone.

"I am very sorry," she mumbled.

"She is dead, and so are my father and my brother and my cousin. Victims of a retaliation attack by the Israeli army. My father grew olives, and my brother was only fourteen when they bombed our village. They later admitted they had made a mistake, miscalculation their target, but the missile had already struck. It was too late. My family did not know what hit them. All I got was one line in the Jerusalem Post. 'During the latest retaliation in the West Bank, a civilian house was the unfortunate victim of a missile attack.' No apology. No compensation. Nothing. The house had been in our family for five generations."

"How terrible," Vega muttered, feeling truly moved and shocked.

"There was nothing left of their bodies to bury. They were pulverized."

"Horrible."

"I was driving the truck when it happened. That's the only reason I survived. I never got to say goodbye. My brother wanted to become a doctor." His eyes were now glistening.

Vega almost reached out to touch his arm, but quickly thought better of it and remained silent. The light outside the cabin had now completely died down, so now they were driving through utter darkness. She felt encapsulated in a bubble of steel and glass. Vega pulled out her water bottle from her shoulder bag and took a swig.

"You want a soda?" Moncef asked, suddenly glad to change the subject.

"No, thank you. I am fine." She was reluctant to accept anything from this stranger. He might expect something in return.

"How about tea? I have a thermos bottle with hot tea. There is no rest stop between here and Eilat, so I have to bring whatever I need. Would you like some?"

"No, thank you. I don't want tea," she lied.

"Are you hungry? Do you want a sandwich?"

"No, I'm okay," Vega lied again, hardly able to suppress the outraged rumble of her stomach.

"I am getting hungry. There is a little turnout coming up. It's an overlook during the day, and we'll pull over and have a sandwich. We still have more than two hours to go."

Two hours sounded like an eternity to Vega. How could she get him to keep on driving? "I can pour the tea for you and hand you the sandwiches," she suggested. "That way you won't have to stop."

"But I want to stop. I need to stretch. I've been driving straight for five hours since Sharm-el Sheikh."

Vega's hopes waned, but she was determined to make this break as short as possible.

"Here we are. This is a gorgeous spot during the day. You can see as far as Saudi Arabia across that sea of sand." Moncef pulled the truck onto a turnout, bringing it to a halt with much screeching and huffing from the vehicle's engine. "I'll be right back," he said.

From the passenger seat on its high vantage point, she looked out at the desert sky appearing cold and distant. The stars seemed small and far away. The constellations had changed to the winter sky, and she was not familiar with them.

With a gust of air, Moncef returned to the driver's seat. "It's cold out there tonight," he remarked with a shudder then pulled out a thermos and a bag with sandwiches from behind his seat.

"It is the longest night of the year," Vega suddenly realized. "No wonder it is dark and cold."

"You are right. Today is December twenty first, winter solstice." Moncef looked at her while chewing on a big bite of his cheese sandwich. "Starting tomorrow, the days will get longer again."

"Three more days till Christmas," Vega remarked.

"Will you make it home in time?" he asked with a smile.

"I really don't know." She had to go to the German consulate in Tel Aviv and get travel documents before she could buy a ticket home.

"Are you sure you don't want a sandwich?" He held out a pre-packed sandwich wrapped in cellophane from a deli.

She could see yellow cheese and wilted lettuce between white slices of bread. "Absolutely delicious," was the urgent message her stomach sent to her brain. "Okay," she said and grabbed it. It tasted great.

"You were hungry," Moncef observed.

"Just a little."

He laughed. "You were starving. How long has it been since you last ate something?"

"Thanks for the sandwich. Shall we get moving again?"

"I am in no rush. I am enjoying myself, looking at you eating."

"Sorry, I must have gobbled it down like a pig," Vega admitted.

He laughed again. "Not like a pig, but like a hungry person who can no longer suppress her desire." He leaned over and put his hand on her thigh.

Vega grabbed his hand and tried to remove it, firmly but unsuccessfully.

"Don't be so shy with me," he said softly, "I know what German girls are like." His other hand was now reaching for her head and trying to bend it toward him.

"You know nothing," Vega said sharply and snapped back her head toward the passenger door.

"I know what I need to know," he whispered, "and that is that nobody is going to disturb us here." He grabbed hold of her other thigh and squeezed it while his hand moved upward to fumble with the straps of her overalls.

"Stop this right now!" Vega screamed.

"Why should I? I am just getting started."

"Get off me!" She tried to slap his face and remove his hands from touching her, but he was strong and determined.

"On the contrary," he answered softly.

Vega thought frantically. "What are you trying to do? Rape me?" she yelled, remembering Tara's story of the second officer on the Anaeas Lauro.

The words did have some impact. His head shot up for a second in alarm, but then he relaxed and tried to kiss her neck. "And what are you going to do about it?" he asked. "Run out into the desert?"

"And what if I do?" she shot back at him, not willing to let him see fear or weakness.

"Good luck," he mumbled. He now had her pinned to the backrest of the passenger seat and was trying to peel down the straps of her jumpsuit and bra.

With a quick move, Vega jerked her right arm away from him

and reached for the latch of the passenger door. It was unlocked and opened unexpectedly quickly. If he had not held her down, Vega would have fallen seven feet down from the cabin onto the gravel of the turnout. Surprised, Moncef loosened his grip just long enough for Vega to pull her leg away and swing it out the door. She tore away, ripping her sleeve in the process and jumped into the night. It was a long way down. She landed with her left foot at an awkward angle, wincing with pain at the impact. As she fell down, a thought shot through her mind: She could not run away if he came after her.

Above her, she heard a door open, and an angry voice yelled out, "Stupid bitch!"

Sounds of his feet on the ladder on the other side of the truck told her he was on his way down. Lying on the ground at an awkward angle, she saw Moncef's boots underneath the truck. She watched his feet making their way slowly to the front of the truck, taking his time. He knew she wasn't going anywhere.

Is this how it ends? Vega felt her heart bursting in her ribs. Should she try to run despite her ankle? How far would she get? The steps came closer; he had almost rounded the front of the truck. What should she do? What could she do? She groped around for a rock, a weapon, but the tarmac of the turnout was empty. Maybe she could roll underneath the truck? As she tried to move, the pain from her ankle shot through her body like a flame. She trifled a moan. From the front of the truck she heard a contemptuous snort. "I can hear you, you stupid girl. Do you think you are better than me?" He rounded the corner of the truck and faced her in front of the dark sky. In his hand he carried her bag. Why? Her heart raced at record speed from adrenaline pumping through her veins. Fight or flight? Neither was an option. Moncef walked toward her, looming over her. Why did he carry her bag?

"Moncef, let's talk…" she began.

"That's all you do, talk, talk, talk. You tease, you slut, you whore! You white girls are all the same." He threw the bag at her. Vega grabbed it and held it like a shield in front of her. She closed her eyes and waited for the impact.

Nothing happened. She counted to ten and opened her eyes. Moncef had rounded the front of the truck and was climbing up the ladder again.

**

The truck engine roared to life and the tanker pulled away from the overlook and back onto the road, leaving her on the ground coughing from the exhaust fumes. She watched the red rear lights of Moncef's truck fade into the night with a mixture of relief and terror. The danger was not over yet. She was completely alone, enveloped by darkness and silence.

So, this is how it feels to be left to die. The image of another roadside rest stop flashed through her mind; Tom lying on the side of the road. This time, she was on the other side, down on the ground, wounded, and watching a vehicle disappear into the distance, leaving her behind

Maybe I deserve this, she thought. This is karma, my penance. How foolish of me to think I could get away with what I did to Tom. Running away to remote and unreachable places was not enough. I should have known. It's the symmetry of the universe. Whatever I did, will be done to me. So, are we even now? Is this how it ends? Is this what the voices on the mountaintop had predicted?

Creepy noises filled the nighttime desert. She heard animal sounds and cracking sounds from the wind, the sand, shifting rocks. No cars came out at night if they could avoid it. Hitting an animal could cause an accident miles away from assistance. Vega knew she would have to spend the rest of the night lying right there by the roadside. Nobody would come to her aid.

Shuddering in the cold, she pulled a sweater and a pair of pants out of her bag. She put on layers over what she already wore. They didn't much help against the freezing temperature. Her ankle seared like a stabbing wound. She could not move or even shift her weight. As she glanced across the dark desert plain, the moon tentatively crawled over the horizon, pale and cold. As cold as a German moon.

The night before, she had celebrated the full moon in Dahab with fires, friends, food, and excitement. What a difference a day makes. This day never seemed to end, and it had gone from bad to worse. She scanned the sky for Vega, but Lyra was not visible. Dragging herself to a corner of the turnout, she ignored the sharp pain in her ankle, which had swollen to the size of a volley ball. As far away from road as possible, she rolled out her sleeping bag and crawled inside, shivering. Terror took hold of her. The emptiness and silence of the desert did not comfort her this night. Until now, she had been traveling in a protective bubble, shielded from harm by her naïveté.

The bubble had burst, however, and deposited her on the harsh bottom of reality. She shifted uncomfortably in her bag, trying to adjust her aching bones and her wounded ankle to the hard dirt beneath. No soft sand tonight to mold to the contours of her body.

Her body and mind were raw and agitated from the violent encounter in Moncef's truck. She had become vulnerable to images of both imagined and real dangers surrounding her. A soft scurrying sound. Maybe it was a Jerboa rat, a scorpion, a striped hyena, or a black cobra. They all lived nearby, drawn by the occasional garbage at the rest stop. Vega froze, paralyzed by fear. She could not escape any approaching animal or human predator. She wondered whether her ankle was broken.

What had she been thinking? Should she have stayed in Dahab, borrowed money, or somehow tried to organize a ride to Eilat? Maybe. But she had not wanted to stay in Dahab any longer, not after being robbed. Now, she was stranded in the open desert, on the longest, darkest, and coldest night of the year. She had come to the end of her road. She was out of money, out of steam, and out of faith.

The conversation on the mountaintop at the beginning of her journey seemed far away. It had been a vivid, psychedelic illusion, what else? What had she expected? That some cosmic extra-terrestrial with a good sense of humor would somehow appear and hand her a pyramid, just like Moses had been handed his tablets of the Ten Commandments? Completely ludicrous.

She had her answer: There were no gods; there was just the cold, dark desert and the hard ground to remind her of the nature of reality. What a fool I've been, Vega thought bitterly. What a wild-goose chase it has been. And this is how it ends. Only yesterday, I believed that my life and journey has a purpose, and that I am here for a reason. How could I be so stupid? Did I think the gods or some guardian angel had nothing better to do than to protect me?

As if in response, she heard a hissing sound in the dark. Whatever was out there, she had no defense against it. She felt completely defeated. Not a drop of water was left of the wave that had kept her afloat. She had been left drained and empty. She had finally hit rock bottom.

**

Even the longest and darkest night had to end eventually. At dawn, a friendly couple returning from a diving trip in Sharm-el Sheikh picked up a very cold, stiff, sore, hungry, and grimy Vega from the roadside. They deposited her after a pleasant drive directly in front of the Laromme Hotel in Eilat. Vega limped inside, retrieved her money and possessions, treated herself to breakfast and a shower, and had her sprained ankle bandaged. By ten o'clock she sat on a bus to Tel Aviv where the German consulate, with true Germanic efficiency, promised to issue provisional passport papers within a day.

Limping, Vega had time to shop for last-minute Christmas presents in Old Jaffa: A lion-shaped ring, for her mother; a small silver box with a Persian miniature painting of a hawk hunt on the lid, for her brother; and a colorful Bedouin scarf with gold embroidery, for Isabella.

True to the embassy staff's word, the papers were ready when she arrived on December 24. That same afternoon, Vega sat in an airplane for the two-hour flight to Germany. She felt great relief to be going home. Back to a cold, gray, and wet Germany. But what did she have to show for? A few trinkets, some small souvenirs. This journey was supposed to be a grand quest, an enlightening search. It had started with so much promise, with so much expectation and anticipation. A sacred conversation on a mountaintop had turned out to be nothing more than an illusion during an acid trip. She was not an inch closer to finding the purpose of her life.

However, she made it home just in time for Christmas Eve dinner.

Chapter 35: Home for Christmas

"Such a long, long time to be gone, and a short time to be there!"
Grateful Dead, *Box of Rain,* 1970

Vega walked into her mother's apartment limping like a wounded warrior. She dropped her tattered bag from the Bedouin market on the carpet. Her clothes were dirty, torn and full of sand. Lisa didn't mind. She ran up to her daughter crying. "You're home, I can't believe you're home. What happened to you? Are you hurt?"

"I'm okay, just a little worse for the wear. A sprain. I'll be fine. At least I made it." Vega said tearfully; she was so glad to see her little family. Lisa kept hugging her, tears streaming down her cheeks. "I thought I'd never see you again. I didn't know where you were. You coming home is my best Christmas gift ever," she sobbed. Vega felt embarrassed and ashamed that she had worried Lisa so much. She had only written that one postcard from Eilat.

Daniel wanted a hug as well. "What happened to you, Daniel. You look so grown up?"

"What happened to you Vega, you look all beat up?" he shot back.

Vega winced. "Yeah, a little. I need some tender loving care."

Vega realized five people, instead of three, sat around her mother's dining room table for Christmas Eve dinner. They hastily pulled up another chair for the unexpected, prodigal daughter, who had returned from the desert. Lisa and Daniel eagerly introduced their new partners. Lisa's boyfriend Albert was a retired dentist and hobby photographer, with thinning brown hair. Vega's brother Daniel had found a girlfriend, named Michaela.. Michaela's long, wavy, blond hair lay around her shoulders like a cape, and her blue eyes seemed to twinkle.

The new family members inquired politely about Vega's trip, but she never had a chance to answer, so the conversation quickly drifted toward the food. Michaela had contributed a cake, and Albert had brought a salad. He also passed around photographs from a trip to Sweden with Lisa. Vega had no pictures to show or share. She did not have presents for the two new family members, either. Her heart and head were bursting with the experiences of her journey, relief at being home, and confusion about arriving in the middle of Christmas dinner. All these images danced and floated around in her mind: The desert; jumping out of Moncef's truck; the tiny island of Kastellorizo; the rolling sensation of the ocean beneath her feet; the sunsets in Dahab; the floating market in Port Said; diving in the Red Sea; guard duty in the kibbutz.

While she was gone, life had gone on in Germany without her, and now she felt like an outsider in her own family. To Vega, it seemed like she had only been gone for an instant, but to the family she had left behind a lot had happened. Vega had not been there to share it. She wanted to reconnect with the two people she loved. But they seemed quite fulfilled in their respective new relationships. Albert and Michaela didn't even know her. She made a feeble attempt, "It is hard to believe I am here tonight. Two nights ago, I slept in the Sinai desert on the longest night of the year."

"Isn't the Sinai in Egypt?" asked Michaela.

"Almost," said Vega. "Right now, it is still part of Israel, but it will be returned to Egypt next year."

"Could you please pass the gravy?" asked Albert, and her mother complied with a smile in his direction. "The roast is delicious, so tender, and moist," he added, and Lisa beamed.

"It has been a long time since I have had mashed potatoes," said Vega, and everybody nodded understandingly, but showed no further interest.

"The best Christmas present is that you came home safely, Vega," Lisa said, her voice trembling.

"I am glad to be here. I almost didn't make it," she replied.

"I'm sure it's very difficult to travel in the Middle East," Albert began. "The food must be terrible. You look like you need another helping of potatoes," he concluded, in a well-meaning tone.

Daniel rolled his eyes, and Vega grinned at him. She had not expected to find a new father figure under the Christmas tree.

"Actually, the food in Israel was excellent. I wish you could try some falafel sandwiches," Vega said, but nobody was listening. They were discussing whether to go to Midnight Mass after dinner or to stay home and watch a movie.

"I almost forgot, Vega," Lisa said. The police were here looking for you."

Vega snapped to attention. "When was that? What did they want?"

"Something about Tom, they wanted to 'tie up some loose ends.'"

"What did you tell them?"

"I told them you were in Israel, and I didn't have an address. Then they said something about standard procedure and left."

Vega's thoughts swirled. She had just returned, and already she felt the threat again. How long would she be able to stay? Her body had arrived back within reach of the law, but her soul was still somewhere in limbo. Time had moved slowly in Germany, but it had moved, and now she would have to catch up.

When Vega gave the Egyptian chess set to her brother and told him that it came from a floating market in Port Said, Egypt, he was thrilled. Her mother loved the lion ring from old Jaffa. "I am so moved that you brought me such a precious gift from far away."

Their enthusiastic reaction wasn't quite enough to help Vega overcome the feeling of disconnect. Maybe it will get better with time, Vega thought, but she knew that some strangeness between them would remain.

A wide gap had grown between them caused by a lack of shared experiences. No matter how much she tried, she would never be able to explain what had happened since her departure, nor what had prompted her travels. How can you explain a painting by Vermeer to a blind man? How can you describe Beethoven's Ninth Symphony to a deaf woman? How could she tell her family living in snowy Germany about the endless sands of the Sinai desert? She was a different person now than before her departure. Vega drank another glass of wine and decided to ponder those questions later and instead celebrated her safe return.

**

On Christmas Day, Vega's friend, Isabella, came to visit. She studied social sciences, and over coffee she asked Vega, "How did you do it? How did you shake the addiction? How did you escape?"

She did research with drug addicts and was well aware of the high relapse rate.

"I cut out a part of me and threw it by the wayside at a rest stop off the Autobahn," Vega replied. "It was the hardest thing I ever did, but it saved my life."

And it cost Tom his life, she thought.

"Just like that?"

"It didn't happen quickly. Actually, I waited almost too long. I should have thrown Tom out much earlier, but it was hard to let go of my first love. I thought our relationship deserved a happy ending. But being with Tom was my first brush with death. I guess my survival instinct made me step on the emergency break just in the nick of time."

"I remember you looked like death back then. I couldn't get through to you."

"Yeah, I came pretty close."

"Do you ever think about him now?" Isabella asked.

"I think about him every single day." He haunts me, she thought.

"Wow, every day"

"I don't want to look back, and I don't want to open old wounds again. I am much better off without him. I found the other great love of my life: Art. Without art, I would probably still be a junkie," Vega said.

Art was her ticket into the world of perception and the imagination. Art led her on a journey that would never end, to past eras, distant countries, and the world's greatest cultures. Unlike people, art never disappointed. It helped to make sense of life. In addition, it had no negative effect on the liver.

"It's been quite a journey," she continued. "It certainly has not been a straight shot, after I kicked out Tom."

"You should write down your story, Vega. Maybe it would help others who struggle with addiction."

"I don't really feel the urge to do that. I don't want to think about Tom or drugs any more. That chapter of my life is over. Finished. File closed."

Or so she thought.

**

With her closest relatives wrapped up in their own lives, Christmas fatigue and restlessness set in for Vega. Her ankle healed and returned to its normal size. On the evening of December 28, she set out to visit the *Mousetrap*, the club in the city center.

Standing under the strobe lights, listening to David Bowie's *Heroes*, Vega saw Heidi, who had told her about the Anaeas Lauro job. They strode toward each other.

"You are back," Heidi said.

"Yeah, I just got back." Vega realized her voice sounded tired.

"How was it?"

"It was great," shouted Vega over the booming bass of David Bowie's band.

"I didn't think you would actually go," Heidi admitted.

"Why is that?" Vega shrugged her shoulders to indicate her question in sign language in case the music drowned out her voice.

"All by yourself and in the middle of the semester, I didn't think you'd have the guts," Heidi yelled back.

"I worked it out with my professors. And I wrote a paper on Bellini for Art History and one on three generations of Bedouin women in the Sinai for Anthropology."

"Wait a minute. The ship didn't go to the Sinai."

"I jumped ship and went by land."

"And your professor gave you permission for that?"

"He liked the idea. He thought it would be a good life-experience."

"Only in the Humanities would you get away with something like that," Heidi snorted.

Vega did not get a chance to respond because just then Klaus walked up. It was an evening for reunions. "Merry Christmas, Vega. How long have you been back?"

"Four days. I got back on Christmas Eve."

"And you already have Christmas fatigue? Being out on the town," he observed. Klaus still knew her pretty well.

Vega shrugged. "Only a week ago, I slept in the Sinai Desert."

"The Sinai? Wow. Were you mostly in Israel or Egypt?"

"I spent most of my time in Israel. First, I lived in a kibbutz, then worked at a hotel by the Red Sea, and finally hung out with the Bedouins in the desert."

"Did you overcome your German guilt trip, traveling in the Jewish homeland?" Klaus asked casually. Typical of him to ask such a question, Vega thought. He always cut right to the point and didn't waste time with small talk.

"You still know me pretty well," she conceded, giving him a slight smile. "I admit that was part of my agenda. I was never proud of being born German and always wanted to leave home."

"I know what you mean; but weren't you taking the guilt a little too far?"

"I went to Israel feeling very humble, traveling as a German in the land of the Jews. They suffered so much at the hands of our ancestors."

"They weren't exactly our ancestors."

"The Nazis were the generation of our parents."

"We shouldn't feel so guilty. We were born years after the war ended," Klaus observed.

"I know that, but we carry our country's history with us, whether we like it or not."

"So you worked in a kibbutz."

"Yes. I was confronted with the attitude of the Israelis, the children of the Jewish immigrants. They are imposing a lot of suffering on another ancient people who are just trying to continue their own way of life in their homeland."

"The Palestinians."

"Yes, the Palestinians are treated like second-class people in Israel."

"You sympathize with the Palestinians?"

"I now understand why they are fighting, but that does not make their methods acceptable. The fighting is violent and relentless. But they have nothing left to lose."

"So you got over your guilt trip, after seeing how badly the Palestinians are treated." Klaus concluded.

"No, I didn't." Vega thought about Tom and how guilty she still felt. She would never get over leaving him dead on the roadside. For a while she had shared her universe with Tom. They had lived in a world of dreams and mysteries together. It wasn't real, but it had been a magical place full of promise. She felt, she would never find that world again, nor anybody to share it with. Tom had been the one, the only one for her. She had loved him, and she had killed him.

Right at that moment, Vega noticed a man striding quickly toward them. She swayed, unstable on her feet.

Tom emerged from the crowd.

Chapter 36: Concurrence

"The time of coincidences is over. What could fall to me now that was not already my own?" Friedrich Nietzsche, *Thus Spoke Zarathustra*

Was he a ghost? Did her subconscious play tricks on her? She wasn't drunk or on drugs. How was this possible? Tom, or whoever he was, walked straight toward her.

"Klaus, I need your help," Vega said urgently.

It couldn't be him, but she recognized his walk, his hair, his eyes, his jeans shirt.

"What is it now?" Klaus asked, seeming irritated.

"Please, I really have to get away from that guy. He's over there." Vega pointed toward the man who looked like Tom.

"What did you do to him?" Klaus asked.

"Long story. I'll tell you in the car. Can we please go? Now! You know I don't have a car, anymore."

"Is he trying to hurt you?"

"Yes! We really have to go. Now!"

If this person really was Tom, he had every reason to hate her and seek revenge. Her heart began to jump in her chest. She had come so far, run so far, only to encounter him here, in her hometown disco, where they used to dance together. She felt slightly dizzy and she wondered if it was fear or pleasure. Was she happy to see him or scared for her life? Was she relieved he was alive, or was she afraid it would start all over again?

"Okay, but this is the last favor I do for you," Klaus said, then added, "I am doing it just because it's Christmas."

"Fair enough."

They ran across a wet road toward Klaus' Renault. Tom was close behind. Vega and Klaus jumped into his car. He started it, and pulled away. Vega watched as Tom flagged down a taxi.

"Vega, is he is following us?" Klaus asked.

"Yes. Can you try to lose him?"

"Is this a car chase? What did you do to him?"

Vega sat quietly for a moment, her heart racing, her breaths came in short, shallow gasps. At last, she had to confront her worst fear. "I threw him out of my car," she admitted.

"While you were driving?"

"Kind of."

"Was he injured? He could have died."

"I thought he did die."

Klaus accelerated the Renault and said, "You get me into the worst situations. Remember driving up that mountain in Switzerland, high on acid, trying to find some godforsaken village of your childhood? It was a suicide mission."

"I am sorry. I know it was crazy."

"Did you ever find that pyramid you were looking for?"

Vega glanced behind them. The taxi was only two car lengths behind. "No. It was a wild-goose chase. Can you drive a little faster?"

Klaus sped through the wet and empty streets. Christmas lights dimly illuminated the entrances of houses. He took a sharp turn. The taxi followed right on their tail.

"Is that why you ran away for so long? You thought you had killed him?"

Vega didn't answer. What could she say? He was right. As usual, running away hadn't worked. She was right back where she had started.

"After tonight, Vega, I want you to stay far away from me. I don't have a death wish."

"You make it sound like I meant to kill Tom."

"I'm just done."

"Sorry, Klaus, for putting you into crazy situations."

They pulled up at the curb on Filderstrasse in front of Vega's home.

"Now what?" Klaus asked.

The taxi pulled up behind them. Tom got out.

Vega's heart began to pound harder. She heard a ringing in her ears, as if the situation had become too unreal to comprehend. What would Tom do? "I'll run inside, Klaus, and you can leave," she said.

Tom walked up to their car. "Vega, I just want to talk to you," he demanded.

Realizing it was too late to make a run for it, she sat and looked through the windshield, away from where Tom stood. "Get away from me," she said through the closed window. Klaus sat, tensely grabbing the steering wheel.

Tom leaned closer to the car and placed his hands on the window. "Open the door," he insisted.

"No," Vega screamed.

"Get away from the car," Klaus shouted.

"Tell your boyfriend I don't have a weapon. I mean no harm. I just want to talk for five minutes."

"I am not her boyfriend," Klaus protested.

"Take your hands off the car and remove your jacket," Vega said sharply, opening the window a crack.

Tom stepped back and put his hands into his jacket pockets.

"Take your hands out of your pockets," Klaus yelled.

Tom obeyed, shrugged off his coat, and held his hands up in the air. One of them was clenched in a fist.

"What are you holding in your hand?" Vega asked through the slit in the window. Her voice sounded hoarse. Did he hide a knife in his fist?

"Something I want to give to you," Tom's voice was a near yell.

"Keep your voice down. I don't want to wake up the entire street." A light had flicked on in one of the dark houses.

"Open your window. I won't hurt you, even though you left me to die."

Vega opened the window a little more. Cold, wet air streamed in.

"What do you want from me?" she asked. A sharp hot pain shot through her body, despite the cold. It hurt seeing Tom so close to her.

"I have something for you. I made it in prison. I learned a trade while in jail."

"What trade?"

"I'm a glasscutter."

"No more drugs?"

"No, I've been clean for many months."

"I'm glad you are better. I am glad you are alive, but I did what I had to do. Please leave me alone." She was shaking from the cold and uncontrolled feelings of fear and regret. "I can't have anything to do with you anymore. It's too hard, it hurts too much." Vega broke down crying.

"I understand, but I thought about you every single day in jail."

Vega didn't respond. She also had thought about Tom almost every day. But usually it had been the image of his dead body. Now he was standing right next to of her. Her first love, who still made her feel warm and weak inside. She hadn't killed him after all. And he apparently didn't want to kill her. Had he forgiven her, or was this some trick, some devious way to get back at her?

As if in response he held out his hand and opened it. In his palm, sparkling in the weak glow of the streetlights, sat a small crystal pyramid.

Epilogue

"When you're down on the lower levels of the pyramid, you will be either on one side or the other. But when you get to the top, the points all come together, and there the eye of God opens." Joseph Campbell, *The Power of Myth, 1988*

With the small glass pyramid at her side, Vega drove on a country road to the University of Tübingen. Under a cloudy sky thoughts of chance and destiny went through her mind. She had been looking for her proof, her sign, in all the wrong places. Now that she had it, what did it mean? How had Tom known about her quest for the pyramid? He had claimed it was just coincidence.

The time for coincidences is over, Nietzsche kept telling her. If not coincidence, then was this pyramid her answer?

The pyramid has been a mythical symbol since the time of the ancient Egyptians. The earliest step pyramid helped them to ascend and be closer to the gods.

In the great seal of the United States, the pyramid represents the unifying symbol that brings together the country's different points of view. Culminating in the eye of god, it transcends the limited perspective of the private universes of individuals. The pyramid creates a transition between an earthly and a higher realm. Could this mythological interpretation be true, Vega wondered

The rational explanation for Tom's survival and choice of creating a pyramid for her was simple. He had been found by the Highway patrol after she took off. They had given him Narcan to bring him down from the overdose, and they had taken him to the hospital for the gash in his head. From there, he was sent straight to jail for numerous probation violations. Incarcerated, Tom became sober and learned the trade of a glasscutter. After the cloud of drugs lifted, he felt remorseful. He understood why Vega had left him and he felt bad about putting her in danger. Tom told the police his injury was an accident. But he was still hurt by her action, setting up the scene to look like an overdose.

In the workshop in jail, he made the glass pyramid because he simply thought she would like it. It also reminded him of the pyramid they had seen in Amsterdam, spreading serenity in the Cosmos club, as well as the pyramids they had talked about in the vertical time zone at the forest lake. In addition the pyramid, like a prism, was a brilliant shape to cut out of glass.

Was it chance or destiny that he had come up with this particular shape for her? How much of life's script was written by fate? How much by random occurrences? Did meaning and purpose exist? Maybe life was just a jumble of chances and coincidences, senseless happenings with no rhyme or reason. Was she just a plaything of the capricious moods of the universe?

Vega could not face the possibility of heartless gods shaping human lives according to their arbitrary whims like they did in Francisco Goya's *Black Paintings*. Driving through the Schönbuch Forest past the monastery in Bebenhausen, she considered the question.

As if in response to her thoughts, the sky opened up and a violent thunderstorm exploded. Sheets of rain and cracking thunder accompanied nearly simultaneous lightning. She pulled over and sat by the empty roadside, shaken by the intensity of the cosmic reaction.

Is this a cosmic affirmation? she thought. Leave the fireworks to the gods. They're putting on a good show. The rain poured down so hard she could see absolutely nothing outside her window. The windshield wipers gave up fighting the intense elemental forces. She was confined inside her car and inside her head.

A lightning bolt struck right next to her, and an idea lit up her mind like a light bulb.

What if she could will a guiding force into her life? What if she made it happen through the sheer strength of her convictions? What if she could create her own gods? What if she gave her life beauty, meaning, and purpose because without these qualities life was unbearable? What if this was the real function of faith? What if this was what the church demanded from its believers? To have faith beyond reason because there is no God beyond the one we create for ourselves. Faith wills gods into existence because without faith there is no God. Maybe this explained the meaning of Zarathustra's question: "The time of chance is over. What could fall to me now, that was not already my own?"

As if on cue, and as suddenly as it had started, the thunderstorm ended. Calmness arrived all around her. Fresh, clean air flowed into her car as she rolled down the window, and she took a deep, cleansing breath smelling the wet earth. Sunrays filtered through the shiny forest with its lush polished leaves. Sun beams broke through the rapidly dispersing rain clouds, appearing like beacons, setting off sparkles in the wet puddles on the asphalt.

Another cosmic reaction? Had Vega just witnessed a demonstration of the concept of the human body as the equivalent of the universe? "He who realizes the truth of the body can then come to know the truth of the universe," the tantric texts of ancient India explain the connection between micro- and macro cosmos.

Had her inner thoughts just become a catalyst for the cosmic powers to reveal themselves? Was the microcosm in her mind connected to the macrocosm above? The Greek philosopher, Hermes Trimegistus, in the 3rd century BC claimed: "As above, so below." Had she just witnessed a link between inside and outside, or was it just another coincidence? "The time of coincidences is over," thundered Nietzsche. Apparently, coincidence existed where Vega chose to see it and destiny where she chose to believe it.

I guess, I have my answer, she thought. If I want to see connections, I have to create them. If I want life to have meaning, I have to give it meaning. If I want gods to accompany my life, I have to will them into existence. If the time of coincidences is over, then everything I encounter is a reflection of myself, karma, or eternal cause and effect.

The responsibility for her life and happiness had bounced back into her own lap. As the voices on the Swiss mountaintop had proclaimed, she must struggle with the chill of infinite freedom and the threatening arbitrariness of life.

The responsibility for her health and happiness had fallen back to her. As the oracle told her, she already knew what to do. As she drove out of a dip in the road, she felt a big weight being lifted off her shoulders. Actually, she had lifted it off herself. It didn't matter who lifted it. The sky was overcast, but the flittering leaves on the poplar trees bordering the road sparkled silvery in a faint breeze. Cool air flowed through her open window. She let go of her thoughts of Tom and allowed her breath to flow in unison with the green landscape.

Vega felt confident that she could make her universe a place of purpose as Nietzsche had hoped, even though the opposite was just as likely, as Goya had feared.

If it was up to Vega, her private universe would posses purpose, kindness and beauty.

ABOUT THE AUTHOR

Cornelia Feye received her M.A. in Art History and Anthropology from the University of Tübingen, Germany. She lived in New York City for five years and worked as an educator at the Jacques Marchais Museum of Tibetan Art in Staten Island. After moving to California she taught Eastern and Western Art History at several colleges in San Diego. Her museum experience includes the Mingei International Museum, the Museum of Man, and the San Diego Museum of Art, as well as the Athenaeum, Music and Arts Library in La Jolla, where she served as the School of the Arts and Arts Education Director for ten years. Feye's art mystery *Spring of Tears* was published in 2011 and won the San Diego Book Awards in the mystery category. Her second novel *House of the Fox* is set in the Anza Borrego desert and San Diego. Her publications include art historical essays and the catalog entries for the Athenaeum Music & Arts Library's *Selections from the Permanent Collection, 1990-2010.*

For other books by Konstellation Press please visit:

Konstellationpress.com

For other books by the author and for images mentioned in the novels please visit:

Corneliafeye.wordpress.com
Facebook: SpringOfTears